GARDEN
LAKES

JAIME CLARKE

BLOOMSBURY READER

LONDON · OXFORD · NEW YORK · NEW DELHI · SYDNEY

This edition published in 2016 by Bloomsbury Reader

Copyright © 2016 Jaime Clarke

The moral right of the author is asserted.

Bloomsbury Reader is an imprint of Bloomsbury Publishing Plc

50 Bedford Square, London WC1B 3DP

www.bloomsburyreader.com

Bloomsbury is a trademark of Bloomsbury Publishing plc

Bloomsbury Publishing, London, Oxford, New Delhi, New York and Sydney

ISBN: 9781448215645
eISBN: 9781448215638

Visit www.bloomsburyreader.com to find out more about our authors and their books.
You will find extracts, author interviews, author events and you can sign up for
newsletters to be the first to hear about our latest releases and special offers.

You can also find us on Twitter @bloomsreader.

For my brothers, Jeremy and Jared
—and in memory of John Kalien (1921–2010)

Contents

Chapter One

It would be the hottest day of the year. The temperature would climb steadily toward a new page in the record book, some 125 degrees by two o'clock, obliterating all previous records. We wouldn't learn of the devastating effects—Sky Harbor International being shut down because of melting runways, the body count among the elderly whose air conditioners had failed—until our return from Garden Lakes, and by then the story would be mythic, a legend we would hear over and over as we grew older.

Our concerns that morning were not of the weather. We were weary not only from having risen with the sun, but from having spent the preceding month sauntering by the bulletin board outside of Principal Breen's office, anxiously awaiting the posting of the roster of those select juniors who had been chosen for a fellowship at Garden Lakes. Historically, Garden Lakes fellows had gone on to good colleges or to celebrated careers, and while for some the opportunity was merely a jewel in the crown, for others it was an academic life jacket, keeping them afloat until the fall semester of their senior year, the one last chance to bring up the old GPA.

1

The delay in posting the list had been due to vandalism to the statue of Saint Francis Xavier in the chapel courtyard. Someone spray-painted the head lime green, and a rumor reached the administration that the vandals were juniors. Principal Breen threatened to cancel the summer leadership program if the responsible parties didn't come forward. We juniors let our displeasure be known and were relieved when a pair of freshmen took responsibility (though they would later claim they had been pressured into accepting the blame) and the roster was published the last Monday of classes.

And so as we boarded the red and white school bus, RANDOLPH COLLEGE PREPARATORY stenciled unevenly on the sides, the relief we'd felt the previous Monday had been replaced by sheer amazement. Simply, those of us who had been selected for Garden Lakes still had the feeling that the whole thing was an illusion, that we'd be prohibited from realizing the honor; but once we glimpsed the school bus, looming like a time machine in the parking lot, we believed. Even if we'd had a crystal ball, we couldn't have guessed what lay in front of us. Before that morning, we didn't know how to flatter or cajole or threaten; or how to use suppression, silence, or misdirection in the service of motive. We did not believe in altruism (as far as we understood it)—self-sacrifice was for those who had cashed in their ambition; our understanding was that personal achievement would lead to success in all facets of life, and that such personal achievement could be obtained through hard work and dedication. But our fellowship at Garden Lakes would change that, poisoning us, widening our arsenal for achieving objectives and forcing our will. The story of our fellowship would be as legendary as the heat that summer, the two stories told in the same breath. But as we took our seats, all we had on our minds was privilege and the chance for distinction.

2

Duane Handley jumped on the bus first. Hands, who would one day lead his family's sixth-generation brewery to ruin, was the star guard on our basketball team. Even as an underclassman, he'd stood out among everyone else in our class. He was taller, more muscular, and always smiling, which didn't go unnoticed by the students at our sister school, Xavier College Prep. He even seemed smarter than the rest of us: Hands had discovered that if you took British Literature instead of American Literature, you could cross the street to Xavier, since Randolph offered only American Lit. (Crossing the street only in the figurative sense, as a cement walkway with fencing had been erected over Central Avenue; we all took to calling it the Bridge of Sighs, named for our reaction to the hordes of blue and green plaid skirts coming and going.) Xavierites figured this out too, and soon American Lit classes at Randolph were filled with pleasant smells rather than odors, and you learned to preregister rather than risk getting wait-listed.

Dave Figueroa sat next to Hands. Figs and Hands had been best friends since Lincoln Elementary, where they'd teamed to win the annual talent show with their air band, Line One. Figs lip-synched the lyrics to Journey tunes while Hands pounded out the backup music on an unplugged keyboard borrowed from the nearest high school band department. The two seventh graders tapped to play air guitar lead and bass would ride their talent-show glory to the end of their days at Lincoln.

Figs, who would later in life succeed in covering up an embezzlement at the firm where he worked, was renowned for another reason: the sophomore class trip to Mazatlán, Mexico, over spring break, a trip sanctioned by Randolph as a way to throw students into the fire together, to make sure that they thought of themselves as a unit, a measurement of loyalty to their alma mater. For reasons that no one could point to, the sophomores didn't have the cohesion that classes before had, but as Figs and Hands and the others blazed through Mazatlán over spring break, working their way down Avenida Camarón Sábalo, to Gus Bar, to Mundo Bananas, to Mr. Tony's, their bond grew.

How they got from there to a nondescript house brimming with girls named Rosa in the Naval Zone was the subject of much debate. Some thought they were going to a house party, others thought the ranch house was a roadhouse. A party of young men, some they recognized and some they didn't, shuffled around the dirt front yard. They were eventually shuttled into the backyard, where the breeze from the Canal de Navegación picked up, blowing a typhoon of plastic cups and blue plastic bags in circles around them. Everyone except Figs went inside.

Some assumed Figs had reconsidered, though, when they heard him in the musty hallway. A sound like thunder shook the walls, which no one noticed, breaking from their business only when the doors to their rooms flew open, Figs standing breathless and wide-eyed. "*Federales,*" he tried to scream. A panic gripped the house, the Rosas heading for a door leading to the basement, grabbing their camisoles and lace panties. Figs led a charge out a window in a back bedroom, jumping through the screen headfirst, landing miraculously on his feet. The sophomores laughed about "that night at Rosa's" thereon after. But while they laughed vigorously at what happened in Mazatlán, they were secretly horrified by what would've happened if they'd been rung up by the Mexican police. They imagined they'd still be in jail, or worse. Needless to say, everyone was grateful to Figs for standing lookout, and it wasn't a coincidence that he was elected junior class president the following year, a unanimous vote.

4

The sole rift between Figs and Hands, which, had we known about it, might've provided the frame of reference that would've saved the fellowship that summer, occurred two months before the end of their eighth-grade year, on the graduation trip to Disneyland. As Figs and Hands attended school in a district with a dismal high school graduation rate, the feeder elementary schools felt compelled to treat graduation from the eighth grade with the pomp and circumstance of a high school graduation, renting a room at the Phoenix Convention Center and decking it out with ribbons in the school's colors to give that statistical percentage of students who wouldn't graduate from high school the look and feel of a real graduation. And prior to graduation, the "senior" class went on a bus trip to Anaheim for a weekend at the Magic Kingdom, all paid for by sponsors.

Figs was lucky to make the trip. Two weeks earlier, he'd been busted selling lunch tickets to sixth graders, having lifted a box when the print shop delivery driver asked Figs to keep an eye on his van, which the driver kept running for the air-conditioning. Unbeknownst to Figs, the school called the print shop to report the missing tickets, which were numbered with red ink, in order to get credit on the next shipment. So when students began presenting the same missing numbered tickets in the cafeteria, it didn't take long for the lunch lady to shake down a fifth grader for information.

The principal expressed his disappointment in Figs, but Figs didn't feel it. While he affected contrition, he felt a certain invincibility—his eighth-grade head had swelled to the point that he believed his and Hands's presence at Lincoln made people *want* to come to school. This overestimation didn't manifest itself in arrogance—Figs had time for you no matter who you were or what grade you were in—rather, it became an endeavor he aimed to excel at. His popularity at school was a job that he loved, a job he hated to leave when the bell rang at three thirty, and one he couldn't wait for when his alarm rang at seven a.m. He did understand what he'd done wrong—not in financial terms, but in terms of jeopardizing his status. The lunch-ticket stunt was to him victimless and had provided some much-needed pocket money, and he knew the principal would let him off. Which the principal did. The principal would, however, have to notify Figs's parents, which was okay with Figs, as his parents, who loved him and whom he loved, were so devoted to their jobs that the only communiqué from Lincoln that would've garnered any attention was one saying that Figs was flunking out. His parents had witnessed Figs's self-discipline grow, elementary school after elementary school, town after town; and so they never worried over him, offering their advice only when it was solicited, which was next to never.

The principal knew this too and flirted with holding Figs back from the Disneyland trip, but Figs lobbied a number of his teachers, who intervened on his behalf, citing an otherwise stellar academic and social record. So Figs was permitted to go, which was a relief, as Figs had been keeping secret his knowledge that Hands's girlfriend, Julie Roseman, was breaking up with Hands to go out with him. This bit of treachery had developed innocently. Julie and Hands had been an item since the first of the year; it was reputed (and true) that Julie had been dating a freshman at the high school where her older sister went. Hands and Julie started to fool around at her parents' house after school, though, and soon Julie had called it off with the freshman, inaugurating the trifecta of her, Hands, and Figs.

Figs welcomed Julie as a part of his friendship with Hands. On the days that Hands didn't have basketball practice, the three would end up in Julie's pool, engineering the trampoline so they could jump from the roof and bounce into the deep end. Sometimes they'd invite others from Lincoln, but most times it was just the three musketeers.

Julie tried to interest Figs in some of her friends, and Figs was interested in a peripheral way. But he had a girlfriend in Seattle that he'd met on a family camping trip to the Grand Canyon and to whom he'd continued to sign letters "Love, Figs," and so he forced himself to stay within reasonable limits, imagining that his girlfriend was doing the same.

But the letters from Seattle were fewer and fewer, until they stopped altogether. A succession of panic-induced phone calls yielded no return call. Figs had revealed to Hands his plan to move to Seattle after high school with his parents' consent. The silence from Seattle, however, shattered those plans, and he consoled himself by showing up unannounced at Julie's, raiding her father's liquor cabinet, and chugging from a half-drunk bottle of Jack Daniel's, taking long gulps, letting the amber liquid fill his cheeks, flushing it down his throat while his mouth filled again with the smoky flavor.

Julie cleaned up the vomit in the bathroom while Figs lay comatose on the white leather couch in the living room. She called Hands and said he should come right away, but sometime between Julie's call and Hands's arrival, it happened. It had probably already happened, or the seed had been planted, but before Figs puked and passed out, Julie had been touched by the look of loss in Figs's eyes. She'd never seen anyone so undone by love—not even her parents, the only model of love that she knew. And so when Hands pushed open the front door to find Julie sitting cross-legged on the love seat, staring at Figs's lifeless form, he had no way of knowing Julie had fallen in love with Figs.

7

Figs was to find out some weeks later, when he showed up at Julie's for what he thought was a pool party. He found Julie pool-side, alone. The clear pool water was still. "Last one in," Julie said, and they scrambled out of their clothes. The pool cast a shimmering light, and before Julie's sister and her boyfriend appeared, Figs realized that Julie loved him. The three had spent so much time together that they had a sort of telepathy. They'd also established boundaries, albeit unspoken, and Figs thought it strange when Julie brushed up against him on the underwater bench in the shallow end. She had never breached his space in that way, and he shrugged it off as having something to do with the fluid dynamics of swimming. But when she brushed him again, this time on her way out of the pool, Figs couldn't help but read the signal, confirmed days later on an afternoon at Julie's parents' house when Hands had practice.

Figs reasoned that just kissing wasn't cheating; anyone can kiss anyone, he thought. Then he imagined Hands, his best friend, kissing Julie, and it took several hours to beat back the rage that built inside him. Figs wondered if he had been in love with Julie the whole time, and revisited his argument with Hands when Hands broke up with his girlfriend Kristina on her birthday. Figs had tried to convince Hands that breaking up with Kristina for Julie was a mistake, a bad decision guided by only one principle: Kristina wouldn't let Hands go any further than taking off her shirt, and Hands was ready to try more.

Figs knew Hands would remember that exchange, gentle as it was—Hands prevailing without further protest from Figs—when he found out about Figs and Julie. Figs had a trump, but he didn't want to have to use it. A couple of weeks before, when Julie was at a doctor's appointment, Hands had convinced Figs to go with him to Kristina's house. Hands was vague about who would be there, and what they were going to do. It ended up being just the three of them, with Hands and Kristina disappearing into one of the back bedrooms when Figs went to the kitchen for another Dr Pepper. Figs watched an hour or so of cable and then left. Hands called him later that night, asking what had happened, saying he and Kristina hadn't been gone but a minute, that Kristina had wanted to show him something in her parents' room, which Figs knew was the official version should a version ever be needed. But it didn't come up the next day at school, and Hands and Kristina passed in the hall like strangers.

Figs and Julie fixed on her house as the venue for admitting their relationship to Hands. Figs had expected some shouting, possibly a fistfight. As music filtered from her sister's room, Julie spoke. The tone in her voice belied her nervousness, and she explained the matter straight through. Hands was puzzled at first, looking over at Figs now and again. When Julie wound down, Hands looked at her and said, "Thanks for being honest," before walking away without acknowledging Figs.

In the week or two after, with nothing but graduation and a long, hot summer ahead, Figs and Julie managed to avoid Hands. His excision from their routine was easy, and the ease was disconcerting.

The day of graduation, Figs met Hands outside the auditorium (he never knew if it had been arranged by Julie or was merely an accident), and after an awkward moment where Figs asked about his parents, Hands looked him square in the eyes and said, without hurt or malice, "I would have never guessed at your disloyalty." He offered his hand, and Figs shook it, Hands's words haunting him all through graduation, through the long summer, through Julie's family's surprise departure for Texas. He parsed that phrase out loud when alone and silently when in the

9

company of others. He researched his past for any history of disloyalty and came up with nothing. He didn't see it at first, his reflexivity keeping his spirit buoyant, but on a particular late-summer afternoon, on a walk past Julie's old house on Garfield Avenue, its windows shaded with the blinds and drapes of the new owners, Figs felt the full force of his betrayal, innocent as it had come about, and its lonely wake devastated him.

He knew what he had to do, and the week before school started, he circled Hands's house, working up the courage to ring the doorbell. Hands answered the door, his face creased by a tan he'd acquired at his uncle's place in Rancho Palos Verdes, outside L.A., where Hands liked to spend part or all of his summer. Months of anxiety poured out and Figs halted a rambling explanation as it wavered into defense and simply said, "I'm sorry."

"I'm over it," Hands said, welcoming him inside. Hands's parents said, "Hello, we haven't seen much of you this summer," and Figs blushed, appreciative that Hands hadn't poisoned his parents against him. They spent the afternoon plotting their course schedule and, like the rest of the incoming frosh, speculating about their chances with the girls at Saint Xavier.

Roger Dixon was the most eager to board the bus. Some of us kidded Roger about how he sat ramrod straight during Mass, or about his symmetrical crew cut, but we always kidded gently because once Roger stopped taking the kidding, or if he thought you weren't kidding but poking fun at him, a beating was doubtlessly in your future. There were a lot of beatings in Roger's past. His father, Colonel Dixon, lived his life by a strict set of guidelines, and he expected Roger, who would later go AWOL in Iraq, to subscribe to the same joyless guidelines.

Mike Quinn was the most reluctant to go. Q preferred to spend his summers in San Diego, or at his family's condo on Catalina Island. But his father, Senator Quinn, thought Garden Lakes was an excellent idea for young men, and Q never had any say in the matter. Q, who would show up at the twenty-year reunion married to a swimsuit model, had long gotten used to everyone kowtowing to his father's every wish, so he wasn't surprised when he discovered he'd been named a fellow. He had learned to bargain with his father, though, and his stint at Garden Lakes was worth a senior trip to Europe, so Q decided he would try his hand at deferring the customary gratification summer brought.

Phillip Sprague wasn't as keen to get away from his parents as he was pleased to have been chosen as a fellow. Sprocket's parents had wheeled him up to the bus, dropping his bag next to his chair, telling him to have a good time. He was a lithe kid, sallow from never spending any time outside, and while his parents didn't consider him a burden, they were overwhelmed with his care. They'd politicked intensely to get Sprocket, who would one day sell his fledgling software company for millions, on the roster, even going so far as to donate a set of the *Oxford English Dictionary* to the Randolph library. For his part, Sprocket was good-natured, and there were those of us who genuinely liked him and didn't treat him any differently than anyone else.

Casey Murfin, the chronic ditcher, helped load Sprocket onto the bus, his small frame struggling behind the wheelchair. Some of us had balked when we saw Smurf's name on the roster, but there was no denying that his father was a powerful businessman whose philanthropy was famous. The Murfin Group controlled the majority of real estate in the Valley of the Sun, the family name minted on signage all over town, which would still be true

11

when Smurf one day successfully slandered a female colleague with whom he'd cheated on his wife.

Warren James fidgeted with his glasses, a new prescription with tinted lenses so he wouldn't have to carry two sets. Warren, who would later be unwittingly implicated in an Internet Ponzi scheme, was the most well-liked of our class, though our affinity for Warren was born more out of admiration for his contemplative nature than camaraderie. In fact, Warren was regarded as the forward thinker among us. True, conversation with Warren was an exercise in patience, a furious replication of questions with a dearth of answers following, but he was not aggressively opinionated, and if you struck up a conversation that you wanted to break away from, that was your own fault.

Vince Glassburn hung back, reclining against his father's cinnamon-colored BMW. He ran his hands through his long black hair, which he wore within millimeters of Randolph's policy about hair not exceeding shoulder length. Assburn, who would die plunging into a frozen lake somewhere between Canada and Detroit, had transferred to Randolph from Minnesota his sophomore year, and it was well known that he burgled houses in his upscale neighborhood and stole whatever he could grab, selling the loot out of the back of his Ford Bronco in the parking lot after school. Most of us had radar detectors whose former owners lived on Assburn's street—or on the next street over—and some of us had expensive neckwear that we'd flaunt at Mass or any other affair that mandated a tie. None of us questioned where Assburn's stuff came from—we didn't want to know. But while we were happy to acquire contraband at bargain prices, Assburn never got what he most wanted: to fit in. There was never an outright edict against him, but for one reason or another he remained an outsider.

Father Matthews conferred with Mr. Hancock and Mr. Malagon, the faculty who administered Garden Lakes. Mr. Malagon, junior to Mr. Hancock by some thirty years and himself a Randolph alum, listened dutifully with his arms crossed, nodding. This was to be Mr. Malagon's first year at Garden Lakes, and he appeared to the rest of us to be taking his duty more seriously than he did the instruction of his history class. Which isn't to say that Mr. Malagon was a bad teacher—students tried to transfer into his class when word spread about how much fun it was. Also, Mr. Malagon's reluctance to put too much emphasis on test scores made him very popular.

Mr. Malagon, whose mysterious exit from Garden Lakes we could never forgive, was popular with the students on the other side of the Bridge of Sighs too. His classroom was situated inside the breezeway in Regis Hall that led to the bridge, and we gawked at the sidewalk outside his window. And Mr. Malagon encouraged us to gawk. He'd gawk too, cracking the window on any Xavier-ites who were dawdling, telling them that they were a major disturbance, sending them on their way in titters. The administration would be particularly interested in these details once their inquiry into that summer began, details we wrongly assumed to be harmless, though we could not have saved Mr. Malagon.

Mr. Hancock, on the other hand, was a sixty-year-old divorcé who was also the school's most feared disciplinarian. There were those of us who became flushed with terror upon seeing Mr. Hancock's shaved dome towering over other students in the hall. Legend had it that Mr. Hancock, whose departure from Garden Lakes would doom us all, had never cracked a smile in his thirty-five years at Randolph, and none of us could dispute it.

The fellows' fathers shook hands with one another (except

those who were professional adversaries, either lawyers on opposing sides of a case, or businessmen toiling in competing industries). Some of the Jesuits spilled out onto the steps for a cigarette, concealing their smokes in the palms of their hands. Several of the priests collected around Brian Lindstrum. Lindy's father and older brother had been killed in a boating accident his sophomore year. Where the stigma of tragedy could've led to ostracism, the school rallied around Lindy, members of all classes adopting a feeling of protectiveness toward him. For his own part, rather than becoming sullen and withdrawn, Lindy immersed himself in his studies, cultivating such a strong love for astronomy that the school's astronomy club asked him to be their new president, an honor usually reserved for seniors. The Jesuits watched Lindy—who would one day die in his sleep, leaving behind a bereaved wife and two small children—board the bus.

"Just like camping," Mr. Malagon said, slapping me on the back as I plopped down in my seat.

Father Vidoni blew the horn, and Assburn and the group of sophomores volunteering as staff in the hopes of being chosen as fellows the following year climbed aboard, the bus still reeking from the basketball team's final away game against Saint Mary's (a loss). Smurf dredged an old, bloodied bandage from between the seats and flung it at Assburn. Mr. Hancock strode through the aisle, making sure everyone was wearing a seat belt, while Mr. Malagon called roll.

"Hands?"

"Here!"

"Figs?"

"Here!"

"Q?"

"Here."

"Smurf?"

"Here, here!"

"Lindy?"

"Here."

"Sprocket?"

"Yes, here."

"Roger?"

"Yes, sir."

"Warren?"

"Here."

"Assburn?"

"Here!"

"Martens?"

Mr. Hancock protested as I answered, the official roster in his hands, unfamiliar with our nicknames. Mr. Malagon reached for it, but Mr. Hancock pulled back. He called roll for the sophomores and all answered accordingly. The two teachers took their seats, Mr. Malagon up front, Mr. Hancock in the back next to Figs and Hands.

The bus pulled out onto Central Avenue, braking at the light at Indian School Road, in front of the First National Bank. We felt like Christopher Columbus, serenaded at court, about to set sail for a new world. To look at us was to remark on our similarities: our white polo shirts, khaki shorts, shoes always worn with socks. But while we might've appeared interchangeable to outsiders, we knew the uniformity of our dress was just a mask for our disparate personalities, though the ambitions that seethed within us remained secret as the bus idled at the light.

The bank sign flashed the time and temperature, which flitted between 100 and 99. The light turned green as the sign flashed 101.

Chapter Two

Charlie stirred cream into his coffee, the rhythm of the spoon against the inside of the cup soothing his seared nerves. He'd spent an anxious afternoon refraining from the impulse to search the Internet for people he'd known in all the places he'd lived. The same impulse visited him in moments of crisis, and each time he vanquished it with the truth that knowing that life had gone on for friends he'd known in Denver and Santa Fe and Rapid City and San Diego and New York City would puncture his precious memories of his time in those places. A small but vain corner of his soul wondered if anyone ever thought of him, wondering what had become of the boy who was there and then wasn't.

Outside, cars raced up and down Central Avenue as the sun descended, setting the interior of the coffee shop aflame. The restaurant had been the scene of many late-night bull sessions after making deadline, which was why he'd chosen it as a venue for reconciliation with Charlotte. Also, he knew his colleagues at the *Arizona Sun* would be at the Christmas party at Mary Elizabeth's, the swank bar at the Phoenician resort that the paper rented for its cozy nooks where office romances that wouldn't last through the winter were kindled.

He longed for Charlotte to clatter through the front door, the diaphanous sunset at her back, her tanned skin ablaze with a warmth he needed to feel. Their last moment together, filled with screaming and the cold touch of her hands shoving him toward the door of her condo on Camelback Road, had left him with a dread he couldn't shake. The scene replayed in his waking hours and menaced his sleep. He thought of a thousand things he could've said, or maybe one true thing. He knew the right words would make a difference, that Charlotte would reinstate their engagement before their mutual friends and families could learn of the rupture, though he could bridge any personal embarrassment. Closure and final decree worried him constantly, and if his job had taught him anything, it was that any dialogue could extend indefinitely if there was affinity between the speaker and the listener. He aimed to reestablish that rapport with Charlotte and anticipated her arrival with a zeal bordering on lust.

But the gloaming settled over the desert and Charlie's hope faded as his reflection took shape in the coffee shop window, a solitary figure at the end of another long year, taking sips from a never-ending two-dollar cup of coffee. He smiled at the waitress, whose curiosity about him had dimmed. He'd delayed an urgent need to urinate out of fear of missing Charlotte's entrance and quickly washed his hands in the cramped, yellow-lit restroom off the kitchen, the air heavy with the smell of greasy meats.

Upon his return, a thin man in his early forties inhabited the space in his booth where he'd hoped Charlotte would sit. Charlie stutter-stepped, the man unfamiliar to him. The waitress, assuming the man was Charlie's long-awaited companion, had served him a cup of coffee, refilling Charlie's idle cup as well.

"Excuse me," Charlie said as he approached. Any other day, he would've guessed the stranger to be an anonymous source who would plead with him to write a story or, as had happened every so often, the angry subject of one of his columns, though those complaints usually took the form of e-mail or hang-up phone calls.

"Hello, Charlie," the man said, smirking. "I hope you don't mind."

"I'm expecting someone, actually," Charlie replied.

"This'll take a minute," the man said. He extended his hand. "I'm Robert Richter."

"Do we know each other?" Charlie asked. He let Robert Richter's hand fall unshaken.

"I work for Tom Gabbard," Richter said, his voice lowering needlessly, as the coffee shop had emptied of everyone, including the waitress.

Charlie searched his mind for any unsavory insinuation he might have made about the county attorney in any of his recent columns, but he couldn't recall any. "This is my personal time," he said. "If you could e-mail me—"

"Why didn't you go to the Christmas party tonight?" Richter asked, his face lit with curiosity. Charlie noticed that Richter hadn't shaved in a number of days, and he began to doubt that Richter worked for Gabbard. "I thought for sure you'd go to the Christmas party."

"Do you have some identification?" Charlie asked. Had Richter actually shown up at the Christmas party? Or had he been following him since he left the office? Richter's casual demeanor suggested the latter, but Charlie couldn't be sure.

Richter comically touched the lapels of his charcoal suit and shrugged.

"How do I know you work for the county attorney?" Charlie asked. People could say they were anyone, he knew.

Richter shook his head. "I work for Tom Gabbard," he said, his gray eyes slitting above a quick smile. "There's a subtle difference, if you catch me."

Charlie didn't, but the freight of Robert Richter's abrupt appearance dashed what small hopes he had that Charlotte would assent to his plea to meet. He'd left specific instructions on her answering machine, calling once and hanging up just to hear her voice. Leaving a message was a bad idea, he knew, but he'd run out of options.

"I'd like to ask you a couple of questions," Richter said, raising his coffee cup to his chapped lips. He reminded Charlie more of a surfer than a . . . what was he? An investigator?

Charlie waved at the waitress to bring his check, an indication Richter mistook as his acceding to the request.

"How important would you say integrity is to what you do?" Richter asked, as nonchalant as asking him the time.

Charlie blinked rapidly, remembering a piece from last Friday's edition about how liars tend to blink more rapidly than those professing the truth. He remembered the piece was not about rapid eye movement's relation to the truth, but was a profile of an outgoing Arizona State University psychology professor beloved by his students for the past twenty years. "The answer seems self-evident," he said.

Richter smiled. "Agreed," he said, nodding. "What's more important, eh? Everything springs from integrity, right?"

The double rhetorical relaxed Charlie; here was no professional, just a hired hack—possibly hired by Tom Gabbard, but possibly not—fishing for . . . what?

"The world is lousy with people who can't understand that concept, though," Richter added. "Your paper is full of them."

19

Charlie wasn't sure if Richter meant the content of the paper or his colleagues, an uncomfortable thought aggravated by Richter's pulling out a pack of cigarettes.

"You can't smoke in restaurants," Charlie warned him more stridently than was called for.

Richter shook free a cigarette and lit it with a fat silver lighter. The waitress materialized and Charlie braced for rebuke, but to his surprise she left the check and ambled back into oblivion.

"I know the owner," Richter said.

Charlie reached into his pocket, wondering if he could still make the Christmas party at Mary Elizabeth's. His colleagues would've outpaced him at the open bar, but their mirth would be a welcome salve to the raw wound of being both stood up by Charlotte and haunted by Richter, who posed two or three more questions that were variables of the first, before stubbing his cigarette out in his coffee cup. Charlie tapped the twenty he'd laid across the check and considered leaving without his change, a gesture he was sure would mean something more to Richter than his just wanting to flee the scene.

"You must think you're the cat's ass," Richter said.

Charlie felt his back straighten. "Excuse me?"

"The youngest columnist in the *Sun*'s history," Richter said. He let out a whistle. "You got something on old Darrell Torrence, something you're holdin' over his fat head?"

Charlie hadn't heard the *Sun* publisher's given name spoken since his days at the *Phoenix Tab*, the weekly where he'd started on the west side of Phoenix after his brief foray into the New York literary scene, the only remnants of which were a stack of *Shout!* magazines, featuring his only published short story, and a box of copies of *Last Wish*, his novelization of the movie of the same name that he'd written for money under the pseudonym

J. D. Martens. In the end, he hadn't possessed the fortitude to ruminate continually on human weakness and desire, to catalog life's ambiguities in the hope of suggesting meaning, and so had ended his career as a fiction writer. He'd settled for the notion that his columns would be his legacy, however small, an archive of his thoughts and feelings, proof that he'd lived.

To everyone at the *Sun*, as well as his admirers and foes, Darrell Seymour Torrence Jr. was known as Duke. Duke the renegade publisher. Duke the decorated World War II pilot. Duke the philanthropist, appearing in the pages of the *Sun* every other week at this charity ball or that, flashing his famously toothy grin.

"Look, I don't—"

"I'm joshing you," Richter said. "I know you earned it. When Mr. Gabbard asked me to talk to you, I remembered your name from the *Tab*."

"Why did Mr. Gabbard ask you to talk to me?"

Richter didn't hear the question, or ignored it. "It isn't every day that someone changes the world, right?"

"No one can change the world," Charlie retorted.

"But they can change the laws, right?"

Charlie nodded involuntary. There was no sense in arguing over what had been the defining moment of his career, Heather's law, named for Heather Lambert, the girl who had been killed in a hit-and-run accident out in Tolleson, the small, predominantly Hispanic community west of Phoenix, by an illegal alien working as a day laborer on a nearby farm. The *Tab* had sent Charlie to talk to Heather's high school teachers and, preferably, to get an exclusive with the girl's parents. Just six months back from New York by way of a road trip to Los Angeles, Charlie had no connections in the local police or in any city hall

21

in any town in the metro Phoenix area, so verifying even the basic facts of the incident required a level of sleuthing that he hadn't yet acquired. It was apparent the real story was that the farmer who had employed the illegal alien was a Tolleson king-pin and that the wheels of justice would turn slowly, if it all, in tracking down the illegal alien, who had fled back across the border after running the red light and plowing into sixteen-year-old Heather Lambert, sending her flying, her body deposited hard against the oil-stained blacktop at the gas station adjacent to the intersection. Charlie had proposed a piece to his editor at the *Tab* implying that if Heather Lambert had been from Tolsun Farms, the gated community on the outskirts of Tolleson, the farmer would already be arrested, an article his editor promised to fire him over if he wrote it.

Charlie surrendered to his assignment and attacked the story not from the human-interest angle—he canceled his scheduled follow-ups with Heather's teachers and classmates and gave up trying to contact her parents—but in pursuit of the truth. Heather Lambert should've been dreaming of endless summer days at the community pool, splashing in the tepid water with her friends, dreading the return to school as the calendar turned from June to July to August. Instead, a wealthy farmer enjoyed the protection of lax prosecution of ambiguous immigration laws (these were the precise words he was able to extract from a prosecutor down-town and ran as a pull quote in his first piece on the Lambert case). Charlie hammered away at the farmer, who engaged a law firm to bother the *Tab* with threatening letters alleging libel, but the *Tab*'s circulation had increased as a result of Charlie's investigation, giving him implicit carte blanche to carry on.

Soon, the farmer began to lose accounts, and his lawyers squawked to the other papers and the local television stations that a junior reporter at a local newspaper was ruining a man's livelihood. The same lawyers protested that the illegal alien had been captured and was being extradited, that justice had been served, which, true or not, didn't quell the outrage toward the farmer, who stood in front of the TV cameras and sheepishly declared that the accused had never worked for him in any capacity and, further, that the accused had stolen the vehicle from the fleet of cars he kept on the farm. The farmer's admission gave Charlie another angle to pursue, and he uncovered that many of the day laborers at the farm were illegal aliens paid in cash. Worse, the illegals were part of a network of laborers whose availability was brokered by a set of individuals who had infiltrated the Hispanic populations around Phoenix. Charlie spent a fruitless few weeks trying to unmask the identities of these brokers, and his editor relegated him to the opinion page because he didn't possess all the facts. By the time his name was known around town, the farmer had been forced into bankruptcy and Heather's law, making the hiring of illegal aliens punishable by jail for each offense, had been swiftly enacted. And not long after that the receptionist at the *Tab* called out that Darrell Torrence was on the phone for him.

"How did they catch Derek Green?" Richter asked.

"I don't know," Charlie said, waving the twenty at the waitress. "Before my time."

"They dealt harshly with him," Richter said.

"Yeah, they don't like it when you falsify your sources," Charlie said.

The waitress finally confiscated the check and the twenty.

"Rumor has it old Duke was so mad he called every paper within a four-state radius and told them not to hire Green."

"Doubt it," Charlie said. A smear of white glinted under the

23

arc lights outside the window, and Charlie leaped out of the booth, breezing past the waitress and out into the crisp evening air. What he had hoped was Charlotte's Volkswagen Passat was in reality a Honda Civic. It made a U-turn in the coffee shop parking lot and cut into the flow of traffic streaming down Central Avenue.

Chapter Three

Though few students would become Garden Lakes fellows, most would pass through its gates as freshmen during the freshman retreat. Garden Lakes itself was in the town of Maricopa, which was far enough south of Phoenix to be in another county, Pinal, which confused the average Phoenician, since the metro Phoenix area was known colloquially as Maricopa County. The gates were the only enhancement to the property that had been paid for by the school, the result of some minor vandalism by marauding boondockers committed during the interim between the stall of the development's building phase and the donation of the property to Randolph by Mr. McCloud, a Randolph graduate and federally indicted land developer whose business had been seized by the government. The bus charged through the gates, opened earlier for the Randolph Mothers' Guild, who were putting the finishing touches on the dining hall for that night's dinner, and whizzed past the only green grass in the whole development, fed by an underground sprinkler system, the palm-tree-studded median separating the channels that allowed cars in and out. The development beyond the palms lay before us like a desert playground. Father Vidoni turned right onto Garden Lakes Parkway, the circular drive that traversed the development, the red and white shell crawling toward the encampment at the western edge of Garden Lakes.

The eastern portion of the development lay unfinished. From above, Garden Lakes looked like a sophisticated crop circle, composed of two paved roads—an outer and inner loop—with a wide river of dirt flowing between the loops, the brick community center bridging the two loops at their southernmost convex. The man-made lake at the center of the development yawned like an open maw that had only its top teeth—the twelve houses that constituted Garden Lakes to date, six on either side of the community center.

A dust devil kicked up and danced along the dry lake bed, petering out near the plug of dirt and rock left of center, the island meant for residents to swim out to, which had occurred exactly once, during a family day for the home builder's employees. Garden Lake had brimmed shore to shore with sparkling water that afternoon. Afterward, the ever-evaporating pool reminded everyone involved with the project of the promises a master-planned community could offer, among them safety in an insecure and increasingly violent world, but also an oasis away from the demands that the world could make and that eventually condemned Garden Lakes to abandonment and despair, the liquid heart of Mr. McCloud's dream drying up permanently under the blistering sun.

Mr. McCloud was steadfast in the face of prison time, which he served after a year and a half of raging against what he came to recognize was the only mortal battle that couldn't be won: arbitrariness with unlimited reserves of cash and power. He had, however, made a provision for his most cherished property. Anticipating the crush of the government's fist, he'd deeded Garden Lakes to Randolph as a charitable gift, to be used by the school as it deemed appropriate.

When the livid government trustee took steps to reacquire the property he argued rightfully belonged to taxpayers, Randolph announced the Garden Lakes fellows program, a leadership camp for juniors. The fellows would be sequestered at Garden Lakes with two faculty members and a supporting cast of sophomores, who would work in the dining hall and assist the faculty members while the fellows worked their project: the drywalling of a house framed by a local home-building company, the labor and framing materials gifted by the home builder. Even though the Garden Lakes program featured academic instruction—a philosophy seminar and a class on grammar and written communication—skeptics argued Garden Lakes was institutionalized slave labor, that Randolph had designs on selling the development for a profit upon its completion—or worse, giving the development back to Mr. McCloud, who would in turn sell it; but over the years, Garden Lakes had become a model for similar programs. (Word reached Randolph that the program had a papal blessing.) In addition, college recruiters who washed up on Randolph's academic shores were curious about which boys were Garden Lakes fellows, causing the sophomore subscription rate to double, each sophomore hoping his volunteered labor would win him a fellowship as a junior.

Father Vidoni honked the horn to announce their arrival. Two eager sophomores whose mothers had brought them directly saluted the bus from the shade of the palm tree waving like a flag from the island, which over the years had been weathered into a dirt cone. A yellow spray of desert dandelion had grown over a squiggle of desert lily, giving the dry lake's lip a mustard-colored mustache. The sophomores jumped over the flowers, dust stirring in their footprints as they made their way to the bus.

To the left lay the sophomore housing; the fellow housing ran in the other direction. The housing was separated by a state-of-the-art dining hall slash classroom slash auditorium slash chapel (slash dance hall for the Singles' Retreat), the building originally constructed as an elementary school for the someday students of Garden Lakes. As the new owners of the development, Randolph gutted the elementary school, customizing it to meet the needs of a desert renewal center. A blanket of prickly pear and barrel cactus, fit snug around a stand of saguaro, encircled the community center, designed to keep out desert predators.

Though no street signs were posted in the development—the reflective green and white totem marking Garden Lakes Parkway had been stolen by the boondockers, who, by now, were in their early thirties—the plans filed with the city called for streets named Palomino Drive, Rockridge Way, Whispering Wind Road, Evening Glow Street, and Lakeland Avenue. Over the years, however, the fellows had rechristened the streets of Garden Lakes: High Street (juniors), Low Street (sophomores); Upper Parkway, Lower Parkway; East Street and West Street. Randolph finally chose Regis and Loyola, easy identifiers correlating to the buildings back on campus where the juniors and sophomores kept their lockers. Each completed house at Garden Lakes had been numbered in honor of a previous class. We numbered our remodel 1959 Regis Street as a tribute to Kevin Randolph, the last Randolph descendant to graduate. Word was Kevin Randolph himself would be attending Open House, the ribbon-cutting ceremony at the end of our fellowship.

Out the window, beyond the community center and past the outer loop, we saw the Grove, the mountain range of dirt and gravel dumped long ago for the landscaping to be done at Garden Lakes, mounds of limestone, pitchstone, basalt, quartzite, sandstone, dolomite, slate, and shale now overrun with weeds and desert critter tracks.

Hands, who would one day lead his family's sixth-generation brewery to ruin, and Figs, who would later succeed in covering up an embezzlement at his firm, had started the rumor that they'd occupy the first house on Regis Street. While this house was the oldest house in the development, it was also the model home built to lure in potential homeowners and had been outfitted with the extras that the other houses lacked: wallpaper, designer faucets, dark-stained wood cabinets (as opposed to the plywood cabinets painted white in the houses by the fellows), wood-slat blinds (not white or crème-colored aluminum), Saltillo floor tile (the other houses had thin, playroom-style carpet, linoleum in the kitchen), and a working electric garage door. All the houses had been furnished by Furniture America, whose president was a Randolph alum. Hands and Figs knew they would be booted down to one of the other houses, as the two model homes were restricted to faculty, but this being Mr. Malagon's first year, and Mr. Malagon being an iconoclast, they thought they had a shot of nonchalantly moving in, bumping Malagon, whose mysterious exit from Garden Lakes no one would ever be able to forgive, down the street. It was this arrogance masked as innocence that galled the rest of us. Hands and Figs knew it profited more times than not (though Mr. Malagon wouldn't be suckered out of the model home).

The bus gasped as Father Vidoni brought the vehicle to a stop in front of the junior abodes. The ride from Randolph had been a long one—not mileage-wise, but encapsulated-in-sweat-and-farts-and-BO-wise. Mr. Hancock, whose departure from Garden Lakes would send us to our doom, refused to let the windows down during freeway travel, citing the noise level as his reason, *reminding us that he didn't need to have a reason.*

29

The floorboard was warmed from travel, and we did our best to form a single-file line and disembark patiently, Mr. Hancock stationed at the back of the bus, with Mr. Malagon up near the finish line, low-fiving us as our duffel bags pulled us out the glass accordion bus doors. We gathered in a semicircle in the street. The sun blasted light through the windows of the framed and stuccoed house that stood along the avenue. The supply shed that housed all the necessary implements rose out of the cul-de-sac, a mistress of hard labors to come.

"Okay, you boys," Mr. Hancock said, "you know the drill. Sleeping arrangements are of your own choosing. There will be no switching houses, so choose prudently. Mr. Malagon and I will take up in the faculty residences." A glimpse between them implied they'd worked out in advance who would live on which side. "Dinner with Mr. McCloud is at five p.m. Mr. Malagon?"

Mr. Hancock had evidently meant to call Mr. Malagon to step back onto the bus, but Mr. Malagon took the question to mean did he have anything to say, and told us, "No fucking around now," a phrase of endearment he'd uttered many times in his class, permitting us to use the same type of language as long as we used it in a clever fashion, never out of anger and never toward one another, and Mr. Hancock's face drained of color.

Mr. Malagon reboarded the bus, standing in the stairwell as the bus pulled forward a short distance, then stopped to let off the sophomores, who milled about tentatively. Mr. Hancock and Mr. Malagon's arrival on Loyola Street was hailed by the sophomores who had not been allowed to ride the bus but had been brought by their mothers, who were unwilling to let their sons off until Mr. Hancock and Mr. Malagon arrived; these mothers – who, for either personal or political or financial reasons, were not part of the Mothers' Guild—waited with the agenda of introducing themselves to the faculty members for the express purpose of Making an Impression on behalf of their sons, who would soon be eligible for consideration for the fellowship.

Mr. Hancock and Mr. Malagon greeted the eager mothers, Mr. Malagon subjecting their sons to random bag checks before allowing them to settle into any one of the four-bedroom houses they desired, the houses farthest from the faculty residence filling up first.

The juniors quickly lost interest in the Loyola Street goings-on. The memory of having stood on that side was too fresh for some, who worried about their worthiness for duty on Regis Street. It was one thing, as a sophomore, to work in the kitchen and in the laundry, studying the assigned texts in the afternoon and before bed, but it was another thing to be charged with the responsibilities of a fellow, the failure of such endeavors to be known ever after; and even if they were completed—and they were never not completed—generations of fellows and alums would submit your contribution to scrutiny, sure to find fault somewhere within the walls of your achievement.

There had been much talk on the bus about possible roommate combinations, incorporating such factors as who was known to be a slob, who was a neatnik, who was most likely to hog the common area, who took long showers, who might spend the bulk of his free time in his room (complete with innuendo as to what he would be doing in his room), and a top-to-bottom scorecard of everyone's BO, provided by Hands and Figs, who both scored counterintuitively low on the scale.

Certain implicit truths had to be factored in once we were faced with the actual decision, the problem much like the problems that confounded those of us who had participated in SAT prep and the mock SAT taken one temptingly beautiful spring Saturday:

There are five three-bedroom houses and twelve students who must live (peacefully and harmoniously) in said houses for forty days and forty nights. The following statements, however, apply:

1. *Q and Assburn cannot be in the same house.*
2. *Hands and Figs must be in the same house.*
3. *No one wants to live with Roger.*
4. *Sprocket must live in the house with wheelchair access.*
5. *Warren and Lindy don't care which house they live in.*
6. *Smurf (secretly) does not want to live with Sprocket.*

These complications were ingrained in everyone's minds, having lived with the various prejudices for what felt like forever, so we assembled in our respective houses as if we were coming home from a long day of work at the mill. Lindy joined Figs and Hands in the house next to Mr. Malagon; Assburn and Roger and Smurf took up in the house next to them. Their neighbors were Warren and Sprocket and me. Q was our lone neighbor for the moment; the final two fellows—Tony "the Terminator" Watson and Jimbo Jergens—would presumably arrive with their mothers and the rest of the Randolph Mothers' Guild.

A tornado of engine noise rumbled as the first of what would be six weekly grocery deliveries arrived, the truck's logo artfully spelling out the last name (in curlicues) of the grocery magnate whose son was a freshman at Randolph, the donation an obvious appeal for consideration of his son's unofficial application to become a Garden Lakes fellow a couple of years hence. Previously, Garden Lakes had relied on one of the faculty members to make grocery trips into town with one of the Jeeps belonging to the property, towing along a couple of sophomores as cart pushers and bag handlers. This proved a burden on the faculty member who stayed behind, though, since the fellows and sophomores alike could smell when they had the upper hand, even if they were unsure how to exercise this transitory rise to power. Occasionally, someone would sacrifice himself, generating a distraction while others raided the dining hall or sneaked out into the desert with a bottle they'd succeeded in smuggling into Garden Lakes.

Mr. Hancock advised the driver that the loading dock was best accessed from the outer loop, the driver and his passenger intrigued by the petite, neatly coiffed mothers and their imported cars. Mr. Malagon yelled that he would meet the truck around, leaving Mr. Hancock to fend for himself among the genuflecting mothers.

One by one the cars on Loyola Street vanished, the bus giving a final honk as it rattled through the gates, the good-bye carrying through the window Q had thrown open to aerate his stale room. He shook out the dark blue comforter donated by Furniture America and folded it, sliding it under his bed.

Smurf, who would one day successfully slander a female colleague at his family's corporation with whom he'd been cheating on his wife, appeared in the doorway, his arm behind his back. "Guess what I found taped under the sink in the bathroom?"

"What?" Q asked, annoyed.

Smurf brandished a tattered copy of *Penthouse* magazine, fanning the worn pages for effect.

"I didn't hear you knock," Q said.

"Roger is in our bathroom, so I used yours," Smurf said. He looked both ways down the hall, a time-honored move known more formally by its nickname, the Randolph Backcheck, and asked Q if he remembered the week Figs was absent from school, his family's impromptu vacation.

"Yeah," Q said, "before finals."

"His family didn't go on vacation," Smurf said. "Figs was in the hospital."

Q, the future husband of a swimsuit model, stopped rifling through his duffel bag and looked at Smurf. Once this tidbit had sunk in, Smurf continued: "Remember that night, the weekend before Figs's absence? Summer Griffith's party in McCormack Ranch Park?"

Q shrugged.

"Well," Smurf started, "remember I went with Assburn? And we turned out to be the only other juniors there besides Hands and Figs? Some sort of senior party. They'd expelled a couple of sophomores with a garden hose before we got there. So anyway, Assburn and I decided to bail and hit the Hump and a couple of other spots. But I forgot my hat—you know the one, the orange fisherman's hat that I got in Mazatlán; some senior chick snatched it, and I let her, thinking I'd get it later. So anyway, Assburn started the car and I went after my hat. I don't find the chick anywhere and start floating between the rooms upstairs and downstairs. No luck. Finally I go out the sliding glass door to the backyard and see the hat bouncing behind this hedge in the back part of the yard, this immense cow-pasture thing. I asked some-one on the patio if they knew the name of the girl who was wear-ing the orange hat, and she said, 'What girl?' So I pointed out the spot of orange in the hedges, and the girl said, 'What orange?' 'Never mind,' I said, and moseyed in the direction of my hat. As I step closer, I hear some noises, some grunting and some smack-ing, and so I'm having second thoughts, but I'm caught in this no-man's-land where everyone who is looking can see me and there's no way to turn around without acting like a complete doo-fus. So I slow up, trying to figure an escape, when Hands comes

34

from the hedges. 'Hey, Smurf,' he says as he passes me. But it's not the usual Hands, you know? He's looking at the ground, and walking fast, not cool like he normally does. I said hey back and figured it's cool to go and get my hat, which at this point I didn't really care about, but, you know." Q shrugged again. "So guess what I saw when I reached the girl who had my hat?"

"I heard this already," Q said. "Robert Samuels told me. He told me not to say anything, though."

"What did he tell you?"

"It's too stupid to repeat." Q went back to sifting through his duffel.

"Samuels doesn't know shit." Q knew Smurf was dying to tell him, but Q didn't want to be baited into asking. He knew Smurf well enough to know that if he was patient, Smurf would blurt it out. "What did he tell you?"

"He told me what happened. I'm telling you, it's too stupid."

"Yeah, but what did he say? Did he tell you about Figs?"

Samuels had told him the same story he'd told a half dozen of us, that Hands had banged the senior chick while Figs watched, masturbating. Q was sure Smurf knew the story, thereby knowing the real reason Figs had taken a week off, too embarrassed to face everyone. But the story had died in its sails when Hands denied it.

"Did he tell you about Figs?" Smurf asked again.

"Hands said it didn't happen," Q said.

"Bullshit," Smurf said. "I saw it."

"You saw it?"

"Was standing right there when it started. I walked in and Figs was smoking pot with some of the seniors, maybe seven dudes and a couple of chicks. They thought I was the cops when I busted through the hedge"—Smurf grinned at this—"but Figs said, 'He's cool,' and they went about their business."

35

"Why are you *re*telling me this story?"

"I'm trying to tell you the *real* story, dude. You're not listening."

"I'm listening."

"So I was talking to this girl about how I needed my hat back when Figs and a couple of the other guys started wrestling around. But I see that they aren't wrestling at all. The seniors are beating the shit out of Figs."

"Why?"

"Don't know."

"What did Hands do?"

"That's what I'm saying."

"What?"

"He didn't do anything. He walked away."

Q looked at Smurf doubtfully.

"Honest Injun," Smurf said, crossing himself.

The story agitated Q. "Go to your own house, why don't you?"

A look of resignation came over Smurf and he drifted toward the door.

"Leave the magazine."

He tossed the magazine on Q's bed and made for the front door.

Down the street, Assburn and Roger settled into their rooms. Assburn, who would plunge to his death in a frozen lake somewhere just this side of the Canadian border, was unhappy about living with Roger but knew there was nothing he could do about it. Recently, Roger had taken to Assburn, inviting him over to his house after school "for some target practice." Roger had ambushed Assburn with the invitation, catching him in front of the gymnasium so that Assburn wasn't ready with an excuse. Truth was, Assburn had nothing to do and nowhere to go. Roger was delighted when he nodded yes.

After an artillery stop at Roger's house, a two-story colonial set behind a fence of oleander ("reinforced with chain link and barbed wire," Roger told him), they made for the shooting range, where Roger's father, Colonel Dixon, was well into his rounds. Assburn admitted that he didn't know much about guns—he'd once shot a Mountain Dew can with a .22 at his uncle's ranch back in Minnesota—but Roger, who would later be absent without leave in Iraq, reassured him, "We've got something for you."

Silence blew through Roger's open-air Jeep on the long ride to the shooting range. It always amazed Assburn that something like the shooting range could exist right outside of Phoenix and he'd never heard of it. He'd felt the same way when he learned that the wedding-cake structure off the I-17 was a castle with underground passages, dating back to the early 1900s. Phoenix seemed to Assburn to be something of an archaeological dig: On the surface it looked like sun and sky and palm trees and glass skyscrapers and desert, bereft of history, like a movie set, but for anyone willing to dig and sift through the sand, odd artifacts and buried history emerged, presenting themselves as dramatically as the Ben Avery Shooting Range.

"Ever shoot clay?" Roger asked.

Assburn shook his head.

"That's okay, my father's over at the targets, anyway," Roger said, unloading the rifles and a box of pistols.

The colonel scarcely registered Assburn's presence as he and Roger set up at the aluminum TV trays provided for the shooters. The riflemen—there were no women—laid their weapons down on the metal tables as their targets were retrieved and replaced by men in yellow vests. Roger put his hand on Assburn's wrist as Assburn went to unzip the case on the rifle Roger had handed to him in the parking lot. "Wait until it's clear," Roger whispered, looking at his father. The colonel pretended to be looking off in the distance at his new target.

"All clear!" one of the yellow vests yelled, and Roger let up on Assburn's wrist.

In the span of an hour and a half, Assburn shot an artillery of rifles: a Remington Sporting 28; a Beretta 687 Silver Pigeon II; a Browning A-Bolt that knocked him back, almost knocking him over, soliciting the only remark the colonel made that afternoon—"Should've brought the old Winchester I gave you for your tenth birthday," he said to Roger, chuckling. Assburn's shoulder ached as he tried to hold his arm steady for the box of Ruger Old Army revolvers Roger opened. Conversation among the shooters was rhythmic, fit in the space between the claps and cracks of rifle fire, but Assburn didn't understand what the shooters meant by things like "sporting recoil pad" and "bore size." His targets were consistently cleaner than Roger's or the colonel's.

By the next morning, Assburn had a hard time believing the previous afternoon had even happened, and Roger passed Assburn wordlessly in the hallway and Assburn mentioned it to no one.

Assburn parted the blinds in his room with his fingers, watching Q as he broached the man-made lake, shielding his eyes while peering out at the landscape. He watched the last of the Randolph Mothers' Guild arrive, parking their cars around the community center. His master plan had been to offer to room with Q if no one else did, but he hadn't counted on the absent fellows. He almost volunteered anyway, but the prospect of Q protesting in front of everyone kept Assburn silent.

The year leading up to Garden Lakes had not gone the way he had figured. Toward the end of his sophomore year, a scrape he had with a senior he'd sold a radar detector to—the senior accused Assburn of trying to resell him his own radar detector, and Assburn didn't know for sure that the senior was mistaken—had led Assburn to the realization that everyone on campus thought he was a lowlife criminal. He'd started his B and E exercises out of boredom and, bolstered by the demand side of the equation, out of a sense of fulfillment. As Assburn punched out a panel of glass in an Arcadia door or ripped out a bedroom screen, he kept his clients' needs in mind, covetous of the looks on their faces when he surprised them with just what they were looking for. But after the senior split Assburn's lip in the parking lot of Lenny's Burger shop while some of his other customers looked on, Assburn desperately wanted to change his image. He knew he could quit thieving; his paranoia about being caught had risen in recent months. He imagined his clients would be able to satisfy their need for discount electronics, jewelry, and guns in the parking lots of any of the public high schools, or through any number of other small-time dealers Assburn had met in his underworldly travels. The more he turned the idea over, the surer he was of his decision. And so when, the first week of junior year, two seniors asked him if he had any women's diamond rings, he announced to them that he was out. The seniors tried to shake him down, accusing him of holding out, but Assburn held fast. He hoped his classmates noticed.

Word did travel that Assburn was out of the game, but it traveled slowly; and the number of Assburn's customers was small compared with the overall student body, so while his customers quit asking him for goods, the perception that Assburn was a juvenile delinquent followed him wherever he went. To his credit, he didn't revert to his old ways. He believed people would come around, if not soon, then by graduation, which was Assburn's personal goal.

A step toward that goal was returning the presidential signing pen that he'd stolen from Q's father.

Since Randolph formed the outermost boundary of our existence, Assburn didn't consider the (possibly legal) punishment Senator Quinn could've inflicted on him. Assburn's only concern was with Q, and how to return the pen without incurring Q's wrath, or exposure to his peers or to the administration.

Various plans had developed during Assburn's guardianship of the pen. The first and most obvious solution was to break back into Q's house during school and replace the pen in the senator's study. But Assburn couldn't reconcile getting caught *returning* something. In the past, he'd been prepared to go down if caught in the act of procuring; he knew an arrest would in all likelihood result in some community service and a parole officer and little else, and he'd relished the idea of the hero or cult status he would achieve if arrested. These thoughts had left him, however, by his junior year, displaced by an aspiration to be thought of as an equal member of his class.

Another plan was to mail the pen back, wearing gloves while assembling the package, careful not to lick the stamps. Assburn had scoped out a mailbox near Biltmore Fashion Park, miles from his house, where he spent one afternoon a month wandering the Sharper Image while his mother had her hair and nails done. But to mail back the pen would correct only part of the problem; Q would continue to disparage Assburn even if the pen magically turned up in the mail.

Assburn knew that he was going to have to return the pen personally. On several occasions, he fastened the pen against his leg with a thick rubber band, but the opportunity to approach Q never presented itself. Assburn found himself walking down Q's street, slowing in front of the gates to his house, hoping Q would see him and call out. But the only one who ever called out to Assburn was the landscaper, a Hispanic who waved at Assburn from his riding lawn mower. Assburn flirted with planting the pen on the landscaper, like they did in the movies, but his multiple trips to Dauphine Street made him reconsider. No doubt one of the neighbors, or their security cameras, could ID him, if it came to that.

Finally the right situation appeared, and Assburn was glad that he'd waited. When he saw his name a few lines above Q's on the roster of Garden Lakes fellows, his hopes surged. Even if Q made noise about the pen, it would only be in front of a limited audience, and during the summer, which would permit the incident—if there was to be an incident—to cool before the start of their senior year.

Assburn removed the pen from his duffel bag. He'd wrapped it in paper towels, sealing it in a Ziploc freezer bag. He stowed the package under the mattress, bouncing on the bed to be sure the bulge was undetectable. Downstairs, Mr. Hancock's voice boomed about the ten-degree savings that ceiling fans afforded, cautioning the boys not to be late to dinner.

The smells from the kitchen filled the hallway: roasted chicken, and dill-seasoned potatoes, and steamed vegetables, and lemon tuna steaks, and rice and beans, and pies—blueberry and lemon and hot apple, begging to be topped with a globe of ice cream or sherbet. The double glass doors at either end of the hallway that bisected the community center sealed us in with the olfactory splendor.

One half of the community center was further divided into two equal rooms—a classroom and a chapel, the rectangle windows of the classroom overlooking the inner loop. The right side of the center held the cafeteria-grade kitchen and pantry, which took up the back fourth of the building nearest the loading dock. The kitchen was well ventilated by the two screen doors, one off the hallway and one on the south side of the building. In the afternoon, scents emanating from the kitchen were known to bring famished desert vermin.

The kitchen was cleverly segregated by a portable wall easily managed by four to six underclassmen. When positioned properly, the wall left about four feet on either side. Placement was dependent upon the event; for the dances at the Singles' Retreat, it was pressed up against the outer kitchen counter (where breakfast and lunch were served); for dinners such as the Randolph Mothers' Guild dinner with Mr. McCloud, the dividing wall was angled diagonally, so the servers—the Randolph mothers—flashed in a dizzy blur from behind the wall like cohosts on a game show.

Mr. Hancock and Mr. Malagon accompanied Mr. McCloud at the large, round, white-linen-draped table in the center of the room. The remaining places were set, and consequently the fellows filled the other tables up quickly to avoid having to sit with the faculty and Mr. McCloud, so quickly that disparate dinner parties arose, the diners making furtive glances at the door to mark what luckless soul would wander in not knowing his dinner was to be ruined by the repetition of "Yes, sir" and "No, sir."

We were to be disappointed, though. Mr. Hancock and Mr. Malagon dined with Mr. McCloud, whose arm shook imperceptibly as he brought the tortilla soup to his lips. Some years older than the portrait of his likeness that hung in McCloud Hall, he appeared haggard. It seemed that Mr. Hancock and Mr. Malagon had trouble sustaining him in conversation. We realized that

Mr. McCloud was barely cognizant of his surroundings, and so we openly gaped at him. We'd never known anyone who had been to prison, and as we scarfed down the delicious entrées ostensibly prepared (everyone knew the dinner was catered) by the mothers of boys whom, since they were underclassmen, we would never truly know, our youth lent us a superiority toward Mr. McCloud, whom we'd joke about later.

The white sun gleamed through the curtained windows, showing no signs of evening. Dessert was served, unleashing a symphony of silver spoons clinking against china plates, such props disappearing with the caterers after the dinner, along with all traces of the opposite sex, their perfumes and hair sprays lingering as some of us took down the dining room and swung the movable wall against its stationary brethren, permitting easy access to the stainless steel counter with its cutouts for hot dishes, a board game missing its pieces, awaiting the blitz of the breakfast crowd.

After dinner, we settled into our houses. Mr. Malagon called some of us out to the sidewalk, inviting us to beat him at a game of beanbag, a wastebasket from his residence standing in for the beanbag board, with its coffee-can crown and slope of polished wood, that Mr. Malagon kept in his classroom. "All or nothing," Mr. Malagon said, arcing four beanbags one after another into the wastebasket from thirty feet. Our sweat-stained clothes began to dry as the sun finally dropped behind the horizon. The catering truck roared away from the community center, its cough fading until all of Garden Lakes was still. The streetlights buzzed and a purple pulse of light shone above the street. It would be another few minutes before the lights would fully engage, and for a moment, there was both nothing to see and nothing to hear except the plop of denim squares weighted with navy beans falling into a plastic wastebasket.

Mr. Hancock strolled leisurely down the street toward us, and everyone except Mr. Malagon and Roger quit tossing beanbags. Some filtered off toward their residences, feigning tiredness or eagerness to get a fresh start for the day ahead. Mr. Hancock reached the beanbaggers, stopping a few feet from the wastebasket as Roger concentrated on his last throw, his first attempts strewn like dead rodents along the sidewalk. Roger moved his arm back and forth, as if weighing his payload, then let the beanbag fly with a flick of his wrist that caused it to sail right of the wastebasket.

"Damn," Roger said, forgetting about Mr. Hancock.

"What's that, Mr. Dixon?" Mr. Hancock bellowed.

Roger looked up from the playing field, startled. He narrowed his eyes as Mr. Hancock continued toward him. Mr. Malagon stepped between them and collected the beanbags and wastebasket. The rest of us dispersed, saluting one another good night and joshing one another about checking for rattlesnakes before jumping into bed, a scare that was more effective with the sophomores than the fellows, since we knew Garden Lakes was fumigated prior to the fellowship program, the perimeter secured with pesticides and herbicides. Most of us had come upon snakes in our lifetime, though, either hiking Squaw Peak or stalking golf balls in the rough, and so we had learned at an early age that there was very little that would deter a rattlesnake from going wherever it wanted to go.

Mr. Hancock and Mr. Malagon spoke briefly on the sidewalk. Hands and Figs tried to listen from Figs's open window but couldn't make out anything other than the sound of Mr. Hancock's low mutters peppered with Mr. Malagon's interjections. We'd know soon enough what they were discussing, though, as rumor spread that Jimbo and the Terminator were no-shows,

44

and that the administration was unprepared for such a situation. There'd never been a fellow who hadn't accepted eagerly—*two* was a historic precedent—and there was no such thing as alternates.

We cursed Q his good fortune, living alone for the summer. Warren and Smurf gathered in Hands and Figs's living room for a bull session after Mr. Hancock's tour of the thermostats. Smurf guaranteed us that Mr. Hancock would force Q to live with him or with Mr. Malagon. Smurf said he'd go to Mr. Hancock first thing in the morning and volunteer to move in with Q, secretly relieved at the idea of getting out of the same house as Roger. We knew Mr. Hancock would not accept Smurf's proposal. It may be that extraordinary times demand extraordinary measures, but Mr. Hancock wouldn't allow any fundamental rule to be bent, breached, or broken, regardless of whether or not the violation solved the problem.

The problem was to have an organic resolution. Lindy, who would die in his sleep in his early thirties, leaving behind a bereaved wife and two small children, knew it first, gazing out his window at the night sky. Lindy watched as Q slipped across the street, his duffel bag slung across his back. He cut across the dry lake bed, retreating to a set of headlights that awoke upon his approach. The headlights dimmed. The sound of tires squealing was drowned by the loud yips of an unseen pack of coyotes. The red flare of taillights was the last anyone would see of Q until school started again in the fall.

Chapter Four

Charlie listened to the outgoing message. The hum of the newsroom receded as he clung to the consonants uncoiling in the lilt of Charlotte's voice. The message assured the caller she was sorry that she'd missed your call, and was eager to talk with you, which Charlie knew was probably true in every case but his. He'd spent the weekend listening to the message after vainly trying to meet up with the *Sun* Christmas revelers, who had disbanded before he could reach Mary Elizabeth's, leaving him to a lonely drink at the bar while the barbacks waded into the vestiges of what looked to have been an epic bash. Nursing his drink, Charlie blamed Richter for Charlotte's no-show at the coffee shop, though he knew his blame was misplaced. Charlotte was intrepid—Charlie was always joking that she'd make a hard-hitting investigative reporter—and Richter's squirrelly countenance wouldn't have deterred her from approaching.

He set the phone back in its cradle as Brennan, his editor, approached in his trademark blustery fashion. Brennan was famous for appearing breathless, as if he'd just eluded capture. "What's the status on the McCloud column?" he panted, leaning against Charlie's desk.

Charlie nodded. "I'll make deadline."

"That's not what I mean," Brennan said.

"What do you mean?"

"I think you know."

Charlie did know what Brennan meant, that the McCloud family had called in protest when they learned about the column being written to mark McCloud's recent passing. The McCloud family matriarch had argued with Brennan to let McCloud rest in peace, and Brennan had privately agreed. Charlie had convinced his editor that because McCloud was a public figure, and a controversial one, the *Sun* was well within its right to cover the passing of one of Phoenix's more notable citizens.

"I think you'll be surprised," Charlie said.

"I never like being surprised," Brennan said before being pulled away by his secretary, who could be seen at all hours of the day hunting Brennan in the reporters' bull pen.

Charlie began dialing Charlotte's number again, undecided if he would leave a message or just listen to her voice, when Billy Gallagher, a lifestyle reporter with a recently coined degree from the Walter Cronkite School of Journalism at Arizona State, breezed by his desk and beckoned him to follow. Such theatrics were usually employed to gossip about which reporters were sleeping together or defecting to another paper or being canned. Charlie watched Gallagher escape into the stairwell and sauntered after him.

"I think Linda noticed," Gallagher said. Linda Macomb, a fellow lifestyle reporter, had the uncanny ability to take a call, write her piece, and converse with someone at her desk all at once. Charlie was intimidated by Linda and gave her a wide berth.

"I don't think so," Charlie said. "She was chasing after Brennan, something about a source that had recanted."

Gallagher leaned against the door to the stairwell.

"What is it?" Charlie asked. Gallagher had married into a prominent Phoenix family that had let him know from the get-go that their daughter was marrying beneath her station, and Charlie had more than once calmed Gallagher's anxieties by kidding that his wife's family's empire was founded on a beer distributorship. "They're drunks, basically," he'd say, which would momentarily cheer Gallagher up before he started worrying all over again.

"I got this private detective on my ass," Gallagher blurted out. "He's asking me questions about the paper. At first I thought it was my prick father-in-law, but this guy, Richter, kept asking about the paper."

Charlie shuddered when he heard Richter's name. "What type of questions?"

"Crazy stuff about what goes on here and about this reporter and that reporter. He even asked about Duke," Gallagher answered. "He asked about you, too. I told him to ask you, and he said he already talked to you."

"I don't think so," Charlie said, wrinkling his brow as if he were drawing a blank. He'd used this ploy before, especially when he was caught out giving contradictory information or realized that whoever he was talking to was about to grasp that he or she had been lied to.

"He said you were uncooperative," Gallagher said.

Charlie smiled. "That sounds like me."

Gallagher smiled involuntarily, worry contorting his face. "Did you talk to him?"

Charlie shook his head. "I have no idea who this guy is." Later, when he reflected back on it, he couldn't rationalize why he'd lied to Gallagher about talking to Richter. He wished he could say his impulse had been to assuage Gallagher's jitters, but in truth his concern was that he was the target of Richter's investigation, though on his life he couldn't guess why.

He spent the rest of the morning in the *Sun* archives, his eyes glancing through past columns for any clue as to why the county attorney would take an interest in him. Charlie hadn't broken any laws, unlike many others whose conduct could only charitably be called lawful. Since the Heather Lambert episode, the law had become a yardstick against which Charlie measured his own behavior, an easier test to pass or fail than the abyss of what was ethical or moral, a test he'd begun to apply to all that had transpired at Garden Lakes. Memories of the high school retreat and Randolph Prep had been on Charlie's mind since he received Father Matthews's call inviting him to lunch at the rectory. Upon his return from New York, Charlie had treated his relocation the only way he knew how: as a move to a new city. He didn't tell the Chandlers, his neighbors from long ago who had acted as his surrogate family and who had gotten him into Randolph, that he'd come back. It was easy enough to avoid his old haunts and familiar shadows so that Phoenix appeared new enough again.

He hadn't kept in touch with anyone from Randolph, though he'd periodically run into someone here and there, most recently Hands, whose wife was the cochair of a breast cancer benefit Charlie attended with Charlotte and her boss, who had sponsored a table. Charlie didn't recognize Hands at first, but the secret they shared from all those years ago forced them into a shy silence, each unclear if the other could rightly recall the promises from the past.

Father Matthews had been Charlie's most fervent Randolph correspondent, writing him a note of appreciation if he approved of one of Charlie's columns, or a gentle but chastising word if he disagreed. His invitation to lunch threatened to elevate their relationship to a new level, one that perplexed Charlie. He wasn't a Catholic, nor was he an alum, having never graduated. And though he passed Randolph twice a day on his way to and from the *Sun* offices, he was never tempted to circle the parking lot or retrace his teenage footsteps.

Gallagher took a half day, grimacing as he brushed past Charlie's desk. He regretted not asking Gallagher what he'd told Richter, if anything. He could imagine Gallagher telling Richter everything he knew or whatever Richter wanted to hear. Charlie knew he couldn't ask now without arousing Gallagher's suspicions. In a long life there are always mistakes made, things to lament, and at thirty-seven Charlie was beginning to feel like he'd already lived forever.

Chapter Five

The Randolph campus was deserted, the students away on Christmas break, a time Charlie remembered as being filled with trips to Vail or California for others, but was just a fermata in the school year for him as he worked on extra-credit projects and wrote papers for independent study in a failed attempt to boost his GPA. As he climbed out of his car, he chuckled at how dire the GPA mess had seemed. He'd had an inkling that life would only be harder after high school, but harder wasn't the right characterization. "Complex" was a better word. But how complex he didn't know then, and on his worst days he pined for the order of rectifying a failing grade with its prescribed and delineated remedies.

Charlie pulled into his former parking spot, the lot repaved and repainted with exacting yellow lines. He crossed the parking lot toward the rectory, circumventing a gold Chevy Impala resembling Brian Velasquez's from back when they were classmates. Beav was a scholarship student from South Phoenix who rode the city bus until his junior year, when he appeared one morning behind the wheel of the gold Impala, which he'd lowered a couple of inches. The thudding bass from the custom stereo made the car pulse. At night, a violet neon light emanated from underneath the car, until the glass tubes were shattered when Randolph installed speed bumps. Beav took enormous static about being the only Hispanic at Randolph, everyone calling him chollo, sometimes in jest and sometimes not. Kids in the other classes referred to him as the beaner, though Beav never let it bother him. Charlie remembered Beav as his biology lab partner and wondered if his dreams of moving to Los Angeles had ever come to be. He was besieged with guilt as he reminisced about Beav, ashamed at all the anti-immigrant sentiment that his articles about Heather Lambert had engendered. An unexpected repercussion of Heather's law had been to give teeth to every racist's call for razor wire along the borders and all sorts of other craziness. Worse, lawmakers had tried to piggyback on Heather's law, and not a single legislative session passed where someone didn't try to introduce a bill in the guise of Heather's law but that was really institutional racism looking for legal cover, such as immigrant teachers with thick accents being removed from their teaching posts for what the Arizona Department of Education termed "incorrect pronunciation" of English words. The previous week's *Sun* had run a story about a group of Hispanic fifth graders who'd had green cards thrown at them while they walked to school.

Father Matthews greeted Charlie as a prodigal son and ushered him from the well-lit carpeted foyer of the rectory and into a dark-paneled room with an oversized oval table made of oak. A tea set had been strategically placed on the table, and Charlie took a chair at Father Matthews's bidding. As his eyes adjusted to the light streaming in from a high window that framed the cloudless winter afternoon, Charlie folded his hands in his lap and answered in the affirmative as Father

Matthews asked a series of benevolent questions meant to put him at ease. He said yes to tea, too, which Father Matthews poured with delicate hands. Charlie watched with fascination as Father Matthews worked like a machine to steep and pour tea for two.

"And do you find your work satisfying?" Father Matthews asked at last.

"Yes, Father." He sipped his tea.

"That's excellent," Father Matthews said. He breathed a ripple across the top of his teacup.

"I was surprised at your invitation," Charlie said.

"Were you?" Father Matthews seemed amused.

"I haven't been back to Randolph in years."

"Perhaps that's why I invited you," Father Matthews said. "Sons of Randolph should not stray so far as that."

"I never actually graduated," Charlie reminded him.

Father Matthews waved him off. His willingness to overlook such an important detail as Charlie's dropping out before his senior year—before he could be called to account for what had happened the previous summer at Garden Lakes—was curious.

"I'm normally skeptical of invitations like these," Charlie said. The air in the room had become clotted with orange and cinnamon.

"Skepticism is not a godly trait," Father Matthews said.

"Occupational hazard," Charlie answered.

"I'm sorry that you must deal with elements that try to mislead you for their own gain," Father Matthews said. "Let me pay you the compliment of direct address." The faint aroma of cigarette smoke stirred as Father Matthews situated himself. "I understand you're working on a column on our dearly departed Brother McCloud."

"I am," Charlie said. It seemed like a hundred years ago that he and the other fellows had sat with Mr. McCloud at dinner. The idea for the column had arisen from the memory of Mr. McCloud at Garden Lakes upon Charlie's reading his obituary in the *Sun*.

"His was a colorful life," Father Matthews said. Charlie imagined Father Matthews likely had to label all kinds of misdeeds as "colorful," including Mr. McCloud's indictment and jail term, as well as the string of bankruptcies and allegations of hidden wealth in overseas bank accounts.

Charlie sat silently sipping his tea, a tactic he'd use when a subject was having a hard time coming to the point. The tea had grown surprisingly cold surprisingly fast.

"May I ask what the thesis of your column is to be?" Father Matthews asked.

"It's a reminiscence about Garden Lakes," Charlie said, surprised at how easily he'd given away information he'd intended to keep secret.

Father Matthews scowled. "But that was twenty years ago," he said.

"Yes," Charlie said, another tactic he'd learned to use when someone was angling for answers he didn't want to give. That the program had been quietly shuttered had been a steady drumbeat in Charlie's heart, and he realized only now how imperative his need to expose what happened was.

"I wonder if anyone will be interested in a column of that nature," Father Matthews said.

"Oh, I've written about all manner of things that people claim not to be interested in," Charlie said, "judging by my mail."

A veil of frustration fell across Father Matthews's face. "Do you think the timing for such a column is right?" he asked.

"Some might think you're exploiting Brother McCloud's death."

"I'm sure some will," Charlie said, and, worried that he was being too flip, added, "I can't control what readers think about these things, Father. There's always someone out there anxious to assume the worst about something or some situation, wouldn't you agree?"

Father Matthews nodded. "I do, my son," he said. "My worry is that you might be creating a situation where a situation doesn't readily exist."

Charlie swirled the residue of his tea and replaced the cup on the tray. Accepting the invitation had been a mistake, and he realized belatedly that he'd only wanted a legitimate reason to visit Randolph.

"Would you like more tea?" Father Matthews asked, his congeniality returning.

"No, thank you, Father," Charlie said.

Father Matthews drank the dregs of his cold tea. "May I inquire into your profession?" he asked.

"Please."

"When you're writing something, a column or what have you"—Father Matthews gesticulated to indicate that he was out of his depth—"how do you know what information to include and what to exclude?"

Charlie thought. "Instinct, I guess," he answered. "When I was with the *Tab*, it was more straight reporting, so the facts were the facts. But with my column, there's more room to ruminate." He regretted inserting this newspaper columnists' joke and covered with, "If you know what I mean."

Father Matthews nodded sagely. "Do you ever struggle with the morality of inclusion?" he asked.

Charlie didn't know what Father Matthews meant and said so.

"I'm sorry. My question is: Do you now and then cross lines by including information that is . . . extraneous?"

"Is there something you want to ask me, Father?" Charlie vowed not to let his perturbation show, though Father Matthews was testing his resolve.

"I'm just inquiring," he said. "I'm wondering at your methods."

Father Matthews wasn't the only one questioning his methods. If Charlotte could borrow Father Matthews's term "morality of inclusion," she would, though it wouldn't bring Charlie any closer to admitting that he'd lied about the illegitimate child he'd fathered at twenty-one. Charlotte had made the discovery by accident, finding a photo he kept tucked away in an envelope in the back of his sock drawer. He never looked at the photo, though he was sure throwing it away would be a sacrilege. But the truth was that he hadn't known of the child's existence until recently and that the girl's mother, a bartender Charlie had briefly known, had kept the pregnancy, birth, and first sixteen years of the girl's life a secret from him. The girl was a stranger to him, someone he could pass on the street without recognizing. Her mother had excluded him from the girl's formative years, the time when the world exercises its influence over you and you become who you become, so in answer to Charlotte's question about why he'd never mentioned the girl, he said, "Why would I?" He argued he was only trying not to complicate their relationship, that he was trying to protect her from the footnotes of his past. But Charlotte was beside herself with rage and grief, saying over and over, "I don't know who you are right now, I don't know you." He pleaded that he was the same person she'd fallen in love with, but this gaffe—though he wasn't willing to confess to anything other than chivalric omission, certainly not immoral exclusion—became insurmountable. An admission of wrongdoing was what Charlotte required, it seemed, but Charlie's instinct was to continue to persuade her of his innocence, that as a fact, the sixteen-year-old girl living in Iowa was of no consequence to the here and now of them and their engagement, an argument that only enraged Charlotte further.

Chapter Six

Sleep came fitfully that first night. The air-conditioning was no match for the weeks of pent-up heat within our residences, and many of us slid our bedroom windows open, the sashes sticking from the dust and dead bugs and spiderwebs encrusted in the metal tracks. The hot night air proved not to be the ally we'd hoped. Also, the open windows were speakers tuned to ominous noises—creaks and croaks and rustling—that frightened us, and our open windows closed, walling each of us inside our twelve-by-twelve tombs.

We woke to the sound of pounding. Mr. Hancock and Mr. Malagon banged on our doors a minute before our alarm clocks could strike four. The thundering of fists made our hearts race, and for a moment we wondered where we were. The blanket of night still hung around Garden Lakes. Fatigued bodies rotated in showers, hurried along by the knocks of their housemates. Once we were out on the street, the sensation of being up at such an early hour was thrilling, as if we were the last human beings left after a terrible scourge. Laughter rang out, all of us dressed in our regulation khakis and short-sleeved white polo shirts, the traditional uniform of a Garden Lakes fellow, and we made our way to breakfast, a variety of cold cereals presented by sophomores who had been awake minutes longer than the rest of us.

Mr. Hancock looked oddly refreshed and urged us to eat our cereal, to have two bowls if we could eat them, and to eat something from the gigantic fruit bowl filled with apples and bananas and oranges and pears. Mr. Malagon advised us to stuff a piece of fruit into our pants as a snack for later, the first official break three hours away.

Our initial surge of adrenaline abated as we paraded into the chapel for the daily prayer. The Garden Lakes chapel was barren of anything remotely religious, save for the pews and the hymnals, dissimilar in every way to the chapel back at Randolph. Absent a confessional and high-windowed ceilings, the Garden Lakes chapel disguised us from one another religiously. At Randolph, it was too clear who was a practicing Catholic—most were—and who was not. And while we were too young to have to cling to differences in religion as a means of separating ourselves from those around us, the demarcation lingered, highlighted in our conscience only at Mass or during chapel.

Mr. Hancock rose. "Let us pray," he began, pausing for the drumming of knees against the carpet as we kneeled, resting our elbows on the pews in front of us. "Our Heavenly Father, bless us this day as we embark on our mission of peace and oneness. Let us value one another and one another's work, for we are all humble servants in your eyes. Let us strive to work diligently and honestly. Let our minds be open. Let us lead by being led and let your word guide us. Amen."

The chorus of "Amen" lacked the reverb it did off the domed ceiling of Saint Frances Xavier, instead evaporating with the noise of us crawling up off our knees. Mr. Hancock called for us

59

to open our hymnals to page 131, to "Before the Ending of the Day," a melodious, fourth-century incantation that Warren had sung repeatedly at Saint Peter the Divine, a Catholic church his mother had once favored in Litchfield Park. The words flowed from Warren's tongue like a language learned through vigorous study: "Before the ending of the day, / Creator of the world, we pray / That with Thy wonted favor, Thou / Wouldst be our guard and keeper now." Warren was suspicious of the rhyme scheme, but as with all things church related, his parents told him it was best not to question the small things. "Make big decisions," his parents said. "Don't spend time on the little questions."

"Before the Ending of the Day" reminded Warren of his uncle, his mother's brother, who had survived a plane crash in his fifties. Walked away from the wreckage as easily as shaking a cold. Up until that day, Warren had sampled many religions. He'd been born and raised in Phoenix, but his parents had migrated from suburb to suburb, staggering through various neighborhoods as renters, Warren's mother never quite content with the street they lived on, or their neighbors. In Glendale, the suburb where Warren was born, a sprawl of farms with livestock, his mother had rejoined her native Methodist Church. Warren's recollection of the Methodists was of their hot chocolate and the giant blue tin of cookies frosted with cubes of sugar the size of diamonds, of which Warren could take as many as he liked.

Across the aisle, Roger, who would go AWOL in Iraq, taking a band of men with him, and be subsequently court-martialed for killing one of them, mumbled the words to the hymn while flipping through the pages of his hymnal, searching not for words of inspiration but for the page number of the book's natural crease. Prior to Garden Lakes, Roger had had no working knowledge about how books were printed, but the colonel had primed him in the rudiments of bindery, about how you could see the individual signatures glued and sewn together if you looked closely at the top of a book. A book's natural crease would fall between signatures; and for the prank to work, the crease had to be avoided.

Roger was unsure of the prank. He wasn't even interested in pulling it, but his father had pulled it in Vietnam, and his grandfather had pulled it in World War II, and his great-grandfather had pulled it during World War I, and it was rumored a relation had pulled it while fighting for the South during the Civil War. Roger thought the prank was lame, but since the plan was for him to go to college and not into the military, his father had reasoned that Garden Lakes would be Roger's only chance to service the peculiar family tradition.

The hymnal seemed to Roger to have many creases. He laid the book flat during the third verse of "Before the Ending of the Day" to examine where it would fall open. The pages fanned like a paper peacock. He thumbed through the signatures, feeling for any resistance. He decided on page 67. Not too close to the front, not too far toward the back. Sixty-seven. Sixteen-page signatures. Sixteen times four plus three. Roger felt confident with his choice. The next step was to make sure Mr. Hancock suspected the theft. He planned to thieve gradually—forks, knives, and spoons, two each, to test the waters. If no one noticed, he'd double the quantity until someone did. He imagined that, like every other resource at Garden Lakes, silverware was a premium and any draw on the supply would be obvious.

Our voices faltered toward the end of "Before the Ending of the Day," the tune accentuated with a less-than-hearty "Amen."

We resumed our seats, and Mr. Malagon and Mr. Hancock ascended to the front of the chapel. We took a collective measured breath, knowing what was next: the official rules and regulations of life at Garden Lakes. Much like on the first day of a new school year, we knew what to expect. Senior tales of life at Garden Lakes had trickled down through the ranks, so even incoming freshmen knew the deal. Our nervousness, however, stemmed not from the official decree, but from the knowledge that with the decree came the end of the ceremonies. Our casual air, tinged with arrogance, dissipated as we wandered through the ever-increasing dimness brought on by the drone of Mr. Hancock's voice.

Schedules run off on colored paper—pink for sophomores and blue for fellows—were distributed. The schedules were virtually identical: rise at four a.m., breakfast at four thirty, chapel at five. The blue schedule called for construction from five thirty until the midmorning break at seven thirty; the pink schedule called for lunch prep. After the break, fellows returned to construction and the sophomores went to the kitchen, this time for dinner prep. Lunch was served to the fellows at eleven by the sophomores, who ate at noon while the fellows were in class. The sophomores cleaned up after lunch and made final dinner preparations until two, at which point the schedules converged on the playing field for sports until four, when the fellows, again served by the sophomores, took dinner. The sophomores ate their dinner at five, after the fellows had retreated to their housing for the reading hour. Once the kitchen closed for the night, the sophomores reported to their pod leaders' housing for tutoring and study from *American Democracy*, the spiral-bound book prepared by Mr. Hancock, a collection of the documents integral to the founding of America and the birth and maintenance of democracy. Free time was slotted for eight, curfew and lights-out at nine.

"I don't have to tell you boys that deviation from the schedule will not be tolerated," Mr. Hancock said. He commanded the sophomores to pick up their copies of *American Democracy* at his house. Each copy was marked with a street number corresponding to the house numbers on Regis Street, indicating the sophomores' pod leaders. The fellows were to verify attendance before tutoring began. "Unfortunately, our numbers work out evenly now," Mr. Hancock said. "Mr. Malagon will now say a few words on that matter."

Mr. Malagon, who had been standing behind Mr. Hancock, stepped forward. "Thank you, Mr. Hancock," he said. "Yes. Undoubtedly you boys know that Mr. Quinn has left us. That was his prerogative. Mr. Hancock and I are not against the exercise of freedom and personal liberty; anyone who doesn't wish to be here, who doesn't feel he can benefit from the Garden Lakes program, is free to leave." Mr. Malagon paused, looking around. "If anyone else would like to leave, please say so." He paused again and our heads swiveled, looking for a telltale flinch or a head hung to mask plans of desertion.

No one came forward.

"Good, men," Mr. Malagon said.

The liturgy ended and we herded into the classroom, the sophomores splintering off for the kitchen to clean the breakfast dishes and prepare, under Mr. Hancock's direction, the meals for lunch and dinner.

A man in his late thirties stood at the front of the classroom, rubbing his face, his stubby fingers mowing the underside of his beard. We grabbed chairs at the four tables that ran the length of the room. Outside the window, the stranger's white pickup truck was parked, two wheels up on the curb, STATEWIDE CONSTRUCTION emblazoned in silver on the side.

We knew *who* the stranger was; we just didn't know his name. The stranger embodied the nonchalance with which we'd described to anyone who didn't know, or anyone who did but would listen, how it was that a crew of unskilled high school juniors could drywall an entire house. Our fathers had listened halfheartedly to our vague talk of sawing and hammering. They knew as little as we did about how a house was built. To them, construction of a house meant deciding on a floor plan, or choosing between lap siding, panel siding, stucco, and brick exteriors. To us, it meant even less. Our confidence was predicated only on the fact that classes before us had done it. We were clueless about what had been completed in the weeks and months preceding our arrival at Garden Lakes: the grading of the site; foundation construction; the framing of the house; the installation of the windows and doors; roofing; siding; a roughing of the electrical, plumbing, and HVAC; as well as insulating the house. Any one of those chores sounded to us the same as drywalling. We were just here to complete the task at hand. And while we knew the project was largely a demonstration of our ability to work together, we also knew Mr. Malagon would be there to chaperone, and we knew that Statewide Construction would oversee the project, driving out to Garden Lakes to inspect the house after each phase.

Mr. Malagon introduced Jack Baker, whose later kidnapping would prove to be our downfall, and the room grew silent. Mr. Baker jumped to life like a marionette, seized with nervous energy, which he walked off by pacing in front of the proctor's desk at the head of the room.

"Morning, gentlemen," Mr. Baker began. His voice reached the far corners of the room, but he talked to the floor as he paced. "I guess you know why you're here. This is my first year doing this, though I've been with Statewide for fifteen years. Some of your predecessors worked with my predecessor, Joe Cotton. He's retired, so you got me." Mr. Baker continued pacing, and it soon became evident that he was not going to look up at any of us. We looked at Mr. Malagon, hoping to share a laugh with him, but he was engrossed in the pages of a white binder foil-stamped with the same silver logo as the truck outside.

"So, here's how it works. You're here for what, roughly forty days?"

Mr. Malagon nodded.

"Plenty of time. There are three phases." Mr. Baker flashed three thick fingers at us. "Phase one consists of measuring, cutting, and hanging the drywall. Phase two is the taping, beading, stapling, and application of compound. Phase three is sanding, texturing, and painting. Phases one and two will require separately managed teams working in unison; each component of the third phase will require all hands for each step. The job will take a minimum of thirty-four days and a maximum of thirty-eight days. Any questions so far?"

Figs, who would later succeed in covering up an embezzlement at his firm, shifting the blame to an innocent department head, which would result in the department head's firing, raised his hand, and to our surprise, Mr. Baker locked eyes with him.

"How long will each phase take?"

"Roughly two weeks. I'm scheduled . . ." Mr. Baker consulted a binder. "I'm scheduled to inspect the site fourteen days from now, with another inspection fourteen days later. Then a final inspection at some point before the event." Mr. Baker's opaque reference to the Open House on the last day of Garden Lakes suggested he was oblivious about what the Open House was, that he didn't know it was the date we were all anticipating, when our parents would drive out to pick us up and marvel at the finished product.

Mr. Baker reached into a box hidden behind the desk and continued talking while distributing a stack of small black notebooks. "These are your job journals. Each man is responsible for his own journal. You should only write in your journal in pencil." He handed out boxes of pencils and tiny red sharpeners stamped with his company's logo in foil. "The job journal is as important to any building job as a hammer, screwdriver, or ladder. I can't stress that enough.

"Now, what goes in a job journal? Page one should be titled 'Living Room.' Skip four pages and name the next one 'Kitchen,' and so forth until there's a section for every room in the house. How many bedrooms is this house, anyone know?"

"Three," Smurf, the future slanderer, said. He stuck his tongue out for our amusement, knowing Mr. Baker wouldn't see.

"Three bedrooms," Mr. Baker said, again consulting his binder. "Upstairs bath. No garage."

"The garage is converted into an extra room," Mr. Malagon said.

"There ductwork for this room?" Mr. Baker asked, seeking the answer more from his binder than from Mr. Malagon.

"The room has windows for cross-ventilation," Warren said. "It's like an Arizona room." Long before he'd be an unwitting accomplice to an Internet scam, Warren had helped his grandparents build an Arizona room onto their house one summer and was familiar with the architectural absurdity.

"So," Mr. Baker said, finding his place again. "A few facts about drywall: A sheet of drywall is composed of a hardened gypsum core wrapped in paper—smooth paper on the face of

66

the sheet, folded around the long edges, and a rougher paper as backing. Drywall doesn't only come in four-by-eight panels. There are different drywall types for different drywall needs. Types of drywall include moisture-resistant drywall, called greenboard or blueboard because of the coloration of its papering. Moisture-resistant drywall can tolerate high humidity and is used primarily in parts of the country where it rains frequently. Here in Arizona we use greenboard for bathrooms, the area around kitchen sinks, and laundry or utility rooms. Anywhere you suspect water will collect or areas that will be exposed to moisture for prolonged periods of time. You should write that down."

A rustling filled the room as we reached into our pockets for our pencils and sharpeners. Lindy's red sharpener skidded across the tile floor, and Roger kicked it back toward him, the sharpener ricocheting off Lindy's foot before Assburn picked it up and handed it back. We turned our journals over and scrawled "Types of Drywall" on the back, employing a skill we had learned in Father Mason's memorization classes, called listing, the theory being that once you listed a series of things in a relevant order, you could recall the items with ease. Based on the partial information we'd received at that juncture, we spaced down under the heading and penciled in "Moisture-resistant," leaving room above the notation for a description of the standard drywall and enough space below for a description of fire-resistant drywall, a type of drywall we guessed was a specialty, the valuable lesson learned in Father Mason's class being that you didn't always get the information in the order of importance.

Mr. Baker continued. "Standard or regular drywall is forty-eight inches wide and comes in panels up to sixteen feet. They come in four thicknesses"—Mr. Baker held up two fingers on each hand—"five-eighths of an inch, half an inch, three-eighths of an inch, and quarter inch. For our purposes, we will be using the thickest board, which is?"

Smurf's hand shot up first in a forest of arms.

"Five-eighths."

"Very good. I was told you guys were smart," Mr. Baker commented without a hint of irony. He moved on, discoursing about what thicknesses provide what kind of fire protection absent the use of fire-resistant drywall.

"What color is fire-resistant drywall?" Sprocket asked, checking over his notes. His immersion in detail would be the wellspring of his success as a software entrepreneur.

Mr. Baker wrinkled his nose. "It's the same color as regular drywall. The only difference is its fire rating."

"And are there variances within the fire-resistant drywall that are similar to the variances of regular drywall?" Sprocket asked.

The rest of us rolled our eyes, used to Sprocket's constant over-self-education.

Mr. Baker rubbed his forehead. "Sure. But we're not going to be using any fire-resistant board, so I don't see—"

"Out of curiosity, then," Sprocket said.

"Okay, sure. Fire-resistant drywall is rated in time intervals—forty-five minutes, sixty minutes, and one hundred and twenty minutes—which is how long the board will resist fire," Mr. Baker answered as he continued to pace the front of the room.

Sprocket was the only one to enter this information into his job journal.

We adjourned to the site as the sun pitched over the horizon, vanquishing the weak morning light that had spread across Garden Lakes. Armed with our job journals and pencils, and with the tutorial from Mr. Baker, we were able to focus on the framed house for the first time as we stood in the moonscaped front yard among the empty pallets and discarded cement bags. A portable outhouse stood sentry near the front door. The drywall was stacked like a gypsum butte along the side of the house. Inside, incandescent rectangles burned across the floors, through the slats of the framing. The smell of wood was overpowering.

With Mr. Baker as a guide, we began the most crucial step: measuring the rooms for drywall. He asked for groups—two groups to make the initial measurements and two groups to recheck the measurements. Our hesitation was born out of our fear that, once formed, these would be the groups we'd be stuck in for the rest of the summer. We stared blankly, some of us standing in shadow, some in sunlight. A couple of us shuffled toward our housemates. Mr. Baker split us into four groups, his mind accounting for Sprocket's inability to navigate the stairs.

Tape measures were doled out to each team. Mr. Malagon supervised the upstairs measurements. Downstairs, we could hear Mr. Baker's instructions to Assburn about which way to measure a wall. Some of us pulled out the store we'd stashed at breakfast, munching fruit and torn pieces of bagel as we measured.

Measurements in hand, checked and rechecked, we reconvened in the kitchen. Mr. Baker, never guessing he was among those who would plot his kidnapping, freed a set of blueprints from a plastic tube he'd retrieved from his truck and bade us to call out the measurements room by room. We drew together in a circle, our job journals open like hymnals, and sang out the measurements as Mr. Baker called for them.

Across the development, sophomores who couldn't boil water were engaged in a crash course in cooking. They learned the distinction between diced and minced, how a tablespoon was not equal to a teaspoon, and that under no circumstances was a teaspoon a pinch. Mr. Hancock distributed photocopies of the same handout he'd been using for over a decade: "One-fourth cup plus one fourth-cup equals _____. One-third plus one-half is _____. There are _____ ounces in a quart. _____ in a gallon." Sophomores who, on the advice of the previous class, had taken an unusual interest in kitchen work at home in the weeks leading up to Garden Lakes passed with ease. Those who remained baffled by how to double the measurements for any given recipe were relegated to the cutting boards and reminded that the kitchen's first-aid supplies were limited.

In addition to meals, the sophs made the daily soups from scratch, soups they'd never heard of, like spicy red bean soup or roasted bell pepper soup or Moroccan potato bean. Mr. Hancock fervently believed that all that life had to teach was represented in soup making. Lessons about action and consequence (a teaspoon of thyme when the recipe called for an eighth of a teaspoon would render the soup inedible), as well as lessons about how certain ingredients complement one another while others, when brought together, ruin the taste of a particular soup. The critical lesson, Mr. Hancock believed, was the notion that digression from the recipe invalidated it. Mr. Hancock's tenure at Randolph had taught him that boys' impoverished kitchen skills—however feminine and unmanly such skills were regarded by society at large—extended to practical matters outside of how to bring a hammer down on a nail, or how to tell a Phillips screwdriver from a flathead. He posited that while the boys may not be headed toward the exacting science of construction—he was sure that none of the boys who passed through Randolph's hallowed halls would ever be a foreman much less an invaluable member of a construction crew—they would need to feed themselves (juvenilia about their wives or, God forbid, their mothers taking care of their cooking aside), and so Mr. Hancock took the occasion to inculcate the same precision required to calculate how many sheets of drywall each room in the framed house would require. Under Mr. Baker's guidance, we scratched calculations into our job journals amid sighs and feverish erasing. Remeasuring of the electrical boxes was called for; strategies for drywalling the bathrooms were advanced and rejected. Pencil shading turned our job journals into coloring books.

Mr. Malagon interrupted Mr. Baker as he was explaining about how corner beads bridged accidental gaps between juxtaposed drywall. "The boys have their seven-thirty break," Mr. Malagon said.

We tucked our job journals into our khakis and trooped to the dining hall for the muffins and juices laid out by the sophs, who also indulged in the feast.

Sprocket and a couple of fellows huddled at one table, poring over their job journals. Sprocket could be heard muttering, "I think the light switch goes here," or, "The outlet is too low." Hands and Figs approached Mr. Baker, who was provided with a cup of Mr. Hancock's black coffee, and lobbed questions about taping sequences, the number of coats of joint compound needed, etc. Mr. Baker checked his watch during a dissertation on skim coating and level-five finishes. Mr. Malagon slipped into the kitchen, and Roger stole closer to the basket of silverware, palming two knives in one hand and a batch of spoons in the other. The sophomores shook out their wrists, stretching their cramped fingers.

Assburn, who would die plunging into a frozen lake somewhere outside Detroit while driving across the ice, smuggling counterfeit game systems into the country, sat by himself, the realization that neither Mr. Hancock nor Mr. Malagon was going to demand Q's return hitting him hard. The first full day of Garden Lakes held so many promises for each of us, but Assburn knew that Q would not return, that he would therefore not be able to return the pen to Q, that the first bead in a long chain of apologies and forgiveness would not be threaded. The rest of us could see Assburn's disappointment, though we hadn't any idea of his dreams of contrition. The day when an accusation could be answered with "Yes, I'm sorry" or "It's true, but I regret it" slipped from Assburn's reach the instant Q disappeared into the darkness.

As the midmorning break expired, Figs squeezed past the dividing wall, which had been pulled parallel with the east wall. A perfume of fruit and spices and warm muffins filled his nose. The Randolph faculty had granted Figs license to areas inaccessible to other students—the photocopier in the principal's office, the sports equipment locker in the gym—and the kitchen at Garden Lakes was just another area Figs felt comfortable broaching. His intention was to propose to Mr. Hancock that a soda and juice break be added between the midmorning break and lunch, a proposal Figs felt sure would be endorsed by the other fellows, but he changed his mind (and direction) when he overheard Mr. Hancock's baritone voice and saw him point a finger in Mr. Malagon's chest: "I said no. And I'm not discussing it."

Figs drew back behind the serving counter as Mr. Malagon reappeared, flushed.

The space between the midmorning break and lunch was filled with Mr. Baker's instruction on the proper methods for cutting drywall, whether you were using a jigsaw, handheld saw, or box knife. A tour of the supply shed familiarized us with the implements we'd be married to for the coming weeks. Sprocket inventoried the shed in his job journal, assigning each item its own page, counting the framing squares, chalk lines, drywall routers, saws, rasps, panel lifters, stilts, hammers, tape measures, screwdrivers, screws, nails, rubber mallets, hawks, taping knives, trowels, paintbrushes, and electrical cords (which could be run to the nearest finished house for electricity), as well as the gallons of joint compound and eggshell white latex paint (Cottage White, officially), which he tallied on the back cover. The cataloging comforted Sprocket. Until after the midmorning break, he'd suffered from a gnawing suspicion that his selection for Garden Lakes was just charity. Sprocket's parents had raised him to endure his disability without bitterness, and he'd come to accept his situation as just one of those things. In that way, Sprocket's thinking was more evolved than our own. At that point we still believed that life could be regulated at our bidding. We knew nothing of luck or chance or fate—we disdained those words as excuses for failure, a poor apology for an absence of will. As far as we knew, desire and stamina was all that counted.

Mr. Baker rushed through his last twenty minutes with us, peppering his instructions with "Don't forget to jot it in your job journal!" Our morale couldn't have been higher as Mr. Baker's truck sailed through the waves of late-morning heat rising from the asphalt and out the front gates, a confidence born from the assumption that each of us was paying closer attention to Mr. Baker than the others. But we had until the next day before we'd be tested, and nothing seals a sense of confidence tighter than the promise of the future.

The sophomores broke in shifts from dinner prep to serve lunch, ladling pasta dishes (including macaroni and cheese) from trays heated by an elaborate steam system built into the serving counter. Lunch at Garden Lakes was traditionally traditional—the closest to cafeteria-style food we would encounter, dinner being an elaboration of Mr. Hancock's moods, which ran the gamut from rich and creamy to spicy and healthful. Dinner was our reward for a long day of labor fueled by carbohydrates and was served to us at our tables by sophomore waiters.

The only wait service afforded us at lunch was beverage service, furnished more in an effort to keep the aisle leading to the kitchen clear than for reasons of decorum. Sophomores fluttered in the background, roaming, waiting to be pressed into service. If a fellow ordered soda, he was also to indicate the brand of soda he wanted. Predictably, Smurf sent his waiter for Pepsi, then, to his table's hilarity, spit the Pepsi out and insisted that he'd ordered Coke.

Those at Roger's table thought he was following Smurf's lead when the waiter asked Roger if he wanted more to drink and Roger ignored him. The sophomore asked again, and Roger started a discourse about drywalling with Figs, who was sitting to Roger's right. The waiter, Dennis Reedy, moved along, asking Figs if he'd like more soda. Roger slurped the last drops from his glass and slammed it against the table, inducing a Pavlovian glance from all the other waiters. Reedy asked Roger again if he wanted more soda and again Roger ignored him.

Roger's tablemates shifted in their seats, sensing that Roger was invoking a shun against Reedy. Everyone at the table knew the shun was without merit, as likely as not, much like the shun he'd invoked against Rebecca Clement, the Xavierite who had spurned Roger's invitation to the winter formal. The first day of classes after the winter recess, Roger and two frosh—Donnelly and Hendrickson—were camped out around the courtyard fountain before the first bell. Rebecca Clement and her friends

74

strolled by on their way to first-hour Spanish. "Hiya, Roger," Rebecca called out. Roger pretended like he didn't hear. Rebecca called out again, and again Roger didn't acknowledge her. Rebecca kept up with her companions, continuing on toward Spanish class, confused by Roger's insolence. Roger gave no standing order, but the next time Donnelly saw Rebecca, he was with two other freshmen, Cooley and Bricketts, and when Rebecca called out to Donnelly, he aped Roger, ignoring her salutation. Cooley did the same in the presence of Fitzsimmons and Anderson, who did the same when Rebecca called out to them in a crowd of freshmen. By spring, half the student body was carrying He-Man Becky Haters Club cards, printed on a dot matrix printer and laminated at the print shop down Central Avenue from Randolph, flashing the cards between classes and in the parking lot after school. Some Xavierites carried the cards as well, and by the Easter break, Rebecca Clement had transferred out of Xavier. Neither Roger nor anyone else spoke her name, but the He-Man Becky Haters Club cards kept surfacing around campus, brandished as a punch line or as a threat.

"Roger, dude, do you want more soda?" Figs asked, while Reedy shied from the table.

Roger carried on with his purported fascination with Sheetrock without pause, and everyone—including Figs—made like Figs had never asked the question. Reedy moved on to another table, terror in his eyes, and Roger rattled the ice in his glass. Another waiter, who had witnessed the shun against Reedy, quickly reached over and snatched Roger's glass without asking him if he wanted more. Roger called out after the waiter, "Pepsi, please," and the waiter returned with a full glass of soda. None of his tablemates spoke as Roger took a long drink and then continued his train of thought about what would happen if you karate-chopped a piece of Sheetrock.

Reedy stepped in Roger's direction, intimating that he wanted to clear up any misunderstanding, but Mr. Hancock appeared from the kitchen with Mr. Malagon, the two not so deep in conversation about the upcoming class that they wouldn't have seen a row had one occurred. Reedy reversed, heading for the kitchen. Mr. Hancock and Mr. Malagon continued their conference at a table vacated by fellows who had trotted down the hall to the classroom early to get the seats in the back row. Sophomores serving themselves lunch repopulated the table as we decamped for class, some of us walking near Mr. Hancock and Mr. Malagon, hoping to catch a sliver of their conversation or to overhear what looked to us like supplication from Mr. Malagon.

We could guess the nature of this conversation. Mr. Hancock was an enemy of change, so when Mr. Malagon, upon being chosen for duty at Garden Lakes, had suggested the academic curriculum be switched from English and philosophy classes (Mr. Malagon successfully argued that, as one of the state's premiere schools, Randolph students were already inordinately well versed in English grammar and the fundamentals of classical philosophy) to a discussion about the great leaders and their decisions in twentieth-century America, Mr. Hancock had balked at the idea. Mr. Hancock's syllabus for American Literature had had exactly zero amendments or additions to it over the years, and he saw no reason to alter a program of learning so successfully implemented.

But the administration heard Mr. Malagon's proposal. Mr. Malagon contended a close examination of the great leaders, not just presidents but men and women of substance, was vital to any true leadership program. Without making known his feelings about the legitimacy of arming fellows with confusing philosophical hypotheses and the keen ability to express their confusion in writing, Mr. Malagon argued a point the administration held dear: effective academia. Every year the administration combed scores of reports filled with colorful charts and graphs to assess and reassess the school's curriculum, spelunking for ways to improve the relevance of a Randolph education. Mr. Malagon pleaded his proposal along these lines.

Mr. Hancock rallied the rest of the faculty on the platform of tradition, pointing out the success rate of past Garden Lakes fellows. His colleagues privately framed the debate as a threat to the more senior, established faculty. Rhetorical questions permeated the teachers' lounge and the halls after school. If the administration disregarded their position, what would stop students from exhibiting the same lack of respect? What message would it send to students to have a proven, successful curriculum undermined by pop academe? And, more importantly, would a vote for the proposal of a junior faculty member signal an end to the administration's confidence in the advice and judgment of senior faculty members?

The questions would remain rhetorical, however. The administration embraced Mr. Malagon's proposition, paving the way for a new course of study at Garden Lakes. The debate, while internal and secret, was leaked to the rest of us through Figs, who worked as an administrative aid during seventh hour. And though we didn't know whether the scrapped English and philosophy classes would have been beneficial, the new course—or rather, the manner in which the new course had come into being—whetted our appetite.

As we took our seats in the classroom, we observed an expression Mr. Malagon had never before exhibited: nervousness.

Mr. Malagon chafed under the promulgation of historical inaccuracies, like the fairy tale that Betsy Ross sewed the American flag, or that Paul Revere ever uttered, "The British are coming! The British are coming!" He had rankled a few colleagues by crafting a class on Hitler aimed at humanizing the Führer rather than portraying him as a one-dimensional black hat. Could Hitler tell you a joke so funny that you'd wet yourself? was the opening line of the unit. "It's easy to recognize evil once it has manifested," Mr. Malagon would say. "A thinking person should be trained to spot the warning signs." Thanks to Figs and his eavesdropping, we knew the proposed class at Garden Lakes was grooved in the same controversial vein, all of which was confirmed when Mr. Malagon launched into a prepared lecture on FDR's administration, fending off a volley from Mr. Hancock, who added helpfully that many of the New Deal programs didn't survive a court challenge, by emphasizing the New Deal's legacy. We watched the interplay like fascinated children.

The sound of sophomores shuffling in the hallway broke Mr. Malagon's concentration, a sound that meant it was time for sports. "More about Mr. Roosevelt and the New Deal tomorrow," Mr. Malagon intoned. "Be sure to read the handout carefully. Did I mention each unit will have a short quiz at the end?" He laughed through our groans. "See you in ten minutes."

Ten minutes later, we met up on the dry lake bed, having raced to our houses and changed for sports, meaning soccer, which, after cooking, was Mr. Hancock's other passion. The sophomores were waiting for us on the makeshift field, their punctuality presumably the result of a harangue some minutes earlier. Mr. Hancock himself appeared in his usual attire, as did Mr. Malagon, who meandered out to the field from class. Mr. Malagon had lobbied unsuccessfully for baseball instead of soccer, but, having lost his treasured philosophy class, Mr. Hancock would not be defeated on this score. He roused fear in the heart of every administrator with the image of teenage boys wielding baseball bats and throwing fastballs through windowed strike zones. Mr. Hancock took the further step of itemizing a list of equipment needed for baseball, complete with slightly inflated prices. He presented this list with a soccer ball tucked under his arm, the only essential equipment needed for a soccer match. The administration rebuffed Mr. Malagon's idea of substituting baseball for soccer; the decision came to him via the same route as his suggestion—in passing—so Mr. Malagon was unaware of Mr. Hancock's rigorous campaign.

The sun blazed down on us. Mr. Hancock passed around tubes of sunblock, and we spread it over our arms, legs, faces, and backs of our necks and ears. We massaged sunblock into our hair like shampoo, as we'd been doing since we were old enough to play outside. The lake bed was polluted with the smell of coconut.

Mr. Hancock, whose departure from Garden Lakes would set off a chain reaction from which we'd hardly recover, divided us into two random teams, mixing fellows and sophomores. Sprocket would be the goal judge, a specialized referee needed for the Garden Lakes brand of soccer: The game would be played half-field because of the scarcity of goal equipment. Mr. Malagon, who turned out not to be what we'd all built him up to be, helped Sprocket maneuver down the slope, and he rode past us carrying two orange pylons from the supply shed on his lap. He placed them an equal distance apart at Mr. Hancock's instruction. Sprocket would call balls in and out. Another position not found in Major League Soccer was the ball spotter, a position of importance that was stationed behind the goal and whose job it was to track down goals and errant kicks so play was not suspended while someone chased the ball down Garden Lakes Parkway. Mr. Malagon and Mr. Hancock would each referee one side of the field, calling out the team captain's name to indicate which team would corner-kick or throw in. The remaining players stood as substitutions on each sideline. Since the half-field made play immediate, the goalies were to step out of the box when their team was on offense.

Figs was the natural choice for captain of his team; so too was Hands. Figs designated Lindy as the goalkeeper for his team; Hands chose himself. Sprocket wheeled himself near the goal line as Mr. Hancock flipped a coin to determine play. Hands— who would one day lead his family's sixth-generation brewery to ruin by distrusting the CFO, whom he considered a rival for his wife's affections—called, "Heads." The quarter bounced on the dirt field, and it was a moment before the dust shrouding the coin settled. Tails. Mr. Malagon and Mr. Hancock withdrew to the sidelines, their breath rattling the tiny wooden balls inside their whistles. Mr. Hancock bounce-passed the ball to Figs, who raised his arms and called, "Ball in," passing it to Smurf, who caught the ball with the side of his foot, the muted thud sounding as if it might have hurt. Smurf, whose expert slander would end his future female colleague's real estate career, showed no sign of pain, though, and crisscrossed the ball away from charging defenders. Smurf passed the ball cross-field to Assburn, and he advanced it toward the goal by faking out Warren. Hands danced inside the goal, his palms sweaty. Each of his athletic feats—buzzer beaters on the basketball court, long balls on the baseball diamond, touchdowns on the gridiron—was prefaced with the same rush, the same sick feeling inside. Hands jogged in place as the soccer ball whizzed side to side across the playing field, negotiating its way toward the goal. Roger ran alongside Smurf, who was trying to corral the ball on a wayward pass from one of the sophomores. The defenders converged when they saw Smurf make a move for the goal. Hands positioned himself with his legs spread wide, ready to pounce. Roger poked the ball away from Smurf, but Smurf leaped over the runaway ball, stopping it with his heel. Mr. Hancock and Mr. Malagon squared off across the field, moving with the action. Smurf passed the ball to Figs right as he charged ahead of the defenders. Figs stutter-stepped and punted the ball at the goal. Hands put his body in the ball's path, and the ball arced off his left arm.

"Out!" Mr. Hancock called.

Mr. Malagon had scarcely put the ball back into play when a scrum broke out. Mr. Hancock's whistle fell from his mouth as he ran toward midfield. Mr. Malagon was bent over Lindy, who was rolling in the dirt, cradling his left arm.

Lindy's screams increased in pitch as Mr. Malagon and Mr. Hancock sorted out what had happened. Defenders closest to the play claimed Roger had deliberately collided with Lindy when it was clear that Lindy had stolen the ball cleanly from Roger. Other players were less sure of the play. Some alleged to have seen Roger flailing his arms, indicating that he was out of control when he smashed into Lindy, who by now was lying prostrate with his eyes closed, he left arm immobile. Roger did not testify in his own defense. He listened coolly as the different versions were replayed, taking count of who was saying what. As Mr. Malagon tended to Lindy—who would one day in his thirties die in his sleep, leaving behind a devastated family—by testing the flexibility of Lindy's left arm, Mr. Hancock pulled Roger aside and asked him what happened.

"It was an accident," Roger said.

Mr. Hancock did not pursue the question and instead turned to Mr. Malagon and Lindy.

"He needs medical attention," Mr. Malagon said.

"More than a sling?" Mr. Hancock asked.

Mr. Malagon nodded.

Figs volunteered to pull one of the two Jeeps around, but Mr. Hancock assured us that only he and Mr. Malagon would ever get behind the wheel of either vehicle. Mr. Malagon pointed out that it was close to the dinner hour, which meant Mr. Hancock was needed elsewhere. "Why don't we have everyone shower up, and I'll run Brian to the emergency room," Mr. Malagon said.

Mr. Hancock hesitated. He knew what Mr. Malagon said made sense, but he speculated as to the seriousness of Lindy's injury (though the distressed look on Lindy's face authenticated the necessity for the trip to the hospital). "We'll set a place for Mr. Lindstrum at the dinner table," Mr. Hancock said, though the remark was directed more at Mr. Malagon than at Lindy.

The half an hour of free time added to the schedule by the abrupt end of sports left us disoriented. Some went to their rooms; others began their showers early, opting to use the time to relax before dinner. Mr. Hancock prescribed ten-minute showers for the sophomores, then herded their wet heads into the kitchen to undertake the evening meal: coq au vin. The sophomores had spent their afternoon cleaving poultry hindquarters, and while the rest of us played cards or grabbed a nap, the kitchen was busied with the shellacking of chicken legs with Mr. Hancock's magical red-wine sauce, a sauce made with one less bottle of wine, said bottle residing in Adam Kerr's bottom dresser drawer. Kerr was generally regarded as one of the more audacious sophomores. He once climbed onto the roof of Randolph to spy an accident that had stopped traffic on Central Avenue (and received a three-day suspension because of it).

Smurf joined Figs and Hands in a quick game of five-card draw. "Everyone's in their rooms," Smurf said about his own residence. He looked at Figs. "Roger's going to get you, you know that, right?"

Figs shrugged and asked for two cards. "I don't see how."

Hands glanced at Figs and then looked away at his cards. "Yeah," he said.

Smurf folded. "Fuckin' guy bulldozed Lindy. Won't be surprised if Lindy's arm is busted to pieces."

There was a knock and the front door opened.

"Never guess what Assburn has," Warren said, pulling up a chair.

"Whatever it is, I'm sure he's not the original owner," Figs said. "You in?"

Warren rapped on the table and Figs dealt him in.

"He's got a mobile phone," Warren said, picking up his cards.

"What—did he steal Hancock's?" Figs asked. The school alleviated parental anxiety by providing Mr. Hancock with a mobile phone, which he kept in a locked box under his bed.

"Guess all that talk about him not being a klepto is bullshit," Hands said. "Figured it was."

"Does it work?" Smurf asked.

"Yeah, he turned it on," Warren said, discarding. "One."

Hands folded.

"Did he let you use it?" Smurf wanted to know.

"Didn't ask," Warren said, uninterested in the story. "You guys see the way Roger knocked out Lindy?"

"I was right next to him," Figs said. "Roger got this look."

Smurf excused himself and the front door opened and closed,

but the exchange about Lindy and Roger continued without a beat, and without consensus. Farther down Regis Street, Assburn denied to Smurf that he had a mobile phone. Smurf called him a liar, but Assburn stuck to his story. "Damn liar," Smurf said again.

The move to the dining hall was less a shuffle toward a meal than it was a rush to keep an important appointment. Fellows walk-skipped to dinner, and we all fell into formation as the waiters brought steaming plates of coq au vin and garlic mashed potatoes.

As promised, a place for Lindy had been set at Figs and Hands's table. The place setting brought stares from the other tables and from the sophomore waiters, who no doubt knew something big was at stake. Roger glided to his table without paying tribute to Lindy's empty chair. He hunkered over his plate and tore into the juicy meat, ravenous.

Mr. Hancock took his seat at the center table, sophomores flanking him. As the meal progressed—seconds on mashed potatoes, more chicken ("It's not chicken, boys, it's coke-oh-van")—Lindy's ultimate disfigurement grew in our minds. We imagined him in a body cast, or worse. Out the windows the sun continued its tyranny of the sky, but we anticipated the pink light that always preceded sundown ("It's all the crap in the air," Lindy had told us) and collectively worried about the ramifications of Lindy and Mr. Malagon's absence after dark.

We held our breath as the sound of talking echoed through the outer hall. Mr. Hancock did not look up from his slice of crushed pineapple–sour cream pie, the delectable concoction we weren't enjoying as we might. Mr. Malagon's frame filled the doorway, blocking out Lindy, who seemed to be struggling in the background, his left arm in a plaster cast up to his elbow. He *was* struggling, but not because of his useless appendage. His right arm was rendered useless too by a cylindrical package wrapped in butcher paper. The package caught Mr. Hancock's attention. Mr. Malagon leaned in and whispered something to Mr. Hancock, causing Mr. Hancock to grimace.

"It's a telescope," Lindy said, taking his seat. A waiter brought a plate of coq au vin and mashed potatoes, while another set down a plate of baked apples sprinkled with cinnamon.

"How did you get a telescope?" Hands asked.

"Mr. Malagon bought it for me," Lindy said between bites.

"Does your arm hurt?" Figs asked.

The whole room was listening to the conversation.

Lindy shook a tumor the size of a roll of quarters in his pocket, the bottle of painkillers rattling like a baby's toy. "Can't feel a thing," he said, smiling.

Mr. Hancock spoke to Mr. Malagon gravely, referencing the package at Lindy's feet, obviously aggrieved. Mr. Malagon concentrated on his dinner, looking up only to take a drink.

Lindy described the hospital, how his mother had raced to the emergency room, thinking that his injuries were life threatening. Lindy became animated when he told the part about the telescope. "Mr. Malagon says we can look at the stars during free time," Lindy said. "Bet they look pretty good out here at night."

"If we're still awake when the sun goes down," Hands said. "Christ, I could use a nap."

At the next table over, Roger was avidly *not* listening to Lindy's tale. He rattled the ice in his glass, unnerving Reedy. Some of us noticed Reedy's unnatural circumnavigation of the dining hall— taking the long way around to the soda machine, hoping to stay out of the willful rotation that threatened to bring him into Roger's airspace.

Adam Kerr brought Roger another drink, staring down at him after he delivered the too-full glass, which slopped over, a dark stain spreading across the tablecloth.

"What are you looking at?" Roger asked in a way that froze everyone within earshot.

"Not sure," Kerr said bravely. "Trying to figure it out."

Roger stamped the top of Kerr's foot with as much weight as he could bring while sitting down. Kerr yelped and hopped on one foot.

"What's going on over there?" Mr. Hancock asked.

"Dixon—," Kerr began, but Hands jumped in: "Nothing, sir. He tripped over Roger's chair. That's all."

Satisfied with Hands's explanation (though perhaps not believing it), Mr. Hancock returned to his conversation with Mr. Malagon, who was forking a piece of pie cut from the reserve kept for the sophomores into his mouth.

Roger glared at Kerr, who in turn glared at Hands. Hands raised his eyebrows, communicating to Kerr that he was not taking Roger's side, but that Kerr should not cross a fellow. Kerr heard the message and limped away.

The fellows adjourned in groups to Regis Street for the reading hour; the hour after dinner but before tutoring allowed for us to read over Mr. Malagon's handout. Although the reading hour was unpoliced, we all honored the rules—each fellow must read in his room, no talking, no congregation in any room—not out of respect for one another's space and time, but because the reading hour was a chance to get forty winks before the sophomores arrived for tutoring.

As the hands on the kitchen clocks reached for eight, the tutoring groups dissolved into informal salons, topics covered including the food at Garden Lakes, disbelief that we'd been at Garden Lakes for only one day, and that it would be weeks before we could contemplate the Open House. Fellows rubbed their tired eyes and yawned symphonically. Word was passed that Lindy was going to set the telescope up in the dry lake bed, and while most of us were fatigued into near muteness, we ventured out, our footprints from the ill-fated soccer game earlier that day transforming the lake bed into the scene of a possible lunar landing, or alien invasion, or so we liked to imagine.

Lindy extended the cheap tripod that came with the telescope. Figs helped him raise it until the telescope rested near eye level, the smooth cylinder bobbing precariously on the tripod's crossbar. Lindy adjusted the eyepiece, tapping the telescope up or down, dialing into the sky's frenetic designs. He located the moon, the glimmer of Mercury deep in the moon's backyard. He called out the constellations as he found them—Hercules, Lyra, Sagittarius, Scorpius—the stars undulating as if the sky were an immense lake, the depths of its black waters limitless. Lindy believed his father and brother floated in the wake of these constellations, watching over him and his mother. He didn't believe in heaven; the concept was too obviously man-made, constructed out of human desire and fear, but he believed in the longevity of a person's essence, and the belief gave him comfort as he searched the skies, his father's tremulous laugh and his brother's endless kidding alive in the stellar oceanography.

Lindy had long abandoned the search for answers as to why his father and brother were struck head-on by another boat, thrown into Lake Pleasant. Lindy was to have made the trip with them, but had been laid up by a summer cold. His mother hated the water and was instead home tending to her sick son when the sheriff's department knocked on their front door. For a time, the details obsessed Lindy: the inebriated pilots of the other craft (who were also killed instantly), his father and brother hitting the water head-first. Did it look to bystanders that they'd dived out of harm's way? The thought of their mouths and noses filling with water, their lungs distended and shapeless like water balloons, slowed Lindy's own breathing. For weeks after the accident, he labored under the torment of what he guessed was an unusually potent virus, but his mother had been stricken with the same disease that prohibited Lindy from waking before noon and from falling asleep before the sun started to rise. Junior year brought an audience of eager ears, but no one approached Lindy about the story. To Lindy, the deaths had become part of his heritage, a personal history too intimate to share with strangers. He and his mother had sworn a pact to carry on, to not let the sudden emptiness in their lives overtake them.

Staring through the telescope a summer later, Lindy felt like he'd kept a promise, the halos and coronas glowing overhead comforting him, affirming that he was a small but valuable part of something larger. Lindy didn't realize he'd expressed this sentiment aloud, an awkward silence descending on the group of stargazers. Even Smurf and Assburn, who had been arguing in whispers about whether or not Assburn did indeed have a mobile phone, quieted.

Warren peered through the telescope. "So what you're saying is that the sky is full of gods," he said.

Realizing that we thought he was talking about the heavens in the abstract, Lindy expounded on Warren's comment. "They're all up there," he said. "Venus, Mars, Saturn, Cupid, Juno, Neptune, Jupiter—depending on where you're standing, they're all hovering, ruling the sky."

"Neptune was Poseidon in Greek mythology," Sprocket added. "All the Roman gods had Greek names." Sprocket was one of the few students handpicked by Mrs. Haberman for

Advanced Latin. "Venus is Aphrodite, Mars is Ares, Saturn is Cronus, Cupid is Eros, Jupiter is Zeus. . . ."

"Same god, different name," Warren said, raising his face toward the moon.

"Yeah," Sprocket said, not sure whether Warren was asking or reiterating.

"You're looking at Gemini," Lindy said to Hands, who had swiveled the telescope north-northwest.

"Cool," Hands said. "It looks like two people holding hands." We lined up behind the eyepiece, all except for Roger, who drifted away from the crowd. Who wanted to watch two people holding hands? Girlish behavior, he thought; just like the horoscopes. His mother liked the horoscopes, which was, as his father would say, case in point. "Now Roger," she'd say, smoothing the paper on the table in front of her, affecting the tone of a sideshow mystic, "you must avoid reckless moves today, which only serve to embolden your critics. Stay calm."

"What's yours?" Roger would ask eagerly, tilting his bowl to spoon out the sugary milk. The horoscopes seemed to young Roger to be real advice—better than advice: It was as if someone could tell the future. His mother had taken the time to explain the signs of the zodiac but could not answer Roger's persistent questions about *how* the astrologers knew what they knew, which amazed Roger as he kept secret count of how many days his horoscope had been dead-on.

"Okay, let's see." His mother scanned the page, gathering her terry-cloth robe around her neck against a blast of air-conditioning. "Here it is. Ohhh, this is a good one: 'Be frugal. Make the least effort for the most effective gain. Going all out can exhaust you before you're finished. Controlled energy, not wastefulness, will see you through the day.'"

Roger would hurry home after school to compare notes with his mother, rereading the horoscopes, which his mother had folded and set on top of the refrigerator. They would freak each other out with stories that proved the horoscopes' veracity, Roger often embellishing for effect.

His father put a stop to the horoscopes his first day of retirement. Roger was startled to find his father seated at the kitchen table, unshowered and unshaved. His mother acted strangely too, busying herself around the kitchen: wiping the counters, rearranging the pea green Tupperware silos that warehoused the family's supply of flour, sugar, and coffee. Was today Saturday? Roger asked himself. A glimpse of the calendar under the giant pineapple magnet on the freezer door confirmed that it was a school day. His father didn't appear sick, though Roger didn't possess the type of bravery required to stare at his father long enough to get an accurate diagnosis.

His father was constantly reminding Roger of his deficiencies. His mother glanced at Roger dolefully when his father was in the room, but rarely said anything against him. Later, when Roger inquired about his father's early retirement from the army, the swift end to what had been described not just by his father but by his father's buddies—who frequently came around on Friday and Saturday nights, staying long after he and his mother had gone to bed—as a brilliant military career, the only derogatory thing his mother had to say was that his father's promotion to brigadier general had been denied because his father lacked the "philosophical qualities" the army mandated of its high command.

The colonel's omnipresence—he was the last person Roger saw before leaving for school, the first he'd encounter upon his return—relegated his mother's luminous personality to the darkened corners of conversation, until she disappeared altogether.

Roger began tagging along on outings to the shooting range, trips that increased in frequency until the colonel was ready and waiting in the driveway when the bus let Roger off, which left his mother longing for the horoscope breakfasts and the long afternoons in the living room, where Roger would act out his day or she would assist in what she could understand of his homework. Those days seemed firmly in the past, and his mother surrendered to the harder, coarser Roger, the Roger who locked himself in his room, the Roger who hardly spoke at meals (when he would take meals in the kitchen and not in his room). She'd ceded all influence in Roger's life to his father, glumly attributing it to Roger's maturation. A boy needed his father if he was to become a man, she told herself.

Roger dodged the light emanating from the classroom window. Peering in, he saw Mr. Malagon and Mr. Hancock deep in conversation. The front door would be open, Roger knew, but what about the kitchen? He had two chances: the door to the dining room and the door at the end of the hall that led to the kitchen.

The hallway was suffused with muted conversation, and Roger realized his first piece of luck: Either Mr. Malagon or Mr. Hancock had shut the classroom door. His cover story, if caught, would be that he'd dropped in for a drink from the drinking fountain, having gotten thirsty from staring at the stars with everyone else, who he'd point out were right behind him. Assembly was sometimes good cover, he knew.

The lock on the door to the dining room caught as Roger turned the knob, his hopes plummeting. What were the odds that the kitchen door was open? he wondered. He knew without doubt that the exterior kitchen door would be locked shut—it could be opened only from the inside anyway. He padded down the hall, past his alibi, the water fountain, knowing he'd need a better story if he was caught wrestling with the kitchen door.

The door was unlocked. The knob turned so quickly Roger held his breath. He checked under the door to make sure he wasn't about to surprise a clutch of sophomores in some last-minute breakfast preparation, but the air coming from under the door was cool and dark. He slipped inside, letting the door fall against his fingers, easing the knob's metal tongue back into place.

Roger's eyes adapted to the darkness, the outline of the por-table wall visible. He felt the sockets of the silverware caddy. Empty. He felt his way along the stainless steel refrigerator, tempted to pull open the double doors in search of a midnight snack, but he kept his focus. His eyes dilated, he maneuvered through the kitchen by sight, zeroing in on the drying rack, which boasted the day's silverware. Relinquishing his plan for modera-tion, Roger clutched as many utensils as his hands could carry. A thump reverberated through the kitchen, quickening Roger's pulse. No alibi would exonerate him now, he knew, and he backed against the door opposite the one that had delivered him, push-ing against the horizontal bar with his backside. The door admit-ted him into the night and clicked shut behind him.

Roger breathed shallowly. In the distance he could make out the voices of the astronomy club. This daring take would be enough to execute the prank and put the whole sordid business behind him. Actually, the prank seemed less onerous once he possessed the silverware. Who knew, it might even be legendary.

Roger took a step and froze. The ground shifted near his feet, the *drip-drip-drip* from the air conditioner suddenly audible. What looked like six or eight pigs rooted through the remains of a prickly pear cactus, the swine having taken no notice of Roger. He heard a low grunting and took another step, choosing a course

92

that would allow escape, but the sight of one of the pigs in profile chilled him: its long snout yawning to reveal its daggerlike teeth. Javelinas. Roger had seen a pack of fifty or so javelinas tear up a wild dog on a cable program (to his then delight). Roger identified the javelinas at the moment they identified him. The tines of the bouquet of forks glinted in the moonlight. Roger knew from the cable program that he was in less danger if the herd did not include newborns, or if a newborn was not grazing nearby. Roger couldn't be sure that he was seeing the whole herd; the trajectory he'd mapped out could well land him in the middle of the herd, like the wild dog on television. He pressed against the door, afraid to let his hands fall to his sides lest the javelinas read this gesture as hostile. He could feel his anger rising. *Fuck this*, he thought. He stomped his foot at the two nearest javelinas, whose grizzled black and gray fur bristled. The javelinas eyed Roger. The rooting and grunting ceased. A musk, earthy and moldy, spread like dye in water. A chill gave Roger a spasm he punctuated by throwing both fists of silverware at the javelinas, sprinting in the other direction. Undaunted, the javelinas gave chase at angles manageable only for animals who bore their load so close to the ground.

Roger crossed the outer loop, the *click-clack, click-clack* of miniature hooves in pursuit. Ahead, the gravel domes of the Grove rose. He imagined himself in some absurd video game, knowing instinctively that he could become surrounded if he were to make the wrong move. He circled the first pillar of gravel, chucking a good-size rock at the pod of javelinas. The rock landed without making contact, dividing the javelinas into two flotillas. Roger sprang from his hiding place. A dark stain the shape of an inverted triangle seeped through the front of his shirt as he skirted the edge of the Grove, hesitant about committing to entry for fear of being trapped.

The lights of Garden Lakes grew faint as Roger charged past the Grove, expelled into the raw desert outside the development. The grunting sounds became intermittent woofing, like a dog barking at passing cars. Roger swooped up a rock in each hand, spinning around to face the pack. But the javelinas had withdrawn, scurrying off into the desert, alarmed by the yips and howls traveling through the bright sky.

Roger let the rocks fall out of his unsteady hands. He looked back in the direction of Garden Lakes, the shadowy points of the Grove obscuring his view, isolating him from the development. The carbon-copy houses appeared fake, a front meant to shake off the cops. He scoured the perimeter, feeling like he'd been lured by the javelinas into a sinister trap. Out of the corner of his eye he saw one of the streetlights along the parkway snap out.

Chapter Seven

Brennan rearranged the set of prism paperweights on his desk, a nervous habit everyone at the *Sun* had grown used to, even fond of. The shiny pyramids skated across the desktop under Brennan's thin, manicured fingers, gleaming under the fluorescence, sprinkling the walls with teardrop rainbows.

"When can I see a draft?" he asked.

"When have I ever shown a draft to anyone?"

Brennan spun the paperweights counterclockwise, knocking them together like steelies in a playground game of marbles. "I'm asking," he said.

Charlie frowned. "Are *you* asking, or is someone else asking?"

Brennan learned forward. "Wait a minute," he said, "what are you accusing me of?"

"I'm not accusing you of anything," Charlie said.

"It sounds like an accusation," Brennan said.

"Do you blame me?" Charlie asked as Gallagher sailed by Brennan's window, glancing into the office. He nodded to Gallagher, who sped out of view. "I know the McCloud family is pressuring you," Charlie said, testing an unsourced rumor

Gallagher had passed along. He gauged Brennan's face for a reaction, but nothing.

"My loyalties are to this paper," Brennan said, thumping his desk for emphasis. "Everyone knows that. Christ." Charlie knew Brennan often feigned umbrage and called upon his reputation when he felt threatened.

"That doesn't mean the McCloud family hasn't been crawling up your ass," Charlie said, switching tack, injecting his voice with sympathy. "I've got a stack of messages from up and down that family tree on my desk."

"They think you have an ax to grind," Brennan said.

"I don't," Charlie said flatly.

"Yeah, well, they're convinced you do."

"Where's their proof?"

"They don't have any," he said. "But they've got their suspicions." Brennan's harried and much-beleaguered secretary knocked, but he waved her off.

"What suspicions?" Charlie asked. Brennan ticked off a series of seemingly unconnected columns Charlie had written over the last year or so: the closure of a private swimming club McCloud had funded with monies he may or may not have gained illegally through a complicated shell game involving the books of American Community; the misfortune of the Tongan families McCloud had imported as landscapers—so many they resided in a community together south of Phoenix—for his assortment of hotels and master-planned communities; the death of McCloud's protégé by a self-inflicted gunshot in the driver's seat of his Lexus in front of a toy store on Camelback Road. The protégé had broken alliance with McCloud upon McCloud's indictment and begun a new company telemarketing genealogy books to those predisposed to pay for such mementos. The company sank into

96

the red and the protégé became aloof, his suicide effectively ending the company and leaving its employees without pay; the average employee was owed in the neighborhood of a thousand dollars.

"Those are all legitimate, newsworthy items," Charlie said. "Is the *Sun* going to start assigning me topics?"

"Hey!" Brennan nearly catapulted out of his seat. "Don't start saying things like that. No way. Have I ever interfered?"

"Some might call this little tête-à-tête interference," Charlie shot back.

Brennan's secretary rapped again, but Brennan ignored her. "The point is that we ran a story on the swim club and we covered the protégé's death in the Metro section, as news—"

"Columns are for comment and opinion," Charlie said. He folded his arms. "That's what Duke hired me for."

Brennan quieted at the invocation of the publisher's name. Charlie knew Duke prized him above others at the *Sun*, and Charlie could threaten to move to another paper if Brennan persisted.

The phone buzzed on Brennan's desk. "I told you I didn't want to be interrupted," he yelled at his secretary through the glass. She motioned for him to pick up the phone. "What? What is it?" Brennan's face contorted. "Richter who?" Charlie felt a heat rise in his chest. Gallagher's paranoia about the county attorney's private investigator had seemed unfounded until Brennan spoke his name out loud. "Okay, yeah, whatever," Brennan said. He cupped the phone. "I have to take this. Promise me you're not going after McCloud."

"I promise," Charlie answered. He stood as Brennan swiveled away, the phone cord falling into the groove in the back of his leather chair. Charlie tried to eavesdrop, but Brennan's voice lowered as Richter came on the line. He heard the county attorney's name mentioned and gently closed the door behind him, the air thinning as he negotiated the newsroom, desperate for enclosure. He guessed what Richter was after, idly wondering if the county attorney was friends with the farmer Charlie had so resolutely forsaken for his own career. Over the years, Charlie had braced for retaliation from the farmer, whose business collapsed under the weight of the Heather Lambert case, but the quiet that followed such a public dustup had been chilling. Charlie had reasoned away the farmer's objections to his assertions that the illegal immigrant had without a doubt been employed by the farmer at the time he plowed into Heather Lambert, who was the perfect victim to tap into the discontent Phoenicians held for illegal aliens. But Charlie hadn't been able to erase from his mind the interview he'd held with one of the employees of the farm, who confided in him that the illegal alien had been a friend of his from Mexico and didn't work for the farmer—the employee had spit the word "friend" in his broken English, and Charlie surmised that the illegal alien was a source of turmoil in the employee's life, maybe even a relative—and that he'd conned the employee into lifting the keys to the farmer's truck under the guise of needing to run a quick errand. That this quick errand was to procure a quarter pound of marijuana could've been verified by even a cub reporter.

Charlie half expected the farmer to produce the employee as a witness in his defense against the maelstrom of bad publicity and innuendo. Charlie had promised not to use the employee's name, and the employee must've been baffled by Charlie's silence, another fountain of anxiety in those heady days at the *Phoenix Tab*. Charlie imagined the employee's indignation at the concealment of the truth or, at the very least, the threat to his employment, an indignation that was left to simmer as the days and weeks rolled on, the papers and airwaves filled with vitriol. Charlie's recklessness grew in the shade of the employee's revelation, Charlie's denunciation of the farmer's practices bordering on libel, but he was driven by self-righteousness, a force not easily overcome by reason.

Charlie had indulged in a bit of self-righteousness at the *Tab* a month or two prior to the Heather Lambert story too. One of the senior reporters was caught falsifying a source for a puff piece spotlighting the struggles of the local chapter of Mothers Against Drunk Driving to heighten awareness leading into the Fourth of July holiday. The reporter had credited a compliment about the chapter to a man on the street who existed only in the reporter's mind. Charlie had suffered innumerable afternoons subjected to the reporter's unregulated rants about this and that. The managing editor was said to be the reporter's best friend in the world, and, worse, the two were neighbors, so Charlie's complaints about the workplace went unheard. Not even the reporter's politically incorrect language—ranging from calling one of the interns "doll" to referring to Mexicans as "spics"—warranted so much as a reprimand from the managing editor. So when Charlie learned of the journalistic shortcut by chance, when the reporter accidentally attributed the fabricated quote to someone who shared the same name as the bartender at a popular watering hole—who refuted the words were his—Charlie seized the chance to ride the reporter in front of the *Tab* staff, including the managing editor. "Just make it up," became a catchphrase he bandied about the office. The reporter began avoiding him, but Charlie's thirst wasn't quenched and he began taunting both the managing editor and the reporter. He'd tell an outlandish tale and finish with "I don't know why I said that, it's not true," before turning to the reporter and saying, "Maybe you can use that in your next piece." The managing editor pleaded with him to tamp down the sarcasm, but to no avail—the office had been infected and soon everyone was taunting the reporter.

When the fevered pitch of his offensive against the reporter dissipated, Charlie's frustrations emboldened him. What began as a casual lunch with the intern the reporter had flirted with turned dark when Charlie filled the intern's ears with the stories of private lust he claimed the reporter had admitted in the intern's absence. He surprised himself with sound bites about deviant sexual behavior he'd only seen in movies or on the Internet. The intern's giggles transformed into rage toward the reporter sometime between their ordering lunch and Charlie's paying the check.

"You can't say I told you, though," Charlie said.

"I'm going to say something right when we get back," the intern said, seething.

"They're not going to take your word for it," Charlie said. He coached her on what to say, convincing her that she'd have to claim that the reporter had touched her in an inappropriate way that made her uncomfortable. The intern questioned the need to lie, but Charlie pointed out how close the managing editor and the reporter were—they were neighbors, for Chrissakes—and she reluctantly agreed. "I'll back you up and say I saw him touch you too," Charlie said. "If it comes to that."

But it didn't. The reporter was fired, and the intern quit shortly after that, maybe buckling under the embarrassment of being the subject of office gossip but probably because she found a better way to spend her free time. That's what Charlie told himself in the quietest moments of the now-still afternoons at the *Tab* offices.

And so the cover-up involving the employee that could've absolved the farmer in the Heather Lambert matter had been an easy elision. Charlie assumed the employee had found work on another farm, maybe in another state, or in another industry. If he was being honest, he had worried that the employee was lying or mistaken. But in Charlie's mind the employee was so far into the distant past he'd become fictive, though he couldn't shake the sickening feeling that Richter had dredged him up for a purpose Charlie's nervous and guilt-ridden conscience was all too ready to supply.

Chapter Eight

Sprocket proved adept in his position as supply manager. With Warren's help, he reorganized the supply shed by construction phase: hanging tools on one wall, taping tools on another, sanding tools on yet another, and on and on. The supply shed had an open front like the illegal fireworks stands on the Indian reservations, providing Sprocket with enough cover to preserve his albino skin, though he slathered himself in sunscreen as a precaution, the front and back of his job journal decorated with his oily fingerprints.

Sweating under the tin roof of the supply shed during construction, Sprocket had occasion to do plenty of reading. Over the years, a library had collected on a low bookshelf in the classroom, and Sprocket would fill the Randolph book bag he'd affixed to the side of his wheelchair with titles like *Encyclopedia of Ancient and Forbidden Knowledge*, *The Astrologer's Handbook*, and *A Treasury of Supernatural Phenomena*. The bag also contained a few volumes of *Super Seek-and-Find* from a subscription his parents renewed yearly for his birthday. The puzzles were a throwback to his pre-accident days, before he crashed his BMX on a homemade ramp in the backyard of the twin brothers who ultimately joined the military, and his parents had kept paying the renewal notices as just another household bill, even though the brightly hued covers grew into a skyscraper in the corner of Sprocket's room after he returned from his stay in the hospital, the puzzles unworked. Sprocket had spent many an afternoon resenting the puzzle books, refusing even to flip through their pages; to do so would be to admit defeat about how his free time could be spent. But then one day he reached for the issue balanced atop the pile, and once he started circling words, he couldn't stop.

The rest of us went about the duties of a Garden Lakes fellow with zeal. A heap of drywall blossomed into a garden of scraps, board cut too small or broken solidly in two by the freight of miscalculation, or by pressure applied in the wrong place, or from navigating a corner too sharply. Regardless, under Mr. Malagon's watchful (but, as it turned out, unhelpful, as his math skills were suspect) supervision, 1959 Regis Street started to look habitable, the dust covering us so thoroughly we appeared ghostly to the sophomores at lunch.

Our sleep patterns adjusted; some of us anticipated the door-bell alarm, waking thirty to sixty seconds before the peal of chimes. A shower routine developed, fellows showing for breakfast in the same order day after day. Mr. Malagon revealed himself not to be an early riser, his eyes still half hooded as he ambled through the breakfast line, hardly distinguishable from the rest of us. Come class time, though, he was rejuvenated, slapping his palms together for effect.

Assburn continued to ignore Smurf's inquiry about the mobile phone in his possession. Assburn, who would plunge through the ice somewhere between Canada and Detroit, sinking to his death along with a load of counterfeit game systems, led a troop of us to his room (after we pledged solemnly not to breathe a word to anyone) and showed us the phone, which was smaller than the brick-size phones we'd seen. We passed the phone around as Assburn regaled us with the story of how he'd stolen it from his father's telecom business. "They're, like, four grand apiece," Assburn said proudly.

When the laws of relay brought news of our secret preview to Smurf, he was irate. He threatened Assburn with a shun and Assburn relented, allowing Smurf to use the phone to call his girlfriend. The shun against Reedy had escalated with the pouring of honey in Adam Kerr's hair while he slept, the penalty for his standing up for Reedy in the dining hall. Kerr was absent during breakfast the next morning but appeared for chapel with a shaved head. Roger snickered at Kerr, and Kerr avoided Roger's glare. Kerr told Mr. Hancock and Mr. Malagon that he'd shaved his head because of the heat, but by lunchtime we'd all heard the story and knew that Reedy had lost his only ally. By dinner, Reedy's nerves were so fragile every sound brought a momentary state of paralysis, as if his next breath, or any movement at all, would bring swift punishment of a kind Reedy could only guess.

Some of us talked about bailing Reedy out, but no one wanted to approach Roger about the reprieve. We'd never observed a shun in a closed environment (at Randolph, the shunee got to go home at the end of the day and had to withstand being ignored only between bells), and some were fascinated with the experiment, knowing the shun would ultimately be rescinded. Which was exactly what happened.

Roger cornered Reedy after tutoring one night, waiting for him at his residence. Reedy had been walking in a group that included Adam Kerr and some others, but they shot through the front door when Roger materialized from the side of their house.

Reedy thought about screaming but knew that even if Mr. Hancock answered his cry for help, Roger would retaliate the following morning (or in the dead of the night, as he had Kerr).

Roger, who would in the future go AWOL in Iraq with a platoon of his men and be court-martialed for shooting one of them, laid out the conditions of Reedy's release: Reedy was to secret a predetermined quantity of silverware from the kitchen, in increments prescribed by Roger. (Reedy had been the first to happen upon the silverware strewn outside the kitchen door and had hurried to wash it and replace the spoons, forks, and knives in their proper places for fear of being blamed by Mr. Hancock.) Reedy was to store the pilfered silverware until Roger called for it. Reedy was also made to understand that if he was caught, he was to take the heat himself, that Roger would deny knowing about it.

"Imagine how stupid you'll sound," Roger said. Reedy got the picture.

The next morning, Reedy moved around the dining hall with his old jauntiness, and we knew the shun had been called off. Hands ceremoniously called out to Reedy at lunch for another soda, and Reedy smiled, buzzing for our table, bringing us all more soda, whether we asked for it or not.

Reedy brought his energy to the soccer field too, though no matter which team he played for—or the makeup of the two squads, for that matter—the scores of the soccer matches were inevitably ties. For the first few days, we thought nothing of the deadlock. Mr. Hancock and Mr. Malagon drew up new rosters daily, no two teams consisting of the same teammates on successive days. If we had thought about it—and we didn't—this could've accounted for the scoring anomaly. Closer monitoring would've detected the silent communication between Mr. Hancock and

Mr. Malagon before a foul was called, or before Sprocket's goal-line calls were overturned, but we were still of the mind to accept things as they appeared.

It was Hands who ferreted out the conspiracy, alerting the rest of us to it during free time as Lindy whirled his telescope around the night sky, hunting for a constellation he was keen to show us.

"Guys need to keep a watch," Hands said. "If you're on the bench, or if you've got a clean view from the field, check for Hancock and Malagon to line up across from each other. They do this right before they call a foul. And they only do it if one team is ahead by two."

We'd never known Hands to exhibit signs of paranoia, but the next day didn't bear out his misgivings. Neither Mr. Hancock nor Mr. Malagon seemed to be looking to the other for calls. Nor did they appear to be acting in concert. Some wondered if Hands's ultracompetitiveness had driven him to delusion, though the even scores piled up. Hands continued to cry conspiracy, but the rest of us lost interest in Hands's theory until that Friday's match. A ball that sailed wide of the palm tree—and was correctly called out by Sprocket—was ruled a score by Mr. Malagon, bringing Figs's team within one score of Hands's squad. Hands conferred with Figs—who had been standing on the sidelines—at dinner that night.

"Who cares?" Figs said. "It's meant to be exercise. Like in a prison yard, you know?" This brought laughs from the table.

Hands snorted. "Let's run laps around the parkway if we want exercise. A match is meant to have a winner and a loser. What's the point of keeping it even?"

"Maybe it's some new teaching method," Warren said. "So no one feels badly about losing."

"Don't be dumb," Hands said, eliciting a couple of laughs before we realized he wasn't trying to be funny. "What would you guys say to a competition for Open House? A match in front of our parents. They couldn't fix that." Hands searched the table for the same fervor he felt for the idea, but met only disaffected stares.

"Yeah, sure," we said, and shrugged.

"Good idea," someone threw in.

We watched Hands work the other tables, his idea getting the same reception; but Hands was undeterred. He knew he was popular enough that no one would protest his idea—he didn't need outright frenzy, just compliance.

"Mr. Handley, what's with all the table jumping?" Mr. Malagon called out.

Hands gave a short oration on "the fellows' desire for a soccer match at Open House." Mr. Malagon appeared immediately sorry he'd asked. "We'll take your suggestion under advisement," Mr. Hancock said without looking up from his asparagus soup, the day's special. Disenchantment shaded Hands's face; he knew the phrase "We'll take your suggestion under advisement" meant something altogether different from what it would have meant had it been spoken by Mr. Malagon. The Open House soccer match would dominate Hands's thoughts over the next week, but his primary attention was focused on an idea hatched that second Friday: a stilt race through the Grove after curfew.

The race was Figs's idea. Hands had inadvertently provided the inspiration, though, as we finished off a ceiling during construction. Figs and Hands each strapped on a pair of stilts that lifted them about three feet off the ground. The rest of us hung the ceiling by standing on drywall benches, adjustable metal sawhorse-like platforms that could hold two drywallers at a time. Sprocket's cataloging and organizing of the supply shed had unearthed two pairs of stilts, and Figs and Hands volunteered to strap them on. The stilts had joints that flexed. "It's like standing on a spring," Figs said, traipsing around the dirt front yard of 1959 Regis Street like a circus performer.

Hands's learning curve was more concave. He took off after Figs but fell in front of Sprocket, who reached out to help him up. Smurf had witnessed this ignominy and cackled from an upstairs window. Figs waltzed through the house, bounding into rooms, yelling, "Just passing through!" as he swept in and out.

Mr. Malagon reined Figs in, though he was enjoying the high jinks. Hands stumbled through the open front door, tripping over a cut two-by-four someone had laid carelessly in the hallway after using it to brace a piece of drywall.

"You okay there?" Figs asked.

"I'll race you anytime in this getup," Hands countered.

And then it was forgotten. Hands acclimated to the extensions and was striding confidently through the house by the end of the working day, looking away when Figs stepped into a hole punched into the earth by a rock that had taken up residence elsewhere. Our enthusiasm for Figs and Hands's stunt waned as the day progressed; we'd practically forgotten that it had happened as we congregated for free time, which Figs and Hands had ritualized by inviting the other fellows to drop in without knocking.

"C'mon, it's Friday night," Smurf begged Assburn. "Let me at least call her and see what she's doing. Hey!" His eyes widened. "Should I tell her to come out, and bring some friends?"

Those playing stud poker at the kitchen table looked up from their cards.

"Are you nuts?" Hands asked. You could never tell when Smurf was joking and when he wasn't. Hands shook his head no to settle the question, excusing the rest of us from having to

108

weigh in on what we knew was a terrible idea, but an idea that tantalized us nonetheless.

"What, then?" Smurf asked. "It's goddamn Friday night."

"So?" someone said.

"So?" Smurf echoed. "So we should do something fun. We can't just work, work, work. *Christ.*" Smurf, who would one day successfully slander a female colleague with whom he'd cheated on his wife, spit the curse out in disgust, realizing what he'd said wasn't true: We would in fact work, work, work, and that would be all.

"What about that stilt race?" Figs asked slyly.

Hands glanced over Sprocket's head as Sprocket dealt. "Anytime, tough guy," he said.

Figs stood. "Why not? If we were quiet about it, we could do it away from the houses," he said. "Maybe down at the entrance. The pavement's better there anyway."

"Why not back in the Grove?" Hands asked, anteing up. "A little obstacle course action."

"No way I can give you the keys to the supply shed," Sprocket said without stopping the fourth round of cards. "No way."

"That's true," Hands said. "There really is no way you can give us those keys." He paused. "We could take them"—he smiled—"but there's no way you could give them to us."

"You want to get me kicked out?" Sprocket asked.

"No one's going to get kicked out," Figs said. "Has anyone ever gotten kicked out? I don't think so. And with Quinn taking off, and the others not showing, they can't afford to kick anyone out."

Some of us nodded in agreement.

"Sorry," Sprocket said.

"Yes!" Warren said, scooping up the pot of plastic poker chips.

Sprocket passed the deck of cards to his left. Warren picked up the cards and shuffled them liberally. "Who's in?"

"This one is just me and Sprocket," Hands said gamely. "For the keys."

Sprocket eyed Hands. "What?"

"If I win, you set the keys on the table and I take them from you. If we're busted, I tell Hancock and Malagon I stole the keys from your room. Everyone in this room will stick to the same story."

"I'll get in trouble for not keeping the keys safe," Sprocket said.

Hands turned to Warren: "Deal."

Luck seemed not to be on the side of the scheme. Sprocket landed all four aces and quickly won the first hand—prompting a call to reshuffle the deck, which Warren did with exaggerated effect. Skill worked against the endeavor as well. Hands's lack of skill as a poker player, that is. Some of us were taken aback by his poor play—we'd all assumed his talent for winning was inherent, so his losing at anything was inconceivable. Consequently, Sprocket beat Hands two games out of three. Hands lobbied for best of five. Sprocket acquiesced under protest, spurred to accept the challenge by the jeers masquerading as encouragement around the room. Hands evened the game at two apiece, but a pair of jacks delivered Sprocket the fifth and decisive game. Hands looked like he was going to propose a best of ten but instead said, "Well, you're a mighty fine poker player, Sprocket. But we need those keys."

Sprocket glanced up from his cards, puzzled.

"Same deal," Hands said. "We get caught, we say we stole the keys from you."

"The deal was *if you beat me*, you could have the keys," Sprocket said, waiting for confirmation from the rest of us, glancing around the room when it failed to surface.

"Aw, c'mon, Sprocket," Figs said. "We're not going to get caught. And if we do, you're not going to be in trouble."

Hands saw that Sprocket was unmoved by Figs's appeal. "No one will care about a stupid little race," he added. "We should just ask Hancock and Malagon, and they'd let us. Maybe I should run over and ask Mr. Malagon," Hands said, standing. "He'll probably want to take on the winner."

Sprocket knew the social consequences if Mr. Malagon assented to the race—and he believed Hands *would* ask, even at the risk of being told no—and surrendered the keys from a hidden Velcro pocket on the inside of the right armrest of his wheelchair, dropping them with a contemptuous jangle on the Formica kitchen table.

There were those who remained behind with Sprocket, either out of sympathy or out of cowardice; the rest of us walked quietly toward the supply shed, which shone under the phosphorescent moon. The Grove was similarly lit, the symmetrical grid of gravel knolls beckoning all comers to test their navigational skills. Figs and Hands suited up first, the vaunted matchup producing cries of "I got next!" from the gallery of faces washed gray by the moonlight.

The ground rules were laid: Contestants were to weave through a specified row of rock. Points would be assessed—one if the contestant grazed any rock pile, two for each fall taken by a contestant. The winner would be the contestant with the fewest number of points against him.

"Ready . . . set . . . go!" Warren signaled the start of the race with a wave. Figs and Hands darted through the maze, in and out of the piles of limestone and slate and shale, some worn into cones by wind, others leveled off by unknown tracks, some human, most animal. None of us acknowledged the orbital train of paw prints that could only have been made by coyotes. The absence of yipping told us coyotes were unseen spectators watching from a distance.

Hands vanished momentarily behind the second rock pile from the finish line, and Figs called out, "Two points!" in a voice loud enough to be heard but quiet enough not to perk the ears of Mr. Malagon or Mr. Hancock. Hands swore through his teeth, knowing he was beaten. Figs galloped to the finish line, a full rock pile in front of Hands, and circled back, weaving toward us so as to avoid Hands's bitter disappointment.

"Two out of three," Hands said, his hands on his knees. He rubbed at the smear of dirt on his khakis incurred from his fall.

"No way," Roger said. "It's my shot at the champ."

We each raced once, though there was no clear champion—Figs beat Hands, but then Roger beat Figs; Assburn beat Roger and then beat me, finally falling to Warren, who was promptly beaten by Roger. Hands was still talking about a rematch with Figs when Warren remarked how late it was. We sneaked back onto Garden Lakes Parkway. The still houses along Regis Street seemed to foretell our doom.

Our alarm clocks read nine thirty, a half an hour beyond curfew, and we each feared being the one to be called on to explain the night's activities. Fantastic improbabilities floated through our minds: *Maybe Hancock and Malagon didn't make a bed check. Maybe they poked their heads inside the door and assumed we were in our beds, exhausted. Maybe we could say we were out stargazing with Lindy.* Some of us set our clocks back a half an hour, creating a digital alibi. We lay awake, though, until we put back those thirty minutes, knowing it wouldn't work.

It was no surprise, then, when Mr. Hancock rang our door-bells angrily, calling out "No showers!" Our blood pumped in our ears, our eyes dry and tired, but we double-timed it to the dining hall, averting our eyes as we entered and took our seats. The kitchen was busy, but no food had been laid out for breakfast.

Mr. Hancock stormed into the room, Mr. Malagon in tow, a sour look on his face, a jury of two called back from deliberations to render their verdict.

Mr. Hancock, on the verge of leaving Garden Lakes with the school's permission, shot Figs a look that stole all our breath. He knew. Someone had ratted us out—Figs in particular—and the pool of suspects began and ended with Sprocket. Possibly Lindy, though Lindy had been leading a pod of sophomores on a celestial exploration through his telescope.

Realizing he had been caught, Figs internally ran through the arguments. He could deny it, though he usually eschewed denial because of its stringency: Once you started denying, you had to keep on denying, regardless of the evidence brought against you. Figs knew unilateral denials were trouble; he preferred the maneuverability of vagueness. He would calmly wait for the case to be presented against him.

Mr. Hancock's glowering unnerved Figs, though. Another thought, one that visited Figs now and again, was that someone—somehow—was onto him about what happened in Mazatlán, that he'd invented the policeraid to make himself out as a hero. The next day and every day since, Figs had known he'd made a mistake. He'd come close to divulging it to Hands, but he knew the information would make Hands coguardian of the secret, and realized his desire to let Hands in on it was a selfish move to lessen the stressful burden. Each time Rosa's or Mazatlán was mentioned, Figs had to call up the mental note cards etched with the details of that night. He had to remember what he'd said about how he'd heard a car pull up, about the quick footsteps on the dirt driveway, about the excited voices speaking Spanish. He'd memorized the details with the same concentration he had his social security number and date of birth, and guarded the information with the same care.

As lucid as the manufactured minutiae was the very real cause of said manufacture. As he paced the backyard that night, the ramifications of not going inside to meet one of Rosa's girls weighed on him. He knew he couldn't let Hands and the others walk out sharing the distinction of having visited Rosa's. The playful taunts weren't what worried Figs. The idea of *not* wanting to visit a prostitute required some sophistication on the part of the mind trying to understand it, and as Figs knew, it was easier to substitute slander and innuendo in the place of understanding.

Panic morphed into desperation. A carload of teenagers arriving at Rosa's prompted the idea of the raid. The sudden absence of the bouncer at the door was the impetus. Figs made up his mind, the strangers in the backyard glancing casually as he charged the door, hollering.

The memory turned Figs's stomach.

But while the occasion of the showerless, foodless breakfast *was* a curfew violation (and it was clear to all of us that Mr. Hancock had been hipped to our derby in the Grove), we wouldn't have guessed in a million years if we had been given a million guesses what had steamed Mr. Hancock and chagrined Mr. Malagon so.

"You boys will notice that Mr. Murfin is no longer with us," Mr. Hancock said.

We scanned the tables, acknowledging one another for the first time that morning, and confirmed what Mr. Hancock had said: Smurf was not in attendance.

"Mr. Murfin has been sent home," Mr. Hancock continued, "for violating curfew."

A silence fell across the room. Our empty stomachs rumbled, our hunger muzzled by our rattled nerves. "Boys, Smurf was kicked out for smuggling in his girlfriend," Mr. Malagon said with dispiriting frankness. Clearly, he'd fought for Smurf and lost. Mr. Malagon wouldn't have considered the offense expellable; Mr. Hancock, on the other hand, would have argued for capital punishment (in which case Smurf was getting off easy). "There are some questions about how exactly Mr. Murfin was able to summon his girlfriend to meet him," he said. "So if any of you boys have anything to add, please feel free to speak up."

Assburn's face glowed with sweat, though he refrained from wiping it for fear of drawing attention. But Mr. Hancock appeared oblivious about Assburn's mobile phone. Warren and a few others glanced at Assburn, but Assburn trained his eyes on the clock on the wall behind Mr. Hancock.

The particulars of Smurf's rendezvousing became known over the course of the next two days: Smurf had instructed his girlfriend to wait with her car hood up outside the gates of Garden Lakes. (This detail was particularly hilarious, as Smurf was often the victim of his own imagination: Once while his parents were on vacation, he fired his father's .357 through his bedroom door, thinking someone was trying to break in in the dead of night. His parents never fixed the spiderwebbing on Smurf's door where the bullet had exited, lodging in the hallway between portraits of Smurf and of Smurf's grandparents.) Smurf waited until ten o'clock and then tiptoed out of his residence on Regis Street, careful not to wake his housemates, padding along Garden Lakes Parkway to the entrance, where his girlfriend was waiting. A perfect plan. Perfect except for Mr. Malagon, who, unable to sleep, was out for a walk. He spotted Smurf, and thinking that Smurf had followed Q's lead and deserted, he reported the departure to Mr. Hancock early the next morning. But Mr. Hancock's search turned Smurf up, asleep in his bed. Mr. Hancock questioned Assburn and Roger, who knew nothing about Smurf's nocturnal voyage. Once satisfied in this, Mr. Hancock hauled Smurf to his residence on Loyola, where he made Smurf phone his parents to come pick him up, which they did before Mr. Hancock woke the rest of us.

We feared Mr. Hancock knew about the stilt race too, but he was prevented from prosecuting by Reedy, who rushed into the dining hall, his bloodless face shaped by terror.

"What is it?" Mr. Hancock growled.

"Laird got bit," was all Reedy said.

"Scorpion?" Mr. Malagon asked, but Reedy's pale look told us it was not a scorpion but a rattlesnake.

The dining hall emptied and we crowded around Laird, a sophomore whose first name some of us didn't even know, who was curled up on the smooth kitchen floor, grabbing his right ankle in anguish. The kitchen smelled of pureed tomatoes.

"You boys stand back," Mr. Hancock said. He and Mr. Malagon kneeled beside Laird. Mr. Malagon ripped Laird's pant leg and we saw spots of blood coagulated around the puncture marks.

"How did it happen?" Mr. Malagon asked.

"I was taking the garbage out," Laird explained, "and it was outside the back door." Laird twitched. "God, it stings."

Mr. Malagon, who would break all our hearts, cautiously opened the back door. "It's gone," he said. "I'll take Laird to the emergency room. Maybe I can talk them into a good rate on visits."

Mr. Malagon's attempt at humor brought a titter from the crowd. "I'll take him," Mr. Hancock said automatically. Mr. Malagon appeared as if he might protest, but didn't. Instead, he rounded us all back into the dining hall, calling on the sophomores to serve breakfast. Mr. Hancock and Laird rolled past the windows while we devoured cereal and fruit as if we hadn't eaten in days. Mr. Malagon disappeared into the hall, reappearing a moment later after having cleared the community center as being free from any sign of the snake.

"I'm going to need some volunteers," Mr. Malagon said. "Fellows and sophomores both. Need teams of three to search the houses and scour the area, beating the brush for this thing. We don't want it sunning on a rock in our vicinity." We looked at one another fearfully. "To be clear," he continued, "I'm not asking you to corner it, trap it, or kill it."

"I'll go," Roger said, hailing Mr. Malagon from a back table. "Count me in."

"Good shoe, Roger," Mr. Malagon said. "Who else? Hands?"

Hands brought his face out of his cereal bowl. "Yeah," he said reluctantly. "Sure."

"Attaboy."

One by one, we volunteered. Not because we wanted to be snake hunters, but because with each raised hand the moment changed from an opportunity to volunteer into an event that would forever divide us into two camps: Those Who Did and Those Who Didn't.

A few of the sophomores, not yet schooled in the ways of coerced volunteerism, elected to stay behind in the kitchen to decipher Mr. Hancock's instructions for caldo verde, a difficult

117

Portuguese green soup whose ingredients included Portuguese sausage and kale. Conscription not being in Mr. Malagon's nature, he did not press the sophomores.

We spread out across Garden Lakes, angst about the day's schedule abetting our search, which we undertook with caution. Under Mr. Malagon's directive, we were to throw open the front door and yell, listening for the clack of the snake's rattle. Cupboards were not to be opened, but were to be banged on; toilets flushed before lifting the lid; each bedroom receiving the door-thrown-open treatment, accompanied with yelling. Beds were to be bounced on before anyone scouted beneath with the sawed-off ends of two-by-fours scavenged from the construction site. "Don't stick your kisser under the bed," Mr. Malagon said.

Sophomores trailed fellows through the front doors of their own houses. The snake hunt momentarily suspended our disbelief that Smurf had been kicked out. His bellowing was plainly absent from our screams and yelling as we tried to flush out the rattlesnake, half hoping for a chance at it, half hoping that it was on its way to Mexico.

The houses on Loyola Street seemed unlived in. The pristine kitchens and unused couches in the front rooms gave the feeling of a model home. A veneer of dust blown in from open windows and open doors had accumulated on the kitchen countertops. Those who had been sophomores at Garden Lakes knew that the downstairs was just a hallway linking the private life spent in the sanctuary of the bedroom to the life of servitude all sophs lived for six of the hottest weeks of the year.

Roger led Reedy (who had become his new best friend, apparently) and Adam Kerr through their residence, violating Mr. Malagon's instructions by boldly opening the kitchen and bathroom cabinets without knocking. Reedy and Kerr stayed back as Roger opened door after door. Being bitten was better than being afraid, he reasoned.

A sweep of Loyola Street turned up nothing. We marched down Regis like a street gang looking for a fight, the air interspersed with tough talk about what would be done if the predator was found. Hands recommended the sophomores be permitted to return to the kitchen, and Mr. Malagon agreed. The relieved sophs hastened inside the community center, leaving us to continue the hunt.

We split up into teams, each inspecting its own house. Mr. Malagon tapped Figs and Warren, who were standing nearest him, to help check his residence. "We'll meet at 1959 to check the jobsite," he said. "But wait for me in the street. No one goes in until I say so." Mr. Malagon's commands fired us up, as if we were war heroes taking back a beachhead or liberating a village overrun by tyrants.

Our labors to turn up the snake in any of our houses were unsuccessful. Assburn charged ahead to his room, yelling as he pushed open the door, listening nervously for any rattling. He wasn't concerned about the mobile phone—though he still wanted to control the number of people who knew about it (we all knew, at this point)—but worried the package with Q's father's pen would be discovered. He leaped from the doorway to his bed, his head coming within inches of the acoustic ceiling finish. He hopped off the bed and swabbed underneath with the board he'd snagged from the pile out front of 1959. Nothing. "All clear!" he yelled, double-checking that the bulge between the mattress and box spring could not be seen or felt.

Mr. Malagon called us all out of our houses for a report.

"Negative," Roger said.

"All clear," Hands said.

"Nada," Assburn said.

"What about Smurf's room?" Mr. Malagon asked.

Assburn and Roger exchanged glances. The door to Smurf's room had been closed, slammed by Smurf in protest as Mr. Hancock and Mr. Malagon stood watch earlier that morning. Assburn had opened his door to investigate the commotion but had been shooed back inside by Mr. Hancock. They'd regarded Smurf's room as quarantined as they swept the house for the snake.

Roger spoke up. "We didn't check."

The sun blasted the rooftops and street with heat. Since none of us wore watches—the schedule our only guide—we would've sworn it was after noon. In reality, it was a little past six a.m. We followed Mr. Malagon, who took the steps two at a time, the way men in their thirties do to test their fading athleticism. Hands and Figs and Roger followed through the house and up the stairs too, others jogging behind.

Mr. Malagon battered the door as he turned the knob. Hands began yodeling, until Mr. Malagon told him to shut up. The snake was not in Smurf's room, the sheets still mussed from what little sleep Smurf must've gotten the night before. An empty pack of Camel Lights lay crumpled defiantly on the dresser, but Mr. Malagon made no effort to throw the pack away, his eyes roving the room. "Okay, boys," he said. "There's nothing here."

A deferential silence fell among us. Smurf was a general pain in the ass, but he could cut the tension in any room. He would've goofed on us for thinking a lowly snake was interested in menacing us, we knew, and this much-needed solace made Smurf's expulsion reverberate. Mr. Malagon lingered, opening Smurf's top dresser drawer as he put one hand on the bedroom door. Figs turned in time to notice Mr. Malagon retrieve Smurf's job

120

journal and fold it into his back pocket. "Let's go," he said to Figs, clapping him on the back.

"We're going to get back on schedule," Mr. Malagon said after we'd all reunited in Hands and Figs and Lindy's living room. "We'll make a search of the jobsite and then we'll work until the midmorning break. Any questions?" There were none. As we let ourselves out, Mr. Malagon pulled Figs aside.

"That was a stupid stunt last night," Mr. Malagon told him. "It would've been you who was thrown out and not Smurf if Smurf hadn't done you one better. Is that what you want?"

"No, sir," Figs said, eyes downcast. He'd assumed this pose before, but this time he felt grateful that he hadn't been tossed out of Garden Lakes.

"Mr. Hancock is going to be keeping an eye on you from now on," Mr. Malagon said. "I can't do on that score other than to alert you to the fact. So watch yourself, okay?"

"Yes, sir."

Mr. Malagon appraised Figs's face and smiled. "Knock that 'sir' shit off," he said. "Everyone else might buy it, but I don't."

Figs smiled back. "Okay."

"Here's a piece of advice, for what it's worth: The only people who like a politician are those who are getting something from him; everyone else hates him. You'll learn that sooner or later, but I thought I'd give you a head start on that bit of wisdom."

Figs didn't understand what Mr. Malagon meant, but nodded as if he did. He knew most adults were appeased by nodding in agreement.

To alleviate our anxiety over the snake—Laird had been given an antidote and returned with nothing more than a sore ankle and a slight limp—Mr. Hancock announced the screening of a movie at seven p.m. in the dining hall (refreshments would be served), and so the reading hour and sophomore tutoring passed slowly, our excitement about the movie overmatching our concentration. We hadn't accounted for the truth that neither Mr. Hancock nor Mr. Malagon would have run to the closest video store and would instead be selecting one of the boxless videotapes stored in the locking compartment under the TV/ VCR combo mounted on a cart that was used to show instructional videos at retreats. So we were dismayed when Mr. Hancock revealed the evening's fare: *The Lost Weekend*, a movie none of us had heard of, starring actors we didn't recognize. But none of us complained, glad to be out of our sweltering houses while the air-conditioning worked to cool our rooms to temperatures that were livable. We were gladder still to be bunkered in the dining hall, forgetting about the day's events for a couple of hours.

Mr. Hancock watched the first half hour of the movie with us, then slipped out the door. Roger crept to the front door, waiting until Mr. Hancock was safely inside his house. He tapped Reedy on the shoulder, and he rose like a soldier and followed Roger into the kitchen. Quickly, they filled a plastic five-gallon bucket that had previously held sliced dill pickles with all the silverware from the silverware bins. Spoons, knives, forks—everything. Those who had seen Roger and Reedy duck into the kitchen pretended not to; the rest of us were too weary to take notice.

By the end of the film, Roger and Reedy had returned, brazenly walking through the front door of the community center. Mr. Hancock reappeared right as the credits rolled, none the wiser. "Twenty minutes to curfew, boys," he said in a businesslike tone. Subconsciously, we appreciated his tone as a constant from our life outside of Garden Lakes. Privately, we aped Mr. Hancock, whose nickname among the brave was Hand Job, addressing one another in parody of his brusque speech. But we obeyed his every instruction. Not to would have reduced him and would've shattered any semblance of what we'd come to regard as our life together, a life forged from the admonishment we'd collectively endured.

Lindy approached Mr. Hancock as the last of us filtered out of the dining hall. Lindy, whose tragic death in his thirties would traumatize his young family, would rather have asked Mr. Malagon's permission to climb up onto the roof with his telescope, but we hadn't seen Mr. Malagon since dinner and presumed he was busy grading our quizzes. "The lake bed is unsafe," Lindy explained to Mr. Hancock, "what with the snake and all."

"The roof isn't much safer," Mr. Hancock said, spying a glass half filled with ice and soda that someone had abandoned under the Coke spigot of the soda machine. "Why not just point that thing out your window?"

"The window faces north," Lindy said, protesting mildly.

"No stars in the north?" Mr. Hancock looked at Lindy dubiously. He sensed that a scheme was afoot, having been ambushed by Smurf's late-night dalliance. Never in his tenure had Mr. Hancock experienced such a flaunting of the strictures of Garden Lakes. Outwardly he blamed modern youth; inwardly he worried his age made him vulnerable to the agitations of the young.

"I'm tracking Lyra," Lindy said. "We've been plotting it on the back of my job journal and—"

"We?" Mr. Hancock asked, hoping to ascertain the conspirators in this unnamed conspiracy.

"Some of the sophomores are interested in astronomy, sir," Lindy said, adding the "sir" in a transparent bid for consent, which, astonishingly, persuaded Mr. Hancock.

123

The rooftop view was spectacular, as Lindy could lie on his back and probe the sky without worry that the telescope would slide from the tripod. He entertained himself watching the itinerant stars shoot against the black sky. Sensing it was near curfew, Lindy dusted himself off. For his amusement, he surveyed Garden Lakes from his new vantage point—the supply shed, the construction site, the empty playing field. A movement in the telescope caught his attention. He focused the lens, startled to see Smurf's face fill up the telescope. He followed Smurf as Smurf hunched behind creosote bushes on the eastern edge of the development, his eyes on the lights in the windows of the houses along Regis Street.

Hands and Figs came upon Warren pacing in front of the locked dining hall door, a hastily markered sign bearing the announcement BREAKFAST CANCELED DUE TO SILVERWARE THEFT taped crookedly above the square window in the door.

"In here," Mr. Hancock said, appearing at the end of the hall.

"Goddamn Roger," Hands murmured.

We were herded into the chapel and directed to sit in the pews. Mr. Hancock promised to send home the first person who spoke without permission. Mr. Malagon watched anxiously from his seat on a folding chair at the front of the room.

"You boys know why you're here," Mr. Hancock said. He was deceptively calm, but Mr. Malagon's countenance evinced the danger we faced. "And since asking which of you is responsible for the kitchen theft is surely a waste of your time and mine, Mr. Malagon is going to search each room in each house while you wait here with me. This will afford the guilty party or parties a few moments before they are exposed, oh"—Mr. Hancock looked at his watch—"about thirty minutes from now."

Mr. Malagon obviously did not approve of Mr. Hancock's

theatrics but restrained himself, instead leaning over and putting his chin in his hands.

"What do you think, Mr. Malagon?" Mr. Hancock said. "Should we give the guilty party a chance for confession?" A dull dread settled over the pews. Mr. Hancock continued without losing the thread of his performance. "I guess it wouldn't hurt to ask," he said.

No one flinched.

Mr. Hancock turned to Mr. Malagon, who stood awkwardly. "It might prove interesting to interview these boys separately," Mr. Hancock said, wrapping up the final act. "I'm certain we'd have the answer to our question then." He turned back toward us. "But we haven't the time." He gave one last look through the pews.

Nothing.

Mr. Hancock nodded at Mr. Malagon, who didn't make eye contact as he passed on his way out.

We found Roger's poise remarkable. Miscellaneous theories ran through our minds. Maybe Roger had dumped the silverware out in the Grove. Or behind the supply shed. Maybe he had buried it in the sand. Each solution would be unsatisfying to Mr. Hancock, we knew, and we secretly hoped Roger had left the silverware under his bed, where Mr. Malagon could easily find it.

Which was what we thought had happened when Mr. Malagon returned with Roger's bag, the clank of silverware preceding his entrance. Consternation replaced the bemused look with which Mr. Hancock had held us during Mr. Malagon's absence, as if he was disappointed that the silverware had been found, confirming its theft and thereby identifying a thief in our midst.

Mr. Hancock waited for Mr. Malagon to disclose the hiding place of the stolen utensils.

"Found it in Casey Murfin's closet," Mr. Malagon said.

The Smurf! A new respect flared up for Roger, whom none of us had considered very clever. Roger's face betrayed little as Mr. Malagon handed the bag to Mr. Hancock, who squinted into the sack. His face clouded with anger. "Mr. Malagon will hold you here until the guilty party steps forward," he said. "You'll make the time up out of your meals." He summoned his kitchen staff and led the sophomores across the hall, discarding the silverware loudly into the stainless steel sink.

Mr. Malagon closed the chapel door. The first glimmer of dawn rose though the window as he spoke. "Let me tell you not only why this prank is unfunny," he said, "but also why it was incredibly stupid." He crossed his arms. "You may not know about the power of cohesion yet, but let me tell you that it is essential to a working environment like this. We enjoy cohesion on campus—we're not walking arm in arm and whistling zip-a-dee-doo-dah, but I think you'll agree that Randolph Eagles are a tight unit. You may be surprised to know that this is not the norm. Life in public school is more scattershot. It's hard to know whom to count on. Believe me, I've taught public high school, and for better or worse, there's a difference in the social fabric.

"And, as you can guess, cohesive communities experience a better quality of life. That would've been the case before today, but now Mr. Hancock is angry, and an angry Mr. Hancock is detrimental to cohesion. Why? Because the only thing more important than cohesion is discipline. And now Mr. Hancock must punish someone for this . . . this idiotic exhibition."

Mr. Malagon's face reddened at having to appear before us as a disciplinarian. Mr. Malagon had a perfect record for never sending anyone from his classroom down to Principal Breen's office, but this record was kept perfect only by the tacit understanding that while fear of punishment had been diminished (if not obliterated), this alleviation brought a measure of responsibility on our part: We had to know how far to take things.

Roger stood.

Mr. Malagon glanced at Roger. "Yes?"

"I know who is responsible," Roger said.

We couldn't guess what Roger was up to. That he would confess in open court was too incredulous even for Mr. Malagon, who looked skeptically at Roger.

Mr. Malagon waited patiently, a clamor from the kitchen piercing the air. "Well?"

"I'd rather tell you in private," Roger said.

Mr. Malagon narrowed his eyes. "Very well," he said. "Step out into the hall."

Roger stepped out of his row, pushing past Warren and Assburn, and fell in behind Mr. Malagon, both sidestepping Sprocket, who was dozing in his wheelchair.

None of us wanted to break the silence, afraid of what was going to happen next. We didn't care if Roger was kicked out of Garden Lakes. We would've gladly doubled up to cover his contribution if the labor would've guaranteed his removal. When we learned that Roger wasn't going to be censured after all—he hadn't even copped to the theft, but instead ratted out Reedy, who willingly admitted that he'd taken the silverware as a joke— Figs said he would float the plot in secret.

The missing silverware was the penultimate crime, as Mr. Hancock and Mr. Malagon discovered when the sophomores were brought back in for chapel. (Breakfast had been canceled as a penalty, but also because the sun was rising rapidly and we all knew we were about a day behind on the construction.) Mr. Hancock bade us to open our hymnals, and the cacophonous sound of butter knives falling against the tile floor rang in our ears.

Reedy appeared close to passing out as Mr. Hancock lunged for him amid a torrent of curses. Some of us noticed Roger's contentment and pleasure at seeing Mr. Hancock explode. And he later chortled when we learned of Reedy's fate: Mr. Hancock forced him to move into his house, doubling Reedy's reading assignments and conscripting him to be his manservant. The slump in Reedy's posture and the lag in his step affirmed the severity of this discipline.

Mr. Hancock did not return and chapel was abbreviated by the weekly grocery delivery. Mr. Malagon took command of the sophomores while they checked in the groceries, allowing the rest of us to pass through the kitchen, grabbing an orange or banana or a bagel or muffin on our way out to the construction site.

"I need four volunteers for garbage," Mr. Malagon called out. We weren't clear if he meant us or the sophomores—the garbage detail was normally handled by the sophs, who collected the refuse from the community center and from each residence, riding with Mr. Hancock to the front gates, where the plastic bags were heaped like a black igloo along the side of the road for the early-Monday pickup. As could be expected, Figs and Hands volunteered directly, commandeering two sophomores as aides-de-camp. Their mission was interrupted by the exodus of the grocery truck, however. The truck revved and soldiered away from the loading dock, lightened of its load. As the truck gained its footing on the paved outer loop, we all saw it at once: the head of the rattlesnake crushed into one of the encrusted tracks, its tail and rattle swaying hypnotically in its final throes. We stood waiting for its scaly body to lunge, to make one last attack, sure that it was feigning weakness to draw us closer, wanting us to play a hand in our own misfortune.

**

128

No one was happier than Reedy when Mr. Malagon announced Mr. Hancock's departure two days later. Rather than calling everyone together, which may have caused confusion and upset, Mr. Hancock excused himself after curfew to attend a family funeral. Some of us heard the Jeep's engine and parted the slats in our blinds to see a pair of headlights, followed by a set of receding taillights. We had no way of knowing about the conversation that had preceded Mr. Hancock's exit—Mr. Hancock's proposal for bringing in a substitute, Mr. Malagon assuring Mr. Hancock that he could hold down the fort until Mr. Hancock's return the following Sunday. We imagined Mr. Malagon relished the opportunity. He may even have had inklings of heroism, how he'd run Garden Lakes solo for five days.

"Mr. Hancock's leave of absence is not without precedent," Mr. Malagon explained to us at breakfast the next morning. Apparently, Mr. Hancock had once been hospitalized for an allergic reaction to a bee sting sustained during sports, though in that instance he'd been gone only overnight. To cope with Mr. Hancock's vacancy, revolving teams of fellows would alternate between kitchen duty and construction. "I'll float between the groups," Mr. Malagon said. "We'll keep to the schedule the best we can, though the sophomores will have to join us for class." We groaned, not really caring. "Oh, and you may have to get accustomed to grilled cheese and tomato soup." Mr. Malagon clapped his hands together and grinned.

We welcomed the change in routine. While it had been only about a week and a half since we left the civilized world, the monotony of the schedule had slowed time to an unbearable pace. A minute was an hour, just as it was when we were in class or serving Saturday detention. Not knowing which team we'd be working on each day added the necessary mystery to pry our eyes open, our alarms shrieking from our bedsides. We were also eager for the chance to prove that our selection as fellows wasn't a mistake, that we were worthy of the honor.

Splitting shifts in the kitchen wasn't the only emendation. To the delight of all, Mr. Malagon announced the lifting of curfew. "I'll trust you to know when you should call it a night," he said. "However, I retain the right to reverse this policy should it be abused." The sophomores enjoyed the changing of the guard, however ephemeral the new regime might be. Banter around the kitchen increased during meal prep, fellows teasing sophomores and vice versa.

Mr. Malagon accepted the sophomores' offer to aid us in construction, too. We agreed to suspend the soup program temporarily (the soups to date were rotting in their containers in our refrigerators anyway), so the sophs would be free to lend a hand, mainly on cleanup but also to make uniform our various fastening techniques, some of us hammering a nail every foot or so, others spacing them even farther apart. And while the surplus workers underfoot created an element of bedlam, we were glad for the help.

Mr. Malagon rewarded our cooperation by sending out for pizzas one night, retrieving the mobile phone from Mr. Hancock's residence to place the order. The girl who delivered the pizzas was a blond angel draped in red and blue, her baseball hat sporting the pizza company's logo pulled down over her eyes. The dining hall fell silent as Mr. Malagon signed the credit card receipt. "I thought it was a prank," the delivery girl said, her voice transporting us back to the real world, reminding us of our mothers and sisters and girlfriends.

"Well?" Mr. Malagon said.

We'd forgotten about the pizza. Those of us closest to the door scrambled after the delivery girl to help with the boxes.

We could still smell her perfume as she pulled away, leaving us in her fragrant wake. We munched, relaxing for the first time since we arrived. Mr. Malagon joined us in telling dirty jokes (though he drew the line at Roger's racist sprinkler joke), later excusing himself to work on the next day's lecture. He advised the sophomores to keep up with their reading, but without the threat of quizzes, tutoring turned into bull sessions about the Randolph faculty, or boasting about Xavierites we knew, most of which we knew was bullshit, though the sophomores ate it up.

The tutoring pods broke up early and Hands suggested a game of poker, but Figs quashed the suggestion as too boring. Warren, whose unwitting complicity in an Internet scam would bilk millions from the elderly, volunteered to get the beanbags from Mr. Malagon, who had disappeared for the night, but Figs demurred. Roger challenged everyone to some Indian wrestling, and we cleared the furniture out of the front room and played several matches, Roger's powerful thighs beating each of us handily. Warren gave Roger the most trouble, his long legs making it difficult for Roger to flip him over.

Sprocket watched from the sidelines, initially cheering on Roger's opponents, but ultimately becoming bored by the predictable outcomes. It was barely eight o'clock when we tired of wrestling.

"Let's drop in on Mr. Malagon," Hands said. "Maybe he has some booze." The idea of sharing a beer with Mr. Malagon didn't sound as far-fetched as it probably was, but we would never know, since the idea never moved past debate.

It was well after one in the morning when we finally crawled into our beds. The four-thirty alarms hectored us from our nightstands. Assburn had slept less than any of us, though. He had fought the onslaught of sleep, making sure his residence was still before creeping out the front door, the package with Senator Quinn's pen tucked in his pocket. He hurried across the lake bed and through the heart of East Garden Lakes. Assburn located an outcrop of rock and dug with his hands until he'd hollowed out a space big enough to fit the package. Packing the dirt over the pen, he heard a shuffling noise in the darkness. He called out Roger's name instinctively, but no one answered. He listened for the sound again, but the quiet spooked him further and he ran back to his room, swallowing his heavy breathing as he neared Regis Street.

Smurf, that unparalleled future slanderer and adulterer, waited until Assburn had faded into the night and then pulled on the corner of the freshly buried package until the earth let go, sand and silt caving around the hollow as the package came free of its hiding place. He turned it over in his hands, wondering what it contained.

Assburn woke relieved. Even the realization that he'd missed breakfast and would have to rush to catch up with the rest of us in chapel did not ruin his exaltation. Burying the pen in the desert was like undergoing a successful operation to remove an invisible tumor, one Assburn saw every time he looked in the mirror.

Mr. Malagon acknowledged Assburn's tardiness with a nod, but under Mr. Malagon's reign of self-government, hunger would be Assburn's only punishment. The rest of us took note and wondered what would happened if, say, Assburn had missed chapel. Or class. We valued our newfound freedom too much to test Mr. Malagon, though. We'd be back on the old schedule soon enough, the days grinding away under the burden of Mr. Hancock's omnipresence.

132

We labored to stay awake during chapel. Mr. Malagon, whose betrayal we'd never forgive, refrained from asking us what had kept us up so late. His response to our tiredness was to sing louder, his surge of energy underscoring our lethargy.

The day wouldn't get any easier. Mr. Malagon reminded us that Mr. Baker, who would be our hostage before it was all over, was set to return that Saturday, to inspect the first phase of construction and give us guidance about the next phase. With the aid of the sophomores, we were able to bring ourselves back on schedule; but the walls of 1959 Regis Street, pocked as they were with openings needing drywall, lashed us to our work. We moved in a delirium, each minute warmer than the last as the sun rose.

Mr. Malagon was chastising Sprocket for napping in the supply shed when Roger's fist glanced off Warren's jaw in one of the upstairs bedrooms. As a testament to how exhausted Roger was, the blow hardly fazed Warren, who in turn collared Roger, dragging him to the ground. The wrestling match overturned a pair of drywall benches, a tape measure resting on one skittering into the corner. The combatants rolled into a drywall lift holding an unfastened panel against the ceiling, and a few of us rushed over to steady the brace, which wobbled and then came to rest.

Mr. Malagon burst through the crowd as Roger regained his composure, standing and delivering two successive punches to Warren's midsection. "Cool it, Roger," he yelled, but Roger was deaf to the instructions and continued to go after Warren, who was no less committed.

Mr. Malagon instructed Figs and Hands to remove Warren from the room. Without hesitation, they locked their arms around Warren and whisked him down the stairs as he screamed epithets at Roger. Roger headed for the stairs, but Mr. Malagon detained him, pushing him into a corner. Some of us slunk away

133

as Mr. Malagon shouted for Roger to calm down. The fight had stirred the dust, and a gray haze floated through the room.

The subsequent minutes were spent interrogating both Roger and Warren, but Mr. Malagon learned only that the fight had started over Roger's co-opting Warren's tape measure. We found this explanation implausible (as did Mr. Malagon), though none of us knew of a beef that existed between Roger and Warren. The lameness of the fight's impetus infuriated Mr. Malagon. He strode through the house, knocking a cut piece of drywall to the ground, calling out, "Any boy who is not inside his residence within five minutes will find his parents here to pick him up."

We milled around for a minute, bewildered. Was he serious? There was work to be done before Mr. Baker's arrival. Any deviation from the schedule jeopardized the Open House. We'd witnessed Mr. Malagon's ire only once before, the time Garth Atlon made birdcalls from the back of the classroom every time Mr. Malagon mentioned Lady Bird Johnson during a lesson about LBJ and the Great Society. The first birdcall soared under our laughter—Mr. Malagon's, too—as did the second and third times Garth put his hands to his mouth; by the fourth time, we were completely distracted from the lesson. Mr. Malagon called for Garth to quit, giving Garth his famous stare, which meant it was all right to goof off but now it was time to work. But Garth was dialed in, the birdcalls tickling his fancy, and Mr. Malagon's stare couldn't reach him. Mr. Malagon beaned Garth with an eraser from the grease board, an impressive throw that silenced us all. Garth snapped to and the lesson continued, though Mr. Malagon was visibly shaken.

Sprocket was the first to accede. He wheeled out of the house, then up the ramp and inside his residence. The rest of us pretended to drift toward our houses, though we were mindful of

Mr. Malagon's clock. Five minutes later, the streets were vacant, our tools scattered throughout the rooms of 1959, abandoned miduse.

Our residences were flushed with a foreign light, everything bathed in a paleness we never had cause to witness. The way the light fell across the kitchen counters, against the backs of sofas, and inched up the stairs lent the houses a new demeanor reminiscent of our own houses on a Sunday afternoon, thoughts of school on Monday held at bay for a few hours longer. Through the window we saw first Roger and then Warren released from custody, Roger breezing out of Mr. Malagon's front door, stomping into his own house. Warren appeared with Mr. Malagon at his side. The two spoke calmly for a minute or two before Mr. Malagon slapped Warren on the back, sending him back to his residence. We watched Warren until he was inside, curious about what would happen next.

Mr. Malagon vanished inside his house for close to fifteen minutes. When he reappeared, he walked purposefully toward the house next door, where Figs and Hands and Lindy were pretending to relax in the living room, saying little as the drama unfolded out the window.

Mr. Malagon gave a blunt rap before letting himself in.

"How's the arm?" Mr. Malagon asked Lindy.

Lindy stared dumbly at his cast, yellowed from the dust that blew through Garden Lakes, black where his fingers folded into his palm. "Okay, I guess."

Mr. Malagon rocked up on his toes. "Figs. Hands. I'd like to see you boys next door," he said. He turned and left as swiftly as he'd arrived. A surprised Figs and Hands followed in his wake, closing the door on Lindy, who bored under his cast to reach an itch.

As Figs and Hands would later say, Mr. Malagon's house had an uncharacteristic chaos about it, one that hinted that our confinement was related to something other than the fight between Roger and Warren. In fact, Mr. Malagon did not allude to the fight in his instructions to Figs and Hands.

"I'm canceling the rest of the day," Mr. Malagon told them. There was to be no lunch, no class, no sports, no dinner, no tutoring, no free time. "All privileges are suspended, and tomorrow's privileges are subject to how well everyone behaves today." Mr. Malagon spoke in a measured tone, asking for Figs's and Hands's help in maintaining the quarantine. A siege of questions raced simultaneously through Figs's and Hands's minds, paramount among them the question about Mr. Baker's impending arrival the next day. A second question, and one of even more concern, was Mr. Hancock's return on Monday. He would doubtlessly be displeased about the sophomores' tutoring being in arrears.

But Figs and Hands raised none of these questions; instead they nodded and accepted their charge. Hands would patrol Loyola Street, and Figs would marshal Mr. Malagon's rules to the fellows. Hands was grateful for his luck of the draw. He knew the sophomores would rejoice in a day spent lounging around their houses (even the cancellation of lunch and dinner would be cause for celebration along Loyola Street). The fellows, on the other hand, would see Mr. Malagon's edict as an attempt to submarine their fellowship; the exceptional nature of the lockdown would surely bring derision from generations of classes of fellows to come, not to mention that the perversion of the construction schedule was risking our showing at Open House.

We didn't believe it when Figs first told us. Assburn ravenously downed a quart of gazpacho the moment he heard, gulping the soup from its plastic container, searching the cupboards for filched fruit or stale bagels. Roger remained in his room, not even coming out to use the bathroom or to raid the refrigerator.

Sprocket staved off boredom by working seek-and-finds. Warren had sequestered himself in his room, traipsing down for a glass of water, wearing a glum look. He regretted losing his temper with Roger, though he had no intention of apologizing, as Mr. Malagon had urged. Roger was a bully, and bullies get what they give from time to time, Warren had told Mr. Malagon, who hadn't disagreed. "Some situations are better than others for reprisal, though," Mr. Malagon had said. "You want to be careful you don't do as much damage to yourself—or more—by striking back in a setting like this. And now you've both put me in a bad spot. One fight leads to another if it goes unpunished. That's not my rule, that's just the way it is." Warren appreciated Mr. Malagon's position and said so, slinking away to await Mr. Malagon's verdict.

Night fell without word from Mr. Malagon. The light pulsing from behind the blinds in his house implied he was slaving over appropriate sanctions. Roger and Warren came out of their rooms and joined their housemates, who had congregated in their respective living rooms to pass the time playing cards or telling stories.

Figs and Hands made the rounds, checking that thermostats were correctly set. Empty soup containers were piled high in our sinks, crusted with lip prints in drying shades of green and red and brown. We'd rummaged every cupboard and drawer in the kitchen in the search for food. Some brought out the fare they'd squirreled away in their dressers: bagel halves and oranges and biscuits formerly fresh and buttery but now so hard they had to be moistened before they could be eaten.

The sophomores had less sustenance, having been too afraid of Mr. Hancock to pilfer any food. They complained to Hands about their hunger, and Hands said he'd see what he could do, knowing there would be nothing he could do short of sneaking them food, which he wasn't prepared to do.

"Let's go to Mr. Malagon," Figs said when Hands mentioned the sophomores' plea in passing.

Hands argued against the idea. He hadn't been in class the day Mr. Malagon whipped the eraser at Garth Atlon, and was surprised by the quarantine. Nothing had suggested Mr. Malagon was even capable of such drastic measures. Hands secretly coveted Mr. Malagon's reputation, always striving to inculcate the student body with the same loyalty and casual deference they showed Mr. Malagon. Unflappable, they would say—the word Hands had heard Principal Breen use to describe Mr. Malagon. (A trip to the Randolph library gave Hands the definition of "unflappable.") The letdown Hands felt over the end of Mr. Malagon's streak of imperturbability shattered his practiced art of cool.

Typically, Figs was ready to lead the charge on an idea that wasn't his. Figs's intimate rapport with the staff in Principal Breen's office made him a conduit for the groundswell of ideas generated by other students. Some approached him looking for an indication on how the administration would respond. If Figs was enthusiastic, he would talk the idea up among the principal's staff, so that when the idea was presented, the administration felt as if it filled a need left void until that very moment. If, however, Figs was not enthusiastic, the student was spared presenting a proposal that would hurt his credibility. In this way it appeared to us that Figs was serving us, looking out for us the way he had in Mazatlán and a hundred times since, from advocating for a better menu in the cafeteria to lobbying the administration to allow students in academic clubs to be excused from class to meet during school instead of after.

Hands knew Figs's MO, though he didn't mind Figs constantly ingratiating himself with the administration and with his peers. Hands recognized Figs's savvy, and on more than one occasion he had been the direct beneficiary of Figs's ability to form a field of goodwill around himself and anything he deemed worthy. What irked Hands was Figs taking undue credit for a particular idea, or shifting a disproportionate load of the blame onto someone else in the face of failure.

Line One was a good example. The air band at Lincoln Elementary had technically been Hands's idea. He couldn't deny that Figs had done the legwork in recruiting the other members and arranging with Mr. Butcher, the Lincoln music teacher, for the band to borrow the needed instruments (keyboard, drum set, amps for show) from another music department in the school district. And Figs had called practice, helping choreograph the lead guitar's movements around him while he lip-synched. He also came up with flourishes for the drummer and the bassist, and positioned the stage lights to shine on Hands in a flattering way.

Still, Hands couldn't help but feel slighted. He could've made a play for another instrument, or even to be the lead singer, but he didn't. He understood Figs's powers of persuasion. What did it matter whose idea it was? Line One raised everyone's profile, even with teachers. So what if Figs received a smidge more attention for an idea that wasn't his? And what did Hands care if Figs offended a pair of seniors at Summer Griffith's party, resulting in an ass-whipping Figs like as not didn't deserve but Hands did nothing to stop? Hands watched long enough to have his thirst for equality in his friendship with Figs quenched and then slipped away from the crowd. At first he was ashamed of resisting his instinct to jump into the fray, but he realized that he was sick of Figs prancing through life unscathed. He'd never paid any real price for stealing Julie Roseman away from him, though at the point at which Figs and Julie confessed, Hands had covertly been seeing his old girlfriend Kristina for months, so it hardly mattered. But still, Hands liked lording it over Figs, calling him out at graduation, avoiding him for the summer, not thinking of either Figs or Julie while he and Kristina holed up in his older brother's apartment in Florida to live like husband and wife, if only for a couple of weeks. He was over it, and was even missing Figs's friendship by the time Figs showed up on his doorstep, his apology spurred by his admission to Randolph. Hands viewed the beating as a corrective, which restored his conviction in the natural order.

And so it wasn't a surprise when Figs, the expert field commander, led a delegation consisting of him and Hands to appeal to Mr. Malagon to excuse us from the quarantine for dinner. We half believed that Figs and Hands would return triumphant, the dining hall opened up for a buffet of anything we could scrounge from the refrigerator. Some of us could taste the salty meats and the sweet desserts, could imagine washing them down with ice-cold soda, fantasies that were dashed by Figs's and Hands's hunched shoulders as they reported back from Mr. Malagon that the quarantine was in strict effect until the morning. Figs and Hands plopped on their couches, agitated, not speaking or looking at each other. They shifted restlessly while Lindy busied himself pointing the telescope out the living-room window, then finally agreed to an early curfew check, Figs complaining he was tired, Hands echoing the sentiment, grumbling about having to do Mr. Malagon's job for him.

***

We woke before our alarms, our stomachs baying with hunger. We scarcely spoke during breakfast. Our banishment had cowed us, so that we felt thankful rather than angry toward Mr. Malagon, who seemed lively as ever, encouraging us to eat up. "We've got a long day in front of us," he said. A morning prayer after breakfast substituted for chapel so we could train our fresh attention on finishing the first construction phase.

Mr. Baker's truck parked in the littered driveway of 1959 distressed us. Mr. Malagon led him inside, soliciting Mr. Baker about his plans for the Fourth. Mr. Baker chatted amicably about driving to Flagstaff in the morning for a family picnic and fireworks.

We knew Mr. Malagon's conversational ploy wouldn't last forever, and we feared Mr. Baker's opinion about the job we'd done hanging the drywall. To our surprise, Mr. Baker's appraisal of our work was favorable. He pulled a mini T square from his back pocket and took spot measurements in every room, clicking his tongue as he hummed a tuneless number none of us recognized. Our confidence skyrocketed as we followed Mr. Baker from room to room. The upstairs bedroom, the scene of the previous day's title fight between Roger and Warren, remained cluttered with tools and overturned drywall benches. Mr. Malagon stooped to retrieve the tape measure from the corner as Mr. Baker stood back from the far wall and shook his head.

"Too many butted seams here," he said.

We followed Mr. Baker and with his help saw what he saw: two ten-foot panels nailed horizontally along the top of the wall, and five-foot panels on either side of a ten-foot panel nailed along the bottom of the wall. Mr. Baker tapped his finger on the butted seam running down the top half of the wall. "Remember what I said about butted seams," he said. "If you have to have them, put them on the outside, like you did down here." He indicated the two butted seams on either side of the ten-foot panel below. "But this wall has too many."

Mr. Malagon spoke up in our defense. "This was the last room we hung, and we had to improvise. And we thought it would be better to stagger the butted seams, rather than align them on either side of ten-foot panels."

"Well," Mr. Baker said, staring at the wall the way we had to stare at the poster on the back of Mr. Malagon's classroom door to make the figure of the naked lady appear. "We'll have to patch the problem with some superior taping."

Mr. Baker checked off all the electrical boxes, making sure we hadn't walled over any outlets. He identified gaps between panels that would need to be filled in with compound before taping, as well as a corner in the kitchen where the drywall had been damaged by an incriminating indentation the shape of a hammerhead punched wide of a nailhead.

We gathered in the living room for Mr. Baker's phase-two instructions, each of us taking a space along the walls to copy down taping sequences, recipes for mixing joint compound, and the hazards of corner beading in our job journals. "If phase one was the most physically demanding, phase two will require patience. Phase three—sanding, texturing, and painting—will be a walk in the park unless you rush through phase two. It's near impossible to fix mistakes made in phase two once you've started phase three. If you remember that, and do not cheat when it comes to taping and applying the three coats of compound required to stabilize the seams and make them part of the wall, which in turn makes the house one solid unit, you will have finished the job before actually completing the work."

Some of us stopped scribbling when we realized Mr. Baker

was indulging in the poetics of construction. Our focus was so intent on proper construction technique—which is to say we did not want to build a lasting monument to our ineptitude—that only the practical interested us. Sensing this, Mr. Baker veered from the philosophical and continued. As he began an aside on the difficulty of taping inside corners without roughing up adjacent corners, Mr. Malagon excused himself, summoning Figs and Hands to follow. Their excusal was an irritant, though, floating through the dust and heat, working its way into us with each chalky breath. The stress and lack of sleep wrought by the quarantine elicited a smattering of vulgar remarks directed toward Figs and Hands. We were used to Figs's (and to some degree, Hands's) insinuating himself in the good graces of the faculty and administration, and we'd welcomed their initiative on campus; but at Garden Lakes the advantage was an affront to the uniformity of our existence. Simply, their elevation by Mr. Malagon subjugated the rest of us, and it burned us up. We blinked momentarily in their absence, drawn back to our job journals by the resumption of Mr. Baker's voice.

The salve, of course, was that Mr. Hancock's return Monday would put right again the pecking order at Garden Lakes, and Figs and Hands would be taping and beading right next to the rest of us, wiping their brows and griping about the heat. Unbelievably, some of us found ourselves daydreaming of Mr. Hancock's return during the last of Mr. Baker's instructions. But that day seemed far away as Mr. Malagon put Hands and Figs in charge so he could run to town to buy binoculars for us to watch the fireworks, his Jeep rocketing through the front gates. We'd been programmed too completely to realize that, for the moment, we were without supervision, and even Mr. Malagon was pleased to learn that all was well upon his return a few hours later.

Hands and Figs were disputing a call when Mr. Malagon brought us together to watch fireworks the following evening, instructing us to bring bath towels to sit on. The palm trees standing guard to the entrance of Garden Lakes were lit yellow and orange, the last of the sunlight burning furiously. Finally the sun was slain, the red sky dissolved into a pale lake that gave way to the bluish purple of night. We wiped sweat with the backs of our hands. The dirt we stirred caught in our lungs, powdered our shoes.

A cannonade of color flared against the sky as Mr. Malagon passed the binoculars. Lindy angled his telescope at the concentric circles erupting from the show being put on at South Mountain. The muffled *crack-crack-crack* of someone shooting a gun in the air died in the wind.

Mr. Malagon leaned back on his elbows. Some mimicked his pose, while others of us lay flat for a panoramic view.

Outside the front gate, Smurf lay on the roof of his car, his smiling face reflecting the same colors as our own. He could hear odd strains of our conversation—us kidding Warren about bullets fired into the air landing near us, us asking Lindy if we could look through his telescope, Mr. Malagon asking Figs and Hands to make a run to the dining hall with him to get soda, (and the foul joke Roger told in Mr. Malagon's absence); and as the fireworks were spent, Smurf awaited the silence that signaled the beginning of his plan to rejoin our ranks. We trudged wearily toward slumber, for what would turn out to be our last night of peaceful sleep.

Chapter Nine

The arrest happened at home, saving a shamefaced walk
through the newsroom. Charlie was dialing Charlotte's
number again when Gallagher pulled him into the stairwell to
tell him what that day's headline would be, that Darrell "Duke"
Torrence Jr. was resigning as publisher of the *Sun*. Gallagher
didn't know what Duke had been arrested for, but it came to
light that Duke had not been arrested but had resigned, which
only piqued everyone's curiosity. Duke, after all, had a court-
appointed driver to keep him from getting behind the wheel
after a string of DUI arrests. The newsroom quieted as the managing editor huddled with Brennan and other editors in the conference room, the blinds turned. Charlie absentmindedly tidied
his desk. A series of messages from Richter that he'd left unre-
turned, as well as his to Charlotte that she wouldn't return, had
sent his mind into overdrive, and Duke's resignation cinched the
idea he'd spun in the sleepless early hours that everyone was
gunning for him, a lifetime of misdeeds revisiting him until he
fled his airless apartment for the friendly confines of a noisy all-
night diner near the *Sun* offices. He'd successfully managed to
appear at work propped up by caffeine, a high that had

evaporated as the conference room door shut behind Brennan, who cast a disappointed glance in his direction. He reached for a half-torn roll of mints in his top drawer as Gallagher slipped out a far exit. Charlie resisted a similar urge until caffeine withdrawal caused him to stand on shaky legs. He popped a mint and sauntered toward the elevator, running to his car in the underground parking lot, the echo of his squealing tires resounding as the guard at the gate saluted him with two fingers.

The horror of Duke's downfall being a consequence of his hiring Charlie away from the *Tab* was a humiliation that would dog him to the end of his days, he knew. He'd spent countless hours at Duke's feet, in his office and his home, both decorated with the trophies of Duke's many accomplishments: his early days as a runner for one of Arizona's most notorious post-Prohibition liquor distributors; his season as a catcher for the Seattle Rainiers, where he wound up after serving as a fighter pilot in WWII; his subsequent rise through a resume stocked with stints at papers weekly and daily before marrying the daughter of the owner of Desert Newspapers, Inc. His office included photos of Duke with political personages of note, both local and national. Duke's laissez-faire administration of the *Sun* was lauded by some and mocked by others, but everyone at the paper respected Duke and his career.

But the voices coming through Charlie's car stereo as he drove aimlessly from Phoenix to Tempe to Mesa, coursing the freeways, alighting at gas stations to refuel or use the restroom, shredded what respect Duke had held. Charlie's attention divided between the traffic and the volume of information filling his ears about Duke Torrence and his fictional military background, endless updates about the carefully crafted war stories Duke had apparently spent decades constructing. Charlie fought light-headedness as revelation after revelation spilled forth, the fake war plaques, the closetful of tailored military uniforms bearing the rank of colonel, the new information that Duke's youngest brother had been killed in action and the news commentators' speculation that this tragic childhood fact might account for Duke's deceptions. Charlie tuned out the amateur psychoanalysis, as well as the purported detail of Duke smashing his war trophies, but was interested in the innuendo that the investigation had been fueled by the *Sun*'s pursuing a story about questionable expenditures in the county attorney's office.

Charlie's disbelief was overridden by the blow that Duke was the target of Richter's investigation and not him. He'd anticipated a humbling and craved the penance and redemption that was to be Duke's alone. He envied Duke his chance to ask for forgiveness. He'd been prepared to confess to every lie he'd ever told in exchange for forgiveness. Charlie had even convinced himself that religion—the popular curative he loathed the most—was a viable salve and found himself struggling with the handles to the Randolph chapel around midnight, after cruising past Charlotte's darkened windows. The chapel doors had been open to him all the time he'd been a student at Randolph, but he'd graced them only parochially, sitting for the requisite masses while his mind wandered.

But the doors were shut against the pews he'd so freely accessed in his youth. To kneel where he'd previously kicked up his heels in defiance of his Catholic brethren would be sweet relief. He contemplated waking Father Matthews, wondering if anyone in the rectory had heard him wrenching on the chapel doors. He bemoaned his flip answer to Father Matthews's question about whether or not Mr. McCloud deserved forgiveness for the sins he'd committed.

"That's between him and his god, I suppose," Charlie had said. He hadn't been in the mood to parse the subtleties of posthumous forgiveness; but if Father Matthews would answer his midnight calling, Charlie would gladly continue the conversation. He'd admit peremptorily that his columns about McCloud and Garden Lakes were retribution for what had happened that summer, what he'd been exposed to, validating Father Matthews's suspicions. Charlie understood that McCloud was just a symbol of his misery, that at some point long ago he'd been unable to keep his head above the tide of his experiences. He'd taken to journalism as a dare, to see if he could tell unembellished truths, but his emotional reaction to every story more suited the temperament of a columnist. It's what Duke must've seen in him. But there were too many Heather Lamberts in the world and not enough chroniclers to herald their stories. Worse, the number of people like those who contributed to Heather Lambert's death seemed exponential. How did so many find it so easy to live with so much selfishness? It was laughable to him that the customs and laws he'd come to think of as absolute were anything more than ceremonial, talking points when referring to the behavior of others.

Maybe it was inevitable that Charlie had succumbed—his most recent transgression being his promise to Father Matthews that access to Randolph's Garden Lakes files would end his investigation into the past—but as for anyone, convenient blame and excuses easily defeated the notion of personal responsibility, and he realized then, holding on to the chapel doors, what he didn't realize that day in Father Matthews's office: He wasn't a strong enough person to overcome the malice in his heart.

Chapter Ten

Katie Sullivan was a name that didn't mean anything to any of us, though Katie Sullivan was the axis on which the plot at Garden Lakes turned that summer. That she was Mr. Malagon's lover, and that she was a freshman at Xavier, became known to us much later, when the story was laid bare, after Mr. Malagon was fired. The story as it was told to us then was remarkable not just for its spectacular nature, but also because once we worked back through it, our own unwitting complicity in Mr. Malagon's lusty schemes thrilled us.

No one could attest to Mr. Malagon and Katie Sullivan's first meeting. As a freshman, she would not have had any classes at Randolph; and her older sister had graduated before Mr. Malagon began teaching at Randolph. Still, we all knew that freshman girls would travel in packs across the Bridge of Sighs to torment us and to activate our supercharged hormones. So while there was no official link between Mr. Malagon and Katie Sullivan, it was easy for us to imagine a superficial one based on Mr. Malagon's charismatic ribbing of any blue and green plaid skirt he saw bounce in front of his classroom window.

In the administration's version, the relationship had begun

149

toward the end of the school year, in either April or May. The stone-faced administration did not provide any scurrilous details but only reported that the relationship included "inappropriate behavior against the moral code of Randolph College Preparatory." Some whispered that the inappropriate behavior featured weekend jaunts to Mexico, as well as all-day "tutoring sessions" at Mr. Malagon's condominium. Unconfirmed stories placed Mr. Malagon at Katie Sullivan's house after school, before her parents returned from work.

The chief witness against Mr. Malagon was Mr. Hancock, who happily related the incident whereby he discovered Mr. Malagon using the mobile phone to call Katie Sullivan from Garden Lakes. Then Mr. Hancock hauled Lindy, who had suffered unimaginably and who would tragically die young, before the administration and compelled him to recall the events that had occasioned his visit to the emergency room. Lindy reluctantly recounted how Mr. Malagon had disappeared for hours while he waited in the emergency-room lobby, his arm in a cast and sling (which was why Mr. Hancock insisted on driving Laird to the ER for his snakebite). Katie Sullivan tearfully admitted that she had met up with Mr. Malagon on that afternoon after he called her from the hospital. She also accidentally divulged that she was the one who had given Mr. Malagon the telescope—an unopened Christmas present from a faraway aunt and uncle—so Mr. Malagon would have an excuse for his absence. Katie also volunteered that she'd met Mr. Malagon in the mall food court the day Mr. Malagon bought the binoculars for us to watch fireworks.

The most damning testimony came not from Mr. Hancock or Katie Sullivan, but from Figs and Hands. Their testimony concerned the night of the quarantine. Several gave supporting

150

testimony that Figs and Hands had gone to solicit Mr. Malagon's permission to free us from the quarantine for dinner. That we had been denied food was a fact in heavy rotation among the administration in the first days of the inquiry, the truth about our houses being stockpiled with soups—enough to get us through the night—exorcised as a matter of convenience.

Hands's testimony, given separately, mirrored Figs's: that Figs and Hands had approached Mr. Malagon's house on Regis Street with the intention of securing Mr. Malagon's consent for the fellows and sophomores to eat dinner; that upon knocking on Mr. Malagon's door, they could hear Mr. Malagon talking to someone whose voice neither Figs nor Hands recognized; that the conversation halted and a period of no less than one minute elapsed before Mr. Malagon answered the door.

Figs and Hands described Mr. Malagon's demeanor as impatient as he replied to their request. One or the other—Figs accused Hands, Hands said it was Figs—wore a suspicious look that caused Mr. Malagon to bark at them, telling them that their stretch as monitors was over and that they were to report to their house until morning. Figs and Hands were starting down the walkway when they heard a girl laughing. The two wended their way around the house and peered in the windows, spotting Katie Sullivan (though they did not know her name) and Mr. Malagon bounding from room to room in amorous chase.

Figs, who would later successfully cover up an embezzlement at his firm, shifting the blame to an innocent department head, resulting in the department head's firing at the insistence of his father-in-law, who also happened to be his boss, testified that Hands was particularly incensed and that it was he who led them through the unlocked front door, frightening Katie Sullivan, who screamed and scampered up the stairs. Figs and Hands watched

151

the backs of her tanned legs disappear and then demanded to know what was going on. Mr. Malagon threatened to expel them both from Garden Lakes if they did not leave, but Figs and Hands repeated their question. Mr. Malagon reached for his shirt, which lay strewn across the back of the couch, and put it on, saying that if they knew what was good for them, they would leave without uttering a word to anyone. Mr. Malagon then threatened to engineer Figs's and Hands's expulsion from Randolph if they told, Katie Sullivan peering surreptitiously from the top of the stairs. Mr. Malagon's even tone was more menacing than his threat.

It was at this point, according to Figs's and Hands's testimonies, that Katie Sullivan called Mr. Malagon upstairs. Mr. Malagon told Figs and Hands to have a seat. While neither could remember precisely how long Mr. Malagon spent upstairs, it seemed to them both that he was back in a flash, wearing a less combative expression.

"This is no one's business," Mr. Malagon said. "It doesn't have anything to do with anything." He searched their faces as he spoke, hoping for affirmation, but Figs and Hands were too stunned to speak, which Mr. Malagon read as insolence. His face colored like it had the day he threw the eraser at Garth Atlon, but the redness drained and he pleaded for discretion. "It's important that this not get around," he said.

Mr. Malagon's supplication ended when Katie Sullivan reappeared at the top of the stairway. Her red and yellow floral sundress was like seeing color again for the first time, and Figs caught himself before he could say hello and ask her name. Hands stood, staring Mr. Malagon down. "You should get her out of here before someone sees," he said indignantly. Figs stood too, with the purpose of raising the idea of dinner again, but Hands's exit pulled Figs toward the door.

Figs was startled by the intensity of Hands's anger. "He's going to ruin it for all of us," Hands said, pointing back toward Mr. Malagon's residence.

"Are you going to say anything?" Figs asked.

Hands breathed deeply through his nose and exhaled, his nostrils flaring. "If I see her around here again, I will," he said.

"I was going to use it to get us dinner," Figs said.

Hands wheeled around. "Fuck *dinner*," he said. "Don't you get what's going on? Don't you see how he's trying to sabotage everything, wasting our summer and shit-canning our fellowship?"

Figs didn't answer. While he agreed that Mr. Malagon was acting recklessly, he didn't see how it would jeopardize all our fellowships, especially since he believed that Mr. Malagon would make sure that Katie Sullivan exited the premises quietly and without a long good-bye. Figs would later say that Hands's hostilities were partly a result of the whispers of favoritism that they'd both heard but ignored. Favoritism was an asset as long as the person showing you favor was not a lecherous, soon-to-be-fired teacher and interim leader of your summer leadership program. Hands fumed about Mr. Malagon's duplicity, accusing Mr. Malagon of setting him and Figs up for a cover story from the beginning. "He must've known he would need someone to protect him if he was caught," Hands said, spitting the words out. They sulked back to their residence, not letting on what they knew. Only the sound of Mr. Malagon firing up the Jeep to drive Katie Sullivan home later that night brought Hands peace, and he fell asleep, fatigued by bitterness.

Mr. Malagon did not recognize Smurf's car as the Jeep's headlights swept across the blue Toyota parked on the side of the road outside the gates of Garden Lakes. Smurf was not in the vehicle; he had sneaked up to Mr. Malagon's residence when he heard the murky stew of raised voices. Smurf kept hidden as he strained to hear the conversation, making out enough bits to piece together what was happening. He'd overheard Figs and Hands on the sidewalk in front of the house, too, and the whole picture came into focus when he saw Katie Sullivan in the passenger side of the Jeep. She appeared to look right at Smurf, but he realized she was seeing her reflection, checking her tearstained face for smudges.

What Smurf said to Katie Sullivan that weekend he would never say. Some of us speculated that Smurf had threatened to tell the administration about her affair with Mr. Malagon if she did not do his bidding, but blackmail was not Smurf's MO. It was more likely that Smurf, before he successfully slandered the woman at work with whom he was cheating on his wife, had colluded with Katie Sullivan, coaching her on what to do to make Mr. Malagon hers forever. Smurf learned what the rest of us would later: that Katie Sullivan was so sick in love with Mr. Malagon that she had once physically harmed herself when she believed that Mr. Malagon was seeing the Spanish teacher at Central High. What Smurf didn't know was that Katie Sullivan had a plan of her own, one that involved her running away to live with her college-aged friend in North Carolina, a scenario we had to believe Mr. Malagon would've found juvenile. The plan as Smurf had designed it in his mind was simple: Katie Sullivan would keep Mr. Malagon away while Smurf sneaked back into Garden Lakes before Mr. Hancock's return. He would skip breakfast on Monday, as would Mr. Malagon, owing to the eyedrops Katie would mix into a vodka tonic for Mr. Malagon the night before. Smurf would catch Mr. Hancock outside of chapel. Mr. Hancock would be surprised, and Smurf would explain that Mr. Malagon had accepted Smurf's apology and

154

that he and Mr. Malagon had worked out the punishment, which would be executed once school commenced. He would then pay a visit to Mr. Malagon, who would be recuperating from his stomach trauma, and hint that he knew about Katie Sullivan without having to threaten to use the information—he still admired Mr. Malagon and did not want to embarrass or demean him in the presence of others—and voilà! His reenrollment at Garden Lakes would be complete.

Smurf's plan went awry immediately, however, as Roger discovered him in the bathroom in the middle of the night. "I'm back!" Smurf was surprised into saying, to which Roger grunted. Smurf lay awake in his room, adjusting his plan accordingly as the sun's yoke appeared on the horizon. He would let Assburn and Roger be the messengers of his return; it would lessen Mr. Hancock's shock. The key would be to show at breakfast after it had started, long enough for Mr. Hancock to hear the rumor of his return, but not long enough for him to go to Mr. Malagon. Smurf recognized the delicate timing this amendment required and crept downstairs to lie on the couch, where his housemates found him the next morning.

As the rest of us headed to breakfast, Smurf panicked, changing his plan, which he knew was dangerous. He decided to approach Mr. Malagon first, to cement their story. There was a good chance Mr. Malagon would see him anyway, as he had to pass in front of Mr. Malagon's house on his way to breakfast, and it wouldn't do to have him come screaming out of his house, in plain view of the dining-hall windows, drawing Mr. Hancock's attention.

Smurf knocked lightly on Mr. Malagon's door. He knocked again using his knuckles. The house was silent. Smurf pounded on the front door, and the door broke open, pieces of the

155

doorframe scattering at his feet. The living room and kitchen were dark, and Smurf called out Mr. Malagon's name. Fearing that Mr. Malagon had been made sicker than Smurf intended, he thundered up the stairs, sure Mr. Malagon was hunched over the toilet or retching over the side of his bed into a garbage can. Instead, he found cool darkness. He backtracked out of the house, closing Mr. Malagon's door as best he could, though it wouldn't close properly. He did what he could to stifle the panic that somehow his and Katie's plan had been botched. He imagined Mr. Malagon in the hospital, hipped to the plot by an emergency-room doctor in a long white coat.

We noticed Smurf in waves, the murmur of those who looked up from their bowls of cereal provoking the rest of us until we all saw Smurf standing tentatively in the doorway, his eyes roaming the tables for Mr. Hancock. The sophomores steered clear of Smurf, avoiding him as they would a predator. Finally, Assburn, who would later die plunging into a frozen lake somewhere between Canada and Detroit, driving across the ice, smuggling counterfeit game systems in order to raise bail money for his best friend, called out to Smurf, and Smurf took a seat at Assburn's table. What we didn't know then but would find out later was that Assburn had been providing Smurf with a day-to-day summary of life at Garden Lakes in Smurf's absence, a duty he'd performed religiously since Smurf lured Assburn out into the Grove with a note placed under Assburn's pillow, along with Senator Quinn's pen.

We were astounded by Smurf's redemption. Those of us who doubted Smurf's story were the first to realize that neither Mr. Hancock nor Mr. Malagon had made it to breakfast.

The blunder that left Mr. Hancock's absence unrectified was purely administrative—Principal Breen, distracted by surprise divorce proceedings, misunderstood the petition Mr. Hancock made to be replaced once he left Garden Lakes, thinking that Mr. Hancock would let him know *if* Mr. Hancock's family emergency meant a replacement was needed. Mr. Hancock believed a substitute had been sent and was frankly glad to be relieved of his duties with respect to Garden Lakes. The rest of the summer was spent contemplating whether to appeal to Principal Breen about finding a permanent replacement. The leadership program sapped too much of his energies, leaving him spent come the fall. The admission left him feeling elderly, but he could not deny the joy he felt at having the remainder of his summer to entertain any fancy he could dream up, and to be free from a student body that became increasingly foreign each year.

Mr. Malagon, we would later learn, had left to drive Katie Sullivan to North Carolina—with her parents' permission—using the occasion of the trip to try to change her mind about leaving. Mr. Malagon would later claim that he believed Mr. Hancock had returned and that, while he regretted abandoning his responsibilities at Garden Lakes, he wouldn't have endangered us had he known that the administration had failed to send a replacement for Mr. Hancock.

The confusion surrounding both Mr. Hancock's nonreturn and Mr. Malagon's disappearance was quickly muted by Figs and Hands, who called us together in the chapel to suggest that Mr. Hancock and Mr. Malagon were testing us, relying on a campus rumor about just that, though we never thought it was anything more than legend.

"It's in our interest to keep the schedule," Figs said convincingly. "If it is a test, and Mr. Hancock and Mr. Malagon show up at lunchtime, or at dinner, and find us off the schedule, we'll have failed."

Hands concurred. "They'll probably be back by lunch."

"Bullshit," Roger said.

Figs and Hands winced. Figs beat a tattoo on the carpet with his right foot and then looked Roger straight in the eye. "No one is being forced," he said. "Anyone can do whatever they want."

A hush descended. We could not fathom either Mr. Hancock's or Mr. Malagon's absence, never mind both, and so we complied. The sophomores fell into order in the kitchen, Hands volunteering to manage them; the rest of us took up the taping and beading at 1959 Regis Street. Figs attempted to direct who should work in which room, but Roger, who would one day go AWOL in Iraq with a platoon of men and be court-martialed for killing one of them after the soldier was wounded by enemy fire and begged him for a mercy killing, blatantly ignored the commands, the rest of us busying ourselves with tape guns or mixing joint compound at random.

We rushed to the dining hall for lunch, expecting to be greeted by Mr. Hancock's and Mr. Malagon's satisfied smiles, ready to accept our accolades for a job well done. We were disappointed, though, and paraded through the lunch line with a growing anxiety, incited by the worried looks of the sophomores as they dumped macaroni and cheese on our plates, the cheese too runny, the overboiled macaroni disintegrating in our mouths as we ate.

We gave Mr. Hancock and Mr. Malagon the lunch hour to appear, striving for nonchalance, which only reinforced our fear. The lunch hour expired without sign of either teacher. Roger became expansive and voluble, launching into a pointless story about how he had helped his father restore a classic automobile one summer. Those who were paying attention to the tale sat restively, aware of their violation of the schedule, but also aware that there was no one to lead the class.

Hands pulled Figs into the kitchen.

"We have to do something," Hands said.

An army of sophomores marched through with dirty dishes. Hands motioned for Figs to follow him into the hall.

"This whole thing is going to fall apart if we don't do something," Hands said.

"Do you think they're coming back?" Figs asked.

"I don't know," Hands said truthfully. "But if they don't, how great will it be if we complete the fellowship anyway? That's never been done before. This is a chance to distinguish ourselves from all the other classes of fellows."

Figs nodded. "But how?"

Warren and Assburn sauntered into the hallway to have a look at the empty classroom, and Figs and Hands ducked back into the kitchen.

"We tell everyone we saw Mr. Malagon this morning," Hands said.

"They'll want to know why we didn't mention it earlier," Figs said.

"We'll say Mr. Malagon told us not to," Hands said, inventing the story on the spot. "We won't announce it; we'll tell a few people and let it get around."

"What if people don't believe us?" Figs asked.

Hands reached out and grabbed Freddy Cantu, who nearly spilled the tray of leftover macaroni and cheese he was carrying. "Cantu here will back us up," Hands said.

"Back what up?" Cantu asked.

Hands filled Cantu in on his role in the scheme, how it was for the good of all and how Hands would make sure Mr. Hancock and Mr. Malagon knew of Cantu's role, a distinction Cantu appeared to prize. Figs and Hands had their man, then, and they fanned out across the dining room, Figs telling Warren, Hands telling Sprocket, Cantu telling the sophomores, who stood in range of Smurf.

When Smurf heard the story, his worry that his plan had gone askew subsided. Mr. Malagon had come back after all, it seemed, which fit with the narrative he was spinning. "I saw him too," he said. "He looked sick."

Figs awkwardly acknowledged Smurf's confirmation, grateful for the support. With Cantu's and Smurf's independent corroboration, the dining hall emptied, the fellows crossing the hall to the classroom, leaving the sophomores to their kitchen work under Hands's direction.

Without a particular lesson to study—we'd been pondering Woodrow Wilson's Fourteen Points, discussing their aggregate diplomatic effect on the end of World War I, leading up to an exercise about the creation of the League of Nations—we spent the two hours playing hangman on the grease board, the only rule being that the solution had to be the name of a great leader. We reasoned that if Mr. Hancock or Mr. Malagon walked in on this activity, we could claim it had *some* educational value.

But Mr. Hancock and Mr. Malagon did not come, and we shuffled out of the classroom, Figs fetching the soccer ball from Mr. Malagon's house for sports.

Hands realized that without Mr. Hancock and Mr. Malagon, we had our first shot at a fair match. We took the opportunity to draw up the teams that would compete the day of Open House. Hands designated himself captain, and Figs volunteered to captain the opposing team. Hands selected Warren, Smurf, and Roger, filling out his roster with sophomores of varying degrees of skill. Figs chose Assburn, Lindy, me, and the remaining sophomores. Sprocket would officiate the goal line, as usual.

The first match was a lopsided affair with Hands's team winning four goals to none. We opted to play into the dinner hour, best two out of three, Figs's team taking the next game. Hands complained that Lindy's cast was an unfair advantage, Lindy using it in goal to deflect the ball with ease. "He's not that mobile," Figs said. Hands protested, but his team called for them to play on. The final game was tied into overtime when Smurf passed the ball to Hands and Hands drove at Lindy, who deflected goal after goal with his cast. But Hands used his foot speed and misdirection to clear a path to the goal, the ball sailing near Lindy's head.

"In!" Sprocket called out, leaning forward in his wheelchair.

Dinner was served, though the entrée for that night— mushroom meat loaf—was ruined because the recipe was not clear about how long the meat loaves should bake, so the mushrooms layered in the middle that lent the dish its juiciness were dry and rubbery. The sophomores crumbled the meat loaves into the garbage can while the rest of us feasted on a sloppy smorgasbord from the reach-in refrigerators and cupboards.

After dinner, we swarmed around Lindy and his telescope, set up under the palm tree in the lake bed, Lindy dialing the telescope in on a constellation that we were too preoccupied to care about.

"Look," someone said, pointing out a light in Mr. Malagon's window. The yellow glow quelled our anxiety.

"Bet he's resting," Smurf said. "He seemed really sick."

We were too in awe of the light to challenge Smurf's diagnosis. Figs and Hands later testified that at that moment they were only relieved that their lie had turned out not to be a lie. We had no idea that it was Smurf who had turned on the bedroom light when he went to coordinate Mr. Malagon's story to match his own and found the house empty.

161

"Where was he?" Lindy asked, expressing the question on all our minds.

"He didn't say," Smurf answered.

"I'm going to go knock on the door," Roger said.

"I wouldn't," Smurf said.

"I didn't ask what *you'd* do," Roger said.

"Cool it, Roger," Figs said.

Roger sneered at Figs and Figs flinched.

"You think you're special." A prickling ran across Figs's back before Figs realized that Roger was talking to Lindy. "Why are you allowed to have that telescope, anyway?"

Lindy stood up, the front of the telescope dipping, aimed at the well-worn dirt. "Mr. Malagon bought it for me," he said.

"Mr. Malagon bought it for me," Roger mimicked.

"Knock it off, Roger," Warren said. He snatched the telescope and looked through the eyepiece at nothing in particular.

"Yeah?" Roger said.

Figs looked at Hands, who was staring at Roger, waiting for Roger to react. The sophomores quieted.

"C'mon, Roger," Figs said.

"What makes Captain Astronomy here so special?" Roger asked.

"Wow, check it out." Warren turned the telescope away from Roger, training it on a patch of blackness, hoping to defuse Roger's vitriol.

"Check this out," Roger said. He seized the telescope and threw it to the ground. Warren fell back, rubbing his eye. Roger kicked the telescope in the dirt and it skidded toward Warren.

Warren withdrew as the others gathered around Roger and Lindy.

Lindy resisted the urge to reach for the telescope until Roger had stormed off. Roger gave Mr. Malagon's lit window the bird as he passed by, shouting something the rest of us could not hear.

The next morning, Assburn hurried into the dining hall, startling the few of us who had woken for breakfast. "Warren's gone," he said, wheezing. He steadied himself on Figs and Hands's table, grabbing at his side.

Figs asked him what he was talking about.

"You checked his room?" Figs asked.

"Yeah," Assburn said. His breathing returned to normal and he sat down next to Hands.

"And?"

"His bed is made and his stuff is all there," Assburn said, "but he's . . . gone."

"Has anyone seen him?" Figs asked. Sprocket shook his head, as did Lindy and Smurf.

"Christ," Hands said under his breath.

"We'll have to look for him," Figs said. "Something could've happened to him."

Assburn's eyes widened. "What could've happened to him?"

Figs shrugged. "Nothing. Maybe."

"Should we tell Mr. Malagon?" Assburn asked.

"I'll let him know," Smurf said.

A brief investigation confirmed what Assburn had described. No one had seen Warren since the night before. Figs pressed us for any strange behavior we may have observed, but we hadn't noticed any; Warren was nothing if consistent in both his reserved bearing and his inquisitive nature. Any conversation with Warren invariably ended with you telling more than you learned, Warren's ability to answer a question with a question unmatched in our limited experience.

Not everyone was sympathetic to Warren's disappearance.

"Probably went home to cry to his mommy," Roger said. "Little moody bastard."

Figs and Hands lagged behind the rest of us as we headed toward the construction site, composing the roster of a potential search party to comb the area for any signs of Warren. Hands raised the possibility of dissent among those who would have to stay behind and do the work on 1959 Regis Street, a concern that proved prescient when Roger threw down his trowel and taping knife in protest, arguing that the labor should be borne equally.

"We need a few people to look around for an hour or so," Hands said. "What if it was you who was missing?" he asked us.

"I suppose you and Figs will be two of the chosen ones," Roger said.

"Figs is coordinating the search," Hands said forcefully. "I'm going to stay here and continue with the taping."

Surprised by this declaration, Figs stepped up. "And the search party will rejoin the construction after lunch," he said. "We expect the search won't take long."

"Who's in the search party?" Roger wanted to know.

Figs pointed with confidence, as if the matter had been previously decided: Assburn, Lindy, and I would accompany him on a door-to-door search, as well as a search of the surrounding area.

"Bullshit," Roger said. "I want to go."

Smurf jogged up Regis Street with an urgent look. "Mr. Malagon said we should look for Warren," he said, catching his breath.

A wave of murmuring went up.

"You told him that Warren was missing?" Assburn asked.

Smurf nodded. "He's real sick. He looks bad. But he wants us to try to find Warren. And he wants us—he wants *me*—to keep

164

him updated. He said he'll call Warren's parents if we don't find him. He's got Mr. Hancock's mobile phone."

"Where's Hancock?" Roger asked.

"He's . . ." Smurf fumbled. "He's still visiting his family. Mr. Malagon doesn't know when he's coming back."

Smurf's mandate gave Figs's plan weight, and Roger backed off.

"Why not supervise the sophomores?" Hands said to Roger, extending a compromise.

Roger accepted the assignment, returning his tools to Sprocket, who logged them back into the supply shed.

The search party ventured from 1959, poking our heads into each of the houses as we made our way toward the community center. Figs made the decision to enter Mr. Hancock's residence. "If he's hiding out," Figs said, "Mr. Hancock's would be a good place to do it."

Heat radiated from inside the house. The box that had previously contained the mobile phone provided by the administration lay open and empty on the kitchen counter. The house was still. Figs opened and closed every door, while the rest of us moved outside.

"Nothing," Figs said, his hair matted to his wet brow.

As the party moved through the houses on Loyola Street, Figs's demeanor switched from one of pursuit to one of determination. "He's got to be here somewhere," Figs said. He led the search into the Grove and identified what might've been fresh footprints on the ground. "They lead that way," he said, pointing to the desert beyond Garden Lakes.

"What's that way?" Assburn asked.

"The freeway, for one," Figs said.

"We should get some sunblock if we're going to go out there," Assburn said.

Figs shielded his eyes. "Let's go out a ways," he said. "Just to see if these tracks go cold."

We agreed to trek on, though the footprints faded a couple of hundred feet from the Grove. Figs forged ahead with his head bent toward the ground, his eyes roving for signs of life. We snaked along in the sand, led here and there by footprints, none of which looked fresh.

As Assburn renewed his call for a retreat for sunblock, we stumbled onto a rock grouping that had seen recent use. Figs examined the prints, circling the rocks. A variety of trash had collected: Styrofoam cups riddled with teeth marks of indeterminate origin, scraps of candy wrappers, a confetti of plastic and rubber and metal ground down by the elements. A pile of discarded apple peels gave away that Warren had been in the vicinity: Warren's aversion to eating the skin of anything—chicken, fruit, pudding, whatever—was famously known.

Figs argued for pressing on, but Lindy said that if we did, "there'd be four more lost." Figs relented and the party hiked back toward the development, arriving as the construction crew was calling it quits for the day.

"Nice timing," Roger said, peeling at a scab of joint compound on his arm.

"We found something," Figs said. He reported what we'd discovered in the desert. "I should let Mr. Malagon know," he said.

"Mr. Malagon wanted me to report back," Smurf said. "I need to get the handout for class anyway. I'll let him know."

Smurf dashed off before Figs could protest.

"What should we do?" Hands asked.

"Not sure," Figs said. "We'll wait and see what Mr. Malagon says."

"Wonder why Smurf," Hands said. Figs wondered the same.

Smurf had somehow supplanted him, and he could reason only that it was a lesson Mr. Malagon was trying to impart. Figs remembered Mr. Malagon accusing him of being too much of a politician; it would be like Mr. Malagon to send a subtle message by drafting Smurf over him as a confidant.

Mr. Malagon's decision, rendered through Smurf, was that we should wait until morning. "Mr. Malagon called Warren's parents, and they said he sometimes wanders off on his own," Smurf told us.

"His parents weren't freaked out?" Sprocket asked.

"Apparently not," Smurf said.

None of us knew Warren well enough to know whether that statement was true or not, so we followed Mr. Malagon's directive and assembled for class to read through a handout on the First Continental Congress, though we couldn't concentrate on anything other than Warren's disappearance and the pallor that had begun to settle around the development in the wake of Mr. Hancock's continued absence and Mr. Malagon's prolonged illness.

The rest of the day was carried out as per the schedule, the illumination from Mr. Malagon's window spurring us on. Curfew was lifted per Mr. Malagon via Smurf, though none of us took Mr. Malagon up on his offer, instead turning in early to lay awake in our beds, wondering where Warren was and how much longer Mr. Malagon would be bed ridden.

Our anxiety-induced insomnia petered out in the early-morning hours, and most of us woke well after breakfast, scurrying through the deserted streets to the dining hall, hoping that life at Garden Lakes had regained a modicum of normalcy.

Instead we found the tables in the dining hall rearranged to imitate a command center, Figs and Hands attempting to map the local terrain on the grease board, which had been wheeled in from the classroom. The whiff of bacon wafted through the building, awakening our hunger. Over plates loaded with bacon and eggs, we listened as Figs and Hands divided us into teams and assigned each team a quadrant. The search had two phases: The quadrants making up the morning phase would fall inside the outer loop; the afternoon phase, a grid of quadrants beyond the Grove. One team—Sprocket, Lindy, and Smurf—would remain at the community center to receive updates, Lindy stationing himself on the roof with his telescope for a bird's-eye view. Smurf persuaded us that the search had the blessing of Mr. Malagon, who wanted hourly reports on our progress.

We stalked out of the dining hall, charged with our duty. Some of the teams were realigned along friendship lines as we scattered to our quadrants—miffing Figs and Hands, though they did not protest.

The morning search produced the same results as the search from the previous day. Warren was not anywhere inside the walls of Garden Lakes. Those whose quadrants did not include any of the residences, and thus were quickly searched, doubled back to the dining hall, waiting for the others to arrive. Sprocket drew an *X* through each quadrant on the grease board as the teams returned, transferring the information to a reproduction of the map he'd sketched on the inside back cover of a book of seek-and-finds. He split his time between overseeing the search and setting up for the cold-cuts lunch we'd agreed on, determining that all hands were needed in the field.

Lindy encountered Sprocket reaching for a plastic tub of mayonnaise on the pantry shelf.

"Let me get it," Lindy said.

"Thanks," Sprocket said. "Not used to shelves that high."

Lindy offered to lay out the bread and cold cuts, but Sprocket declined his help. "You won't tell on me if I get a sneak preview, will ya?"

Sprocket smiled. "Help yourself."

Lindy made a roast beef sandwich while Sprocket ribbed his sandwich-making abilities, Lindy laughing along at the primitiveness of his sandwich—bread, meat, cheese, mayo—before they shifted into another conversation altogether.

"Let me know if you hear another team come back," Sprocket said, sticking his head into the refrigerator to gather condiments. Lindy said he'd keep a lookout. Sprocket wheeled up to the counter carrying half-empty ketchup and mustard bottles in his lap, placing the opened bottles in front of the new, unopened ones from the pantry. "Smurf is giving the reports, but I'm tracking all the information," he said without self-importance. Lindy chewed his sandwich. "I'm going to miss it here," Sprocket said.

Lindy swallowed the last of the sandwich, wishing he had something to wash it down with. "What do you mean?"

Sprocket looked at Lindy, embarrassed. "I mean, it's nice to be useful. People like you when you serve a purpose," he said bashfully.

"People like to take advantage," Lindy said, feeling protective of Sprocket.

"That's true," he said, "but you can't go around thinking everyone is taking advantage of you. I mean, I don't mind if people want me to do things for them. It's a good feeling." Sprocket caught Lindy staring at his legs, and Lindy averted his gaze. "It's okay, I know what you're thinking. I mean, I know. I know that this"—Sprocket swept his hand around the kitchen, but Lindy understood that he meant much more—"is all artificial. Everyone accepts my handicap here and I'm not made to

169

feel grateful for it, which I *am* grateful for."

"Nobody cares about—"

"Do you know that I have *two* personal assistants at home?" Sprocket asked. "I mean, they come on different days," Sprocket said, realizing the melodramatic tone in his voice, "but the point is I'm so useless at home that I have to have personal assistants as counterparts to my parents, who are on high alert whenever I'm in the room. They actually sit up in their seats. They would've never let me organize the supply shed, they would've never even let me try. And they surely wouldn't let me be in charge of the search party and laying out lunch." Sprocket's voice cracked and he fell silent, staring shamefully at a mustard stain on his pants.

Lindy grappled for words, not wanting to pity Sprocket, though pity was what Lindy felt through and through. It had been a long time since he felt sorry for someone other than himself. "I'm sure they—"

Sprocket interrupted again, looking up with a smile. "I don't blame my parents," he said. "They're typical of what waits for me after graduation. I have to prepare myself for being pitied." Sprocket fingered the stain thoughtfully. Lindy was too moved by Sprocket's analysis of life after Randolph—a life Lindy hadn't begun to contemplate, but a life he guessed Sprocket thought about all the time—to offer any comfort, though he couldn't think of what to say anyway.

In order to prevent any team from getting lost, the desert beyond Garden Lakes was reimagined into pie-shaped quadrants, each team sweeping the quadrant from side to side, meeting up with alternating neighboring teams every ten to fifteen minutes to exchange intel and head counts. The afternoon search brought with it an extra measure of preparation: We took turns passing sunblock around the dining hall, having to raid Mr. Hancock's supply to cover everyone. A squad of sophomores collected and washed the plastic soup containers from our residences, filling them with water so each team member had a quart for the journey.

Smurf escaped to Mr. Malagon's to think. Warren's unexpected vanishing was a monkey wrench in his plan. The secret about Mr. Malagon's disappearance was a pressure that manifested itself physically, his head throbbing. He cradled Mr. Hancock's mobile phone, pressing the on button. He'd call Randolph and let them know what had happened. Maybe the administration would appreciate hearing it directly, rather than from the police or whoever would get involved with the search for Warren. He tricked himself into thinking this for less than a minute, coming around to the realization that he would undoubtedly be expelled from Randolph unless he was somehow able to sustain the illusion about Mr. Malagon, which would keep order, and which in turn would make everyone campaign for Smurf's getting credit for the fellowship.

He looked at the mobile phone as it gave three quick beeps and expired in his hand, the luminous face going dark. Smurf was peering out the window, wondering whether or not Mr. Hancock had a charger (which would be missing from the case upon Smurf's inspection), when Hands appeared on the sidewalk below. Smurf pushed open the window and called down to him. The mobile phone was heavy as a stone in his palm. He could not bear the burden of Mr. Malagon's disappearance alone.

"Come up," Smurf said nervously.

By nightfall, the command center in the dining hall was littered with dirty dishes and the remnants of an unsatisfying dinner of our ever-dwindling supply of leftovers. There had been no new

171

evidence to justify a further search of the outlying area. A committee consisting of Figs, Hands, and Smurf revisited Warren's room with the intent of analyzing the room's contents, but they returned without a conclusion.

"If he were dead, he'd be stinking by now," Roger said, which was funny to no one but him.

A rattling of the window focused our attention. The fronds of the palm tree embedded in the lake bed bent horizontally, blown by a fierce wind. Sand brushed against the window, giving off a sound like static electricity. The sky was the color of ink.

"Whoa," Assburn said.

A barrage resembling artillery fire sounded behind us. We rushed into the kitchen and found Adam Kerr, Reedy, and Cantu pacing. The sweet smell of butternut squash soup hung in the air.

"What is that?" Kerr asked.

Figs climbed up to peer out of the small, rectangular window that overlooked the loading dock. An immense grayness blew across the outer loop, and Figs winced as the building was fired upon again.

"Rocks from the Grove," Figs said. "The wind is really blowing."

The windstorm died down as quickly as it had begun, and we let our curiosity about the storm's aftermath draw us outside, freeing us from the command center without having made a definitive plan for resolving Warren's disappearance. Garden Lakes Parkway was powdered with sand, but Regis and Loyola Streets were clear except for a sprinkling of sandstone that had leaped the community center. We sneaked off in twos and threes to crawl into bed, too worn out to think.

A few of us stayed behind and helped clean up the mess in the dining hall, avoiding all topics of conversation: what should be done about Warren, and what would happen to the schedule. We moved with a fluidity that suggested clearing the tables and washing and drying the dishes was the utmost important job in the world.

A sonorous honking disrupted our concentration. We recognized the honk as that of the grocery truck, and it occurred to us that we had not received any groceries in over a week, the confusion about Mr. Hancock and Mr. Malagon and Warren preoccupying our minds, distracting us from our worry that the previous Sunday had come and gone without a grocery delivery.

"Mix-up because of the holiday," the driver said without apology.

Figs grabbed the clipboard Mr. Hancock used to hold the grocery list and followed the driver outside to check in the groceries.

Adam Kerr and Cantu were finishing up the dishes when Figs asked them to move the groceries from the loading dock into the pantry and refrigerator.

"Where is everybody?" Figs asked.

The kitchen was suddenly empty, as was the dining hall.

"Everyone looked pretty tired," Cantu said.

"You guys look beat too," Figs said, feeling guilty about asking them to help with the groceries. "Why don't we drag this stuff inside and deal with putting it away tomorrow so you guys can get to bed. I'll take care of the perishables."

"No one's been sleeping," Cantu said. He glanced at Kerr, who nodded. "Some of the guys are talking about leaving."

Figs started. "Leaving to go where?"

"Home," Cantu answered.

Figs put his foot up on a mixed case of pickles, mayonnaise, and ketchup. "Who is thinking about leaving?"

Cantu shrugged. "Some of us."

"*Us?*"

"Not us," Cantu said, pointing at himself and Kerr, "but some of the other guys want to go home."

"You mean some other sophomores," Figs said.

Cantu nodded.

"I don't understand—," Figs began, but Adam Kerr cut him off.

"They think maybe Warren was murdered."

Figs brought his foot back down, rocking back. He'd guessed the sophomores' mutiny was about Mr. Hancock's and Mr. Malagon's absence, not Warren's. Figs forced a laugh. "Warren wasn't murdered," he said. He laughed again for effect. Kerr and Cantu didn't look convinced. In the face of their doubtful stares, Figs spoke as rapidly as his mind spun an answer. "The grocery guys found Warren."

Cantu's eyes grew wide.

"Yeah," Figs said. "They said they would've been here sooner, but they ran into Warren wandering around by the freeway and they took him to the hospital."

"What happened to him?" Kerr asked.

"He fell down and hit his head," Figs said. "Dehydration. They said he didn't even know who he was when they found him. But they recognized his outfit." Figs's voice acquired a conspiratorial tone. "We'll let everyone know in the morning."

The story picked up Kerr's and Cantu's step as they finished moving the groceries off the loading dock. Figs reminded them again to keep their secret as they parted ways in front of the community center. He trod down Regis Street and knocked on Hands's door to confer and cement the story, but Hands was passed out from exhaustion.

Hands woke early, refreshed. His dream about a flood that had submerged Garden Lakes amused us as he told it over breakfast. "It was like Atlantis," he said, equally amused.

Someone had erased the grease board and rolled it out into the hallway, packaging it for its return to the classroom, an action that lent credibility to the tale of Warren's rescue by the grocery truck, which by breakfast had circulated, so that Hands quizzed Figs about the details upon his late arrival to the dining hall, Figs having overslept.

"Where did he fall?" Hands asked.

Figs buttered a bagel. "Not sure."

"Did the driver say Warren was bleeding?"

"He didn't say."

Conversation around the dining hall dropped off so we could hear the story.

"Was he really by the freeway?" Hands asked.

Figs took a bite of his bagel, nodding.

Hands drained a glass of chocolate milk, replacing it on the brown ring that had formed on the tablecloth. "Is he going to come back?" he asked.

"Don't know," Figs said.

"It cheered Mr. Malagon up to hear that Warren was okay," Hands said, looking across the table at Smurf.

"Yeah," Smurf said, to bolster Hands's statement.

Figs curbed his feeling of betrayal that Hands had been taken into Mr. Malagon's inner circle, the need to speak confidentially with Hands growing urgent.

"What exactly did the driver say?" Hands asked.

"What I told you," Figs said, dropping his butter knife on the floor. He bent down and retrieved it. "That they found Warren by the freeway and that he had amnesia, or something like that. They didn't say a whole lot about it."

"Maybe we should give him a call and see how he's doing," Assburn said. "You know, to make sure he's okay. We could use Mr. Hancock's mobile phone."

Smurf belched to mask the jolt he felt at the mention of the mobile phone. "Great idea," he said. "I'll ask Mr. Malagon. Though he'll want to make the call himself. You know how he is."

We nodded, knowing what Smurf meant.

A motion proposed by Smurf (which we read as coming from Mr. Malagon) that each of us would be responsible for making, eating, and cleaning up after our own meal—so all hands could report to 1959 Regis Street—was roundly passed. The motion was put into effect and we all chipped in with the breakfast dishes, working with a precision we didn't know we possessed. Figs made several failed attempts to try to isolate Hands, to explain his lie about Warren and to be briefed on the situation with Mr. Malagon, but Hands sensed Figs's anxiety about not being privy to the secret about Mr. Malagon, and for the moment, Hands did not want to share the deception he considered insignificant if it kept order and motivated everyone to move forward with the essential obligations of the leadership program. Also, he knew Figs would ask endless questions about Mr. Malagon, a quiz Hands wanted to avoid. Warren's disappearance was a bigger threat, Hands reasoned, and with the resolution of that situation, there was no reason they couldn't soldier on toward the finish line. The who, what, when, where, why, and how would sort themselves out after, he told himself, and would pale in comparison to our collective achievement.

We sent up a hurrah as we passed under Mr. Malagon's window, letting him know that we were working in solidarity toward the objective laid out on day one. We imagined Mr. Malagon

176

smiling to himself, maybe hobbling to the window to get a look at the parade of conviction.

While Sprocket inventoried the tools that had been deserted a day earlier, checking the list of implements against the master list in his job journal, we broke into teams of five, each team incorporating two or three sophomores. The workforce had swelled noticeably, so that we decided on two overall teams: one to tape and bead the upstairs, and one to do the same downstairs.

We wouldn't get any farther than deciding teams, though, before our intentions were derailed.

"Look who's out of the hospital," Roger said.

We stood still, all of us, as Warren approached, a girl we didn't recognize following a few steps behind him. His clothes were filthy, the knees of his pants blackened by dirt. He clearly had not showered since he'd left. Warren waved hello when he saw us, and some of us waved back, the girl waving too. Warren reached back and clutched the girl's hand, pulling her close.

Chapter Eleven

Warren's eyes brimmed with excitement as we fired questions at him, his sour-breathed answers fogging up the dining hall, though we were too entranced to care. The girl sat quietly, her enormous green eyes taking us in. She, too, traveled in a cloud of dust, but her earthen odor wasn't as offensive as Warren's. She swung her bronzed legs under the chair, and some of us tried harder than others not to stare. She could've been sixteen or she could've been twenty-six; her weathered skin made judging her age problematic.

Warren's odyssey had been triggered by his habitual insomnia, a condition he did not have to delineate for any of us. Though he would not identify the fight between Roger and Lindy as the catalyst, he alluded to it. "My stress level was up here," he said, his hand above his head. He thought a walk might help tire him out, so he stole out of bed and out of his residence, cutting behind the community center and crossing the outer loop. "I was going to walk the loop," he said, "but the moon was so bright that I could see in every direction, so I wandered off toward the Grove."

From the Grove, Warren bounced out into the desert, drawn by the remarkable moonlight. He described meandering in a blinding light, the monotonous landscape drawing him farther and farther away from Garden Lakes.

"Then it got darker," Warren said. He reached into his front pocket and pulled out a homemade gunnysack made of two back pockets from an old pair of Levi's hemmed together, a zipper (presumably from the same pair of Levi's) threaded across the top. He unzipped the primitive pouch and plucked out what looked like a black pill, popping it into his mouth. He extended the open pouch. "They're olive pits," he said.

Hands pinched a pit out of the sack. "Nice and salty," he said, rolling the seed around with his tongue.

We passed the pouch as Warren continued.

"I couldn't see much then," he said, "except for this piece of driftwood about twenty feet in front of me." The driftwood had baffled Warren. "How did it get so far from the water? And what was it before it drifted into the ocean?" The second question had held more possibility for Warren, knowing as we all did that arid parts of the earth were once covered by water. But before he could investigate, a truly unbelievable occurrence had distracted him.

"Right there in front of me," Warren said, hopping out of his seat and tracing an imaginary circle at his feet, "like it was reaching out to me." A thrill ran through us, and he paused, setting the scene. "There's a tall cactus over here"—pointing off to his left—"and a wash just past the cactus. On my right are creosote bushes, all dried out with their flowers turned to fuzz. I turn around to see how far I am from the outer loop and realize that I can't see Garden Lakes at all. I can feel myself starting to panic, and I think I'm hallucinating about vanilla ice cream when this . . . thing"—Warren clasped his hands together and spread them slowly—"starts growing."

Those of us who had had Mr. Bisesto for biology knew what Warren was talking about—the queen of the night, a flower that bloomed one night a year, emitting a strong scent of vanilla. Mr. Bisesto annually told the story of how he once spotted the rarely seen night-blooming flower on a retreat in California.

"So I see this sign and I keep going," Warren said. He walked farther into the desert that night, trekking onto the Tohono O'odham Indian reservation, south of Maricopa. He moved unmolested through the reservation, encountering no one, until he reached a dirt road running alongside to the freeway. Frustrated by the circuitous route he'd taken, he mapped out the easiest path back to Garden Lakes, using the I-10 as a guide.

"But I decide to walk in the opposite direction," Warren said. "I don't know why. I just do. I look one way and go the other, back into the desert." He walked parallel to the freeway, though he moved to the interior of the land, away from the headlights caroming around him. "I ended up getting lost," he said. "I couldn't hear the freeway or see any headlights, but I kept on going. It all seemed like a mistake. That's when I found Axia." Warren gestured toward the girl, who smiled. We didn't understand her name when Warren said it, but were too shy to ask him to repeat it. Axia was *not* Tohono O'odham; she was not even Native American, a fact we did not know until later. We assumed otherwise as Warren continued with his story, about how he came upon a band of Tohono O'odhams—"thirty or forty, a bunch of them kids"—under a ramada. "They had these tools and they were using them to pop the tops off of the cacti," he said. He stood and demonstrated the motion, hoisting an invisible pole in his hands like a shotgun and crooking his elbows.

We foolishly imagined Warren walking into a nest of Indians like the ones we'd seen in Westerns, with scowling faces, their headdresses piercing the air. We knew only two varieties of Native Americans: the kind that wore colorful T-shirts emblazoned with brand names, and the kind from the movies. Warren assured us the group looked "like you and me, except for the color of their skin."

The Native Americans were, in reality, a family that had come together to harvest the fruit from the saguaro cacti and pay homage to their ancestors.

"What, like a rain dance?" Hands asked.

Axia laughed, revealing a snaggled top tooth.

"No, not a rain dance," Warren said. "The Tohono O'odhams are very informal about their rituals. This was the nearest thing to the wine festival ritual that celebrates the new year. I learned about it from Axia. The family didn't speak English."

Figs could feel Hands staring at him from the next table over. He ran his lie about the grocery guys finding Warren frontward and back, parsing his words for the loophole that would set him free from everyone's scorn. If he could just explain everything to Hands, he was sure Hands would say he would've done the same. It was the same as telling everyone that they'd seen Mr. Malagon when they hadn't. Figs would momentarily elude our inquiry, though, as our thoughts were preoccupied with Axia.

Warren continued his tale, how the family brought him back to their olive farm (and how the olive pits we were all sucking on had not been pitted by a machine but had been sucked clean by the olive farmers, which caused us to spit the seeds out; "They've been roasted," Warren said), how he learned Axia was not Native American, but had been traveling around the United States by thumb.

"I left when Axia left," he said.

Our eyes shifted to Axia. We could see the young girl she was through the dirt and grime that clung to her skin and clothes.

We imagined her in a blue and green plaid skirt, the uniform of all the girls in our dreams. Axia's hair hung in clumps, and it could've been any color in the world. She began to fidget, her hands adorned with chewed fingernails moving restlessly in her lap.

"She can't stay," Hands said, breaking our trance.

Warren's look cut through Hands.

"I'm sorry, man," Hands said, "but you know the rules. We've got work to do."

We wanted to protest but knew what Hands said was true. The extraordinary circumstances that had brought Axia to Garden Lakes would have to be ignored if we were to accomplish our goal. We would have to classify Axia as the enemy in order to persuade ourselves that turning her out was the correct thing to do.

Some were more easily persuaded than others.

"Why not let her get a shower and some rest?" Figs spoke up.

"I don't understand why she has to leave," Warren said.

Figs held up his hand to quiet Warren. He turned to Hands. "If we can all agree to keep on schedule, there's no reason why she can't stay," he said. "I'm sure we could use her help." He addressed Axia: "Would you be interested in helping us?"

"She's an excellent worker," Warren piped up.

"Wait, wait, wait," Hands said. "The question isn't if she can stay, but when she'll go."

"Can I smoke in here?" Axia asked. She pulled a tarnished gold cigarette case studded with turquoise from her pocket. Her question emboldened Hands.

"There's no smoking in any of the buildings," he said, sounding eerily like Mr. Hancock.

Axia got up and strode through the dining hall, perching outside the window to light one of her hand-rolled cigarettes.

The sophomores excused themselves to start lunch prep as the exchange reheated. Figs argued that Axia's arrival was an interesting twist to the program, but Hands viewed it as a clear breach of what Garden Lakes stood for.

"How can you say it's a breach?" Figs asked. "The whole point of being a fellow is proving yourself. Here's a chance for us to prove ourselves."

"What will it prove?" Hands demanded to know.

"That no matter the circumstances, we know how to make good decisions," Figs said.

We'd never beheld such a disagreement between the two, and it was hard to know when to chime in or whose side to ring in for. Hands garnered Smurf's allegiance, who agreed that allowing Axia to stay would be a violation of the rule against having visitors. "Look at what happened to me," he said, playing his expulsion for laughs. The joke missed its mark, though, and the debate stalled.

"I don't see any harm in her spending the night," Figs said.

"Me neither," Warren said.

Figs's proposal met with a smattering of approval. Hands was about to object, but Figs spoke over him. "I say we let her shower, get something to eat, and rest. Why don't you"—he indicated Hands and Smurf—"go to Mr. Malagon and see how he feels about her staying."

Realizing his advantage, Hands agreed.

"But first," Figs said, "we have to deal with the schedule."

We bolted back plates of sandwiches, stuffing apples and oranges and bananas and bagel halves into our pockets to sustain us through an afternoon shift at 1959 Regis Street. The sophomores were charged with manning a water line to combat the white-hot heat billowing through the rooms, filling and

183

refilling any container they could find with cold water for our water breaks. Our minds were not on the job at hand, though, but on Axia, who had been given the keys to the house relinquished by Quinn so she could clean up and rest. We imagined her brown body turning under the water, the days' and weeks' worth of filth falling away to expose the girl she'd been before she took up a life on the road. We willed ourselves to concentrate on applying the first coat of compound in an attempt to cover up the constellation of nails spread across the walls in every room.

The afternoon shift was one of our most successful, and we knocked off thirty minutes early as a reward, to allow us to scrub up for dinner. We compared smears of joint compound on our extremities and in our hair to prove that a good shower was warranted, but we secretly wanted to be presentable at dinner.

Hoping to meet up with Hands at their residence, Figs reached over Assburn and handed Sprocket his trowel. "One at a time," Sprocket complained, but Figs persisted, dropping the tools into their corresponding plastic boxes.

Figs was unable to locate Hands, though, Hands's dry towel hanging untouched in the bathroom. He asked Lindy if Hands had come in, and Lindy remarked that he had seen Hands talking to Smurf in front of Mr. Malagon's house. Figs peered out the window in the direction of Mr. Malagon's, but the sidewalk was empty, Hands and Smurf having moved into the house to continue their discussion.

"It's too dangerous now," Smurf said. "We should tell everyone."

"Tell them what?" Hands asked, aggravated. "Tell them that you lied about Mr. Malagon being sick?"

"What about you? You're in this now."

Hands moved them into the kitchen, away from the broken front door.

"I'll say that I didn't actually *see* Mr. Malagon," Hands said. He smirked. "I'll say that it was all coming from you."

"But you said you saw him."

"Figure of speech," Hands said.

"I don't understand why you don't want anyone to know."

"And I don't understand why you *do*. Do you want everyone to think you're a liar? A lie like this will make Assburn look like a saint. Is that what you want, people laughing at you and calling you names?" Hands had never understood why Smurf didn't take more care of his reputation, and he needed Smurf to focus on just that for his threat to take hold.

Smurf leaned against the dusty kitchen counter. He regretted taking Hands into his confidence; the strain of keeping Mr. Malagon's absence a secret had multiplied rather than lessened. "No, I don't," he answered.

"Good," Hands said, softening his tone. "I want the same thing you do: for us to complete our fellowship and then go home. But we have to get rid of that chick." Neither Smurf nor Hands could remember her name. "If they come out and find her here, we're done for."

Smurf took in what Hands was saying.

"Do you agree?" Hands asked.

"Yeah," Smurf said, "but what about letting a few key people know about Mr. Malagon?"

"Good idea," Hands said. "But you know what happens once you let someone know something. Everyone knows. Plus we're not in the position of having to build a consensus. All we have to say is that Mr. Malagon says she has to go and that'll be that. End of argument. Then we can call the school."

Smurf guessed at how tough it would be to keep the secret about Mr. Malagon close once a few people knew. He agreed to

185

go along with Hands's idea and stood next to him as Hands delivered Mr. Malagon's verdict during dinner. Axia's absence had left us dejected—"She's sound asleep," Warren had reported after a collective query—and our egos were soothed by the knowledge that Mr. Malagon had ordered that she leave.

"Should we wake her up and tell her," Figs said angrily, "or should we let her sleep?"

"Mr. Malagon said she could stay the night," Hands said without missing a beat.

The idea encouraged various amorous plots, all of which depended on Axia's waking from her nap. The gulf in communication between Figs and Hands had jettisoned our studies, but we knew we wouldn't be able to sit in our living rooms poring over ancient texts or handouts while Axia luxuriated in Quinn's old residence. Sensing this, or perhaps as a way to sharpen his skills, Hands suggested an after-dinner soccer match. We shouted excitedly when we touched the ball, cheering our teammates, in some cases chanting one another's names.

Hands was the only player who knew the score at the end of the match, taunting the opposing players for another game. We played another three, our muscles aching, some of us bleeding, all of us hoping that Axia would appear to witness our skill and cunning. Even Sprocket was infected with a new enthusiasm, calling "Gooooaaaal!" if we scored, or barking "Out!" if we missed.

We would've played best of five, four out of seven, first one to ten—anything to dawdle long enough for Axia to wake, but she slumbered through the night.

It was nearing midnight when we lay down our disappointed heads.

***

We came to breakfast the next morning, fatigued to the brink of hallucination, to find the sophomores camped around Axia, who was relating an apparently hilarious tale about a truck driver she'd hitched a ride from outside of Albuquerque. Warren sat next to her, punctuating her story with his sharp laughter.

The sophomores took their stations as we shuffled in, serving us an unusually gourmet breakfast consisting of omelets, raisin muffins, hash brown casserole, and handmade sausage patties spiced up with jalapeños and herbs. The sophomores whispered Axia's name in response to our wonderment at the delicious spread.

Figs sat at Axia's table, introducing himself. He stuck out his hand awkwardly and Axia shook it.

"Figs is sort of the captain of the team," Warren said. The rest of us looked around for Hands or Roger, who might've had something to say about Warren's anointment, but they arrived late, stumbling in as Axia, in answer to Figs's questions, told her story.

After spelling her name for us, she admitted it was not her real name. "I read it in a book," she said. Her given name was Virginia Dare, and she had been born in Fort Wayne, Indiana, eighteen years earlier, but had been raised outside of Lincoln, Nebraska ("in a place that doesn't exist for me anymore"), by a couple who adopted her at age two, after her birth parents were killed when their car collided with a cement embankment. The couple that brought Axia to Nebraska, and renamed her Lisa Grayson, as her adoptive mother had a bedeviling aunt named Virginia that she loathed.

Life in Nebraska was grim, and Axia was not permitted to watch television, or play with friends after school, or any of the other activities that we presumed all other kids enjoyed. The household sounded overtly religious, but Axia did not allude to any particular church.

"I didn't find out I was adopted until I was fourteen," she said.

Warren howled. "Can you believe *that?*" he asked us. We helped ourselves to seconds of hash brown casserole, listening all the while.

"The idea that I was adopted set everything in motion," Axia said. Some of us stared at her snaggled tooth, which we thought made her even cuter. "I looked at my adoptive parents like strangers from then on. Every worry that I had about turning out like them vanished."

Her surroundings suddenly felt fake, a movie set against which her life had played out for the last fourteen years. A turbulent two years followed in which Axia disobeyed every word her parents and teachers said. She suffered through a series of groundings, detentions, and suspensions with a smile.

"Did you try to find your real family?" Assburn asked, having come in after the part about how her parents had been killed. Someone threw a crumpled napkin at him.

"What?" he asked defensively.

Axia repeated the information, and Assburn covered with, "I meant your parents' family. You know, like aunts and uncles."

Axia shook her head. "I could've," she said, "but any life back in Fort Wayne would've been as strange to me as the one in Nebraska. None of it belonged to me."

She counted the months and weeks and days and hours and minutes until her eighteenth birthday. Axia asked the Graysons (which is how she referred to them) if she could invite a friend from school over—the only friend Axia had made in four years of high school—but they said no. That simple, one-word, two-letter answer germinated the resentment and bitterness that Axia had been nurturing since she was fourteen, and rather than eat the fried chicken and mashed potato dinner the Graysons had prepared (fried foods being forbidden in the Grayson residence except on special occasions), Axia scooped up as many of her meager possessions as she could fit into a bag. She walked out to the highway and had a ride south within the hour.

Twelve hours later she was stranded southeast of Denver, tired from the amphetaminic blather of her first chauffeur, who had taken her as far as Branson, Colorado. "The end of the line for me," the driver said, grinning under his greasy baseball hat stitched with the word GAMECOCK in camouflage lettering. The second leg of her journey—she was flirting with an idea that she was bound for Mexico—took her as far as Albuquerque, a good test to judge what life in the desert would be like. She did not have a driver's license, and it would be difficult to reenter the United States once she committed to leaving. She took a job at Five Points Bakery, near the Rio Grande. "I would eat my lunch on the riverbank," she said. "It was actually an ugly spot, but I liked to watch the river." She took a furnished room in downtown Albuquerque, then two months later agreed to move in with a coworker who wanted someone to share the rent and utilities.

But the morning after she'd verbally agreed to move, Axia took the money she'd been able to save by eating popcorn for lunch and dinner—something like two hundred dollars—and cushioned the soles of her shoes with the bills. She packed her belongings—fewer in number than at the start—and hit the highway, rolling into Phoenix as the sun set across the valley.

"You came down the I-17," Warren gushed. His subservience around Axia was beginning to grate on all of us, and we started to intuit how it was she had come to Garden Lakes.

The sophomores busied themselves around our tables to hear Axia's story, collecting the dirty dishes with an alacrity only curiosity could incite.

Axia told of catching a ride with a carload of Arizona State students on their way to Mexico for spring break. The students treated Axia to so much beef jerky and Miller Lite that she became sick, vomiting out the window to the loud applause from inside the car.

The spring breakers invited Axia to tour the Mexican side of Nogales with them—they were paying a quick visit to someone named Spanky before speeding off to Rocky Point—but she declined, though she accepted their parting gift of a maroon and gold T-shirt depicting a devil with a pitchfork, the school's mascot. She changed into the T-shirt in the bathroom of the McDonald's on the American side, where she said good-bye to the students, the restaurant overflowing with tourists too afraid to eat across the border.

To quell her stomach, Axia removed a five-dollar bill from her shoe and ordered a large Sprite and a small french fries, finding a seat by the window where she could rest while she ate the skimpy dinner. She spent a few nights wandering the busy streets of Nogales, tempted to cross the border but dubious about what awaited her there. Every experience she'd had—good or bad—was American in nature. The lark of living in Mexico faded as Axia began searching for a way back north, finally grabbing a ride back to Phoenix with an elderly couple who had crossed the border to fill their prescriptions.

"Same as my grandparents," Warren chimed in.

"Woo-woo," Roger said, drawing circles in the air with his finger. He pushed back noisily from the table, and we heard the front doors close behind him.

We watched Roger pass in front of the dining-hall windows while Axia finished her story. "I got as far as Casa Grande, and that's where I went into the fields"—which we took to mean her stint as an olive farmer—"and then I met Warren," she said.

"You've been living with the Indians for *four months*?" Sprocket asked.

Axia shrugged. Hands fidgeted in his chair as others lobbed questions. Figs sensed confrontation and hoped to deflate it. "Give me a hand in the kitchen?" he asked Hands.

Hands frowned. "What for?" he asked.

"I'll go," Warren volunteered before Figs could answer. Irked, Figs traipsed off to the kitchen with Warren at his heels.

Warren took Figs's arm and pulled him into the hallway.

"I'm on your side," he said.

"What?" Figs asked.

"About Axia staying," Warren said. "She should be allowed to stay. What if you and I go to Mr. Malagon and ask? Maybe we could take her to meet him. I'll bet if he could meet her, he would change his mind."

Figs contemplated Warren's plan. He cared less about Axia than he did about Hands's and Smurf's burgeoning importance with Mr. Malagon. Why should they be the only conduits? Figs understood that if he and Warren took the issue to Mr. Malagon, and Mr. Malagon's decision held, he would be at an even greater disadvantage. An alternative plan—one that Figs had been working on overnight—was to reverse his stance on Axia, hoping the recompense for his support for her expulsion would be access to Mr. Malagon. The likelihood that Mr. Malagon would let Axia stay was slight, Figs knew. His inclination was to play the percentages, but if he fought for Axia and won, he would be elevated and not simply part of a triumvirate.

Warren pressed the case for approaching Mr. Malagon on Axia's behalf, but his words were muted by Hands's voice floating into the hallway from the dining hall. "We have to get to work," he said. A bustling followed as we took the cue to stand and collect our dirty dishes. Axia stayed seated, looking passively for Warren, who pushed through us as we filed out of the community center. A shoving match erupted between Smurf and Warren but was quickly broken up by Figs and Hands, each taking their respective fighters to their corners.

"Don't worry," Warren said to Axia. "We're going to Mr. Malagon ourselves."

Hands let go of Smurf. "What?"

"You heard me," Warren said. A wild, chaotic look possessed him.

"Maybe I don't want to stay," Axia said.

"The choice should at least be yours," Warren said, breaking free of Figs's hold. "If you want to leave, fine. But I'm not going to let them"—he pointed a finger at Hands and Smurf—"throw you out. That's not fair."

Warren walked with purpose out of the dining hall. Hands clambered after him, leaving Figs and Smurf in his wake. Smurf had barely spoken—something about Mr. Malagon not being home—when a loud crash rang out. We rushed to the window, expecting to find Hands and Warren engaged in hand-to-hand combat, wondering what had broken. The view from the window, however, was remarkably serene: Roger standing on the lip of the lake bed, shading his eyes; Assburn and Lindy huddled together on the sidewalk, their conversation interrupted; Hands outside the community center doors, lurking in the shadow of the roof; Warren and Lindy gathered around Sprocket in front of Mr. Malagon's house, their sunlit faces searching Mr. Malagon's bedroom window, which had been smashed out when Roger's kick sent the soccer ball over everyone's head, the faintest trail of the ball's trajectory lingering in the air.

We stood breathless, waiting.

Warren lifted a wedge of decorative concrete from the walkway and heaved it through Mr. Malagon's living-room window. Those inside the dining hall couldn't see the window but heard a pop and then a shower of glass. Warren turned to face the others, but everyone looked past him, staring in horror at the two broken windows.

In testimony before the administration, the amount of time that lapsed between the shattering of Mr. Malagon's windows and the confirmation that Mr. Malagon was not in the house varied widely. Some claimed to know right away, which was the truth for all of us, while others said they were shocked to learn later that Mr. Malagon was not laid up in bed, as had been advertised, but had abandoned us. The discrepancy of who knew it and when was due to our reaction to the broken windows, a reaction the administration found incredulous, calling fellows in individually to substantiate what they deemed an outlandish lie: that everyone reported for work at 1959 Regis Street, honoring the teams we'd drawn up before Warren reappeared, working with urgency to compensate for the time we'd lost owing to the search for Warren.

Our focus was acute, driven by the fear of what we suspected about Mr. Malagon, that he had forsaken us for some unexplained reason. We pored over our job journals, comparing notes. Inside corners called out to us to be taped off; we affixed J-trims to the shower stalls and window jambs; outside corners were fitted with bullnose corner beads. We worked with an expertise that had, for any number of reasons, previously eluded us. We worked through lunch. We worked through class time. We worked through sports.

Some of us lagged behind the rest, joining our teams late; and of course Smurf did not reunite with his team at all, though we did not realize he had left Garden Lakes—this time of his own volition—until dinner, when it was the marquee gossip. Intelligence about the events leading up to Smurf's departure, as well as the whereabouts of those who reached the jobsite late, was not clear to us until the administration made its official report. We knew generally about Figs and Hands and Assburn's tardiness; their lateness was noted by Roger, who commented when the three walked onto the job without offering an excuse or even a flippant response, then reported to Sprocket for their equipment and jumped in.

According to the account put out by the administration, the reason for Figs and Hands and Assburn's tardiness involved two distinct and simultaneous events, both put into play as the rest of us set upon 1959 Regis Street.

First, Smurf demanded to use Assburn's mobile phone. Assburn, stricken with the realization that Mr. Malagon had deserted Garden Lakes, agreed. Smurf must've believed he could salvage the situation with one phone call to Randolph, though as I look back, this plan seems impossibly naive. Smurf's testimony after the fact left open for interpretation why he'd wanted Assburn's mobile phone, largely because of the evidence that Assburn's phone had met the same fate as Mr. Hancock's (though it was a sure bet that Mr. Hancock hadn't squandered valuable battery life calling 900 numbers as Assburn had) and Smurf himself said he wasn't sure whom he was going to call—Randolph or Katie Sullivan. Smurf's failure to contact Randolph after leaving Garden Lakes threw a spotlight of suspicion on him, and the administration was never completely convinced that Smurf wasn't working in harmony with Mr. Malagon or covering for him in some way.

Mr. Malagon's own testimony on the matter was sealed, forever unknown.

The second event was unfolding a few houses down, as Figs followed Hands into their residence. "Did you *ever* see him?" he asked as Hands started to ascend the stairs.

Hands pivoted on the bottom step. He eyed Figs coldly, assessing whether Figs was reaching out or digging his finger into the wound. Figs began pacing the living room, signaling the latter. "It was all Smurf," Hands said in a rush of inspiration. "He called me up to Mr. Malagon's room. I wanted to tell everyone, but Smurf thought we'd all hang him. So I went along with it."

"I don't get what the plan was," Figs said, bouncing between the living room and the kitchen. "What was Smurf up to?"

Hands shrugged. "He never said."

Figs stopped pacing. "Where *is* Smurf?"

Figs became the next to know that Smurf had become the fourth deserter after Quinn and Mr. Hancock and Mr. Malagon, climbing into his car, which he'd kept hidden outside the main gates. Figs brought his hand to his mouth as Hands related Smurf's getaway.

"What will you say?" Figs asked pointedly.

Hands stepped down and took a seat on the love seat. He knew it would be his word against Smurf's, and even though Smurf was not present to give his side, his silence was as good as him disputing Hands's story, the room for doubt too great to be overcome by repeating that it was all Smurf's idea. Hands knew he needed an ally. He wondered if he could recruit someone cold. Roger? Not likely. Assburn? Possibly. He knew from Smurf that Assburn's famous cry of innocence over the theft of Senator Quinn's pen was phony, but Assburn had probably disposed of the pen for good by now, and leaning on Assburn might have negative results. He needed someone who was weak minded or, at the very least, weak willed, someone who could be promised something in return for verifying Hands's version of events. He considered Sprocket but could not think of anything he could promise Sprocket for an alibi.

Hands ran through the possibilities. Warren was the best candidate—he possessed an indefinable credibility that others respected—but Warren was too distracted by Axia to be of any use, witnessed by the fact that Warren had stayed behind to help Axia, who had begun cleaning the kitchen and dining hall as the rest of us rushed out to the sound of breaking glass.

Lindy had a workableness to him, but Lindy wouldn't be as strong an ally as Figs, a fact Hands had known from the start.

"I'll tell them that it was all Smurf," Hands said defiantly.

Figs gave a look of surprise, knowing what Hands had figured out for himself, that he needed Figs. "No one will believe you."

"Everyone believed *you* when you lied about Warren and the grocery truck driver," Hands said matter-of-factly, regretting the barb immediately.

Figs winced. Hands's alliance with Smurf still smarted, and while Figs wanted to help Hands, wanted to realign Hands's loyalties, he wasn't going to offer. Hands would have to ask.

Figs suffered through another round of haranguing about Warren before Hands asked. Figs accepted, seizing the moment to secure Axia's place at Garden Lakes.

"You're crazy," Hands said. "Can you imagine what will happen if the school finds out, either now—if Smurf goes and tells them—or at Open House, when all our parents show up?"

"She'll leave the day before Open House," Figs submitted, an olive branch he'd worked out in advance, knowing Hands would raise this particular objection, and further knowing the objection was legitimate. The school couldn't know about Axia; that would be rule number one.

Hands continued to object, though his position was considerably weakened. Finally he acquiesced. "I'm not responsible, though," Hands said. "If something happens, it'll be all you."

"Fine," Figs said, "but if I'm going to be a hundred percent behind your story, you have to be a hundred percent behind Axia staying. That's the deal."

"Yeah, okay," Hands said.

By the time they joined us for construction, they'd worked out all the details, though we heard the story for the first time that night at dinner, Smurf's tire tracks still fresh in the dirt along the shoulder outside the gates. We heard about how Smurf had roped Hands in, how Hands had gotten all his information secondhand, through Smurf. We ate in shock; we'd never known Smurf to pull something so devious. We marveled at his duplicity, impressed by it, but our admiration slowly wore away as we realized the gravity of our new situation.

We had only to look to Figs and Hands for guidance, though. As the sophomores cleared the tables, they made their pitch to keep Garden Lakes afloat until Open House, interspersing their speech with "It's a good opportunity" and "What better way to test ourselves?"

It was agreed that, in order to argue successfully for full credit for our fellowship, the schedule would remain intact, as would all the rules and regulations—including the reinstatement of curfew. We frittered away an hour on a scheme put forward by Hands, who wanted to break us up into pods, each pod rotating duties every day. "That would work," Figs said, "but what if the administration declared us ineligible because we didn't all have a hand in construction?" (The sophomores would quickly see that

197

the emphasis of the coming days would be on the fellowship; anything pertaining to kitchen work or laundry would become background noise.) "We've got nineteen days until Open House. We're pretty much on schedule at 1959. We're a bit behind in our classwork"—Figs and Hands had located the two boxes in Mr. Malagon's closet filled with the handouts and tests Mr. Malagon had planned to use for class—"but it's nothing we can't catch up on."

We didn't see any reason why we couldn't do it. The idea of going it alone appealed to us, and while we bore no confidence in our abilities, we were driven mainly by our collective desire to prove that it could be done. We felt sure we would employ any means necessary to accomplish the goal, and wouldn't they be surprised? We imagined our parents' reactions when they discovered what we'd done, and the reactions of droves of others' parents when they heard. Our determination would be fabled, one for the annals of Garden Lakes, one that would be discussed year after year. And long after, no matter where we were in the world, our immortality would be resurrected every year as spring brought the first whisper of Garden Lakes—who would be nominated, who would be chosen—and if we strained our imagination, we just might hear the awed conversations beginning with "Did you hear about the fellows from the class of eighty-eight?"

"We all have to agree," Figs said, calling for a vote. Figs and Hands raised their hands. Sprocket raised his hand as fast; he hoped to become the class proctor and planned to lobby Figs and Hands (and anyone else) for the commission. Roger flashed his palm and then let his hand fall back down on his knee. Lindy voted yes too.

Warren's hand flew up in the company of hands thrown up by the sophomores, who had straggled in from the kitchen. His vote wasn't just for continuation, but also for allowing Axia to stay, a fact that Figs had tipped him off to, Figs guaranteeing Axia could stay as long as Warren would help counter any arguments against Figs and Hands's proposal to maintain the status quo. The zip in Warren's vote was fueled by his happiness at not having to help Figs twist arms on the Axia front.

"We've got this, boys," Hands said, sealing the pact.

The administration found the incongruous testimony about Axia unbelievable. Some reported that we believed Axia would be asked to leave, that a vote for continuation was a vote for Axia's expulsion. Others thought Axia was to watch over the sophomores and their kitchen duty. What the testimony didn't reveal was our secret longing to have her around, not only because she was a girl, but because we wanted someone to witness our acts of bravery. We wanted someone to cheer us on in success or buoy us after a day of defeat. We liked the idea that there was someone other than us, someone who, for no reason, we felt accountable to. And while we would not have been able to express this feeling in those terms, the Axia issue was dropped once we raised our hands endorsing continuation, and Axia blended into the background.

We were able to abide by the schedule for exactly twelve days.

We welcomed the structure of the daily schedule back into our lives. Conformity to the schedule brought the sense that we were steadily chipping away stone to uncover sculpture.

Eagerness woke us that first Saturday. Axia joined the sophomores in the kitchen and proved as adept as Mr. Hancock, her nearness motivation enough for the sophomores, who toiled with renewed purpose. She also served as another pair of eyes for sports, situating herself on the ever-shifting sand of the island in the lake bed to aid Sprocket in close calls. We offered to substitute her in during play, but she demurred. We did what we could to encourage her to join a team, but she would only let us set up goal kicks for her before and after games, Hands batting down every ball she shot.

We did make one amendment to the schedule, one we knew we could justify: Rather than breaking the sophomores and fellows up into pods for tutoring, we congregated in the dining hall, the sophs reading aloud George Washington's Farewell Address, Chief Justice Taney's opinion in *Dred Scott v. Sandford*, the Emancipation Proclamation, the Gettysburg Address, Samuel Gompers's Letter on Labor in Industrial Society, etc., conversation periodically veering wide of the subject at hand, devolving into joke telling or a bull session about what Mr. Hancock intended by including a particular text in *American Democracy*. Our ability to digest and pontificate on the texts sharpened in Axia's presence, her sitting at one of the back tables, where she listened quietly.

Construction continued apace. We made strides in beading and moved into the taping phase, careful to adhere to the taping sequence Mr. Baker, the future kidnapping victim, had laid out for us: fasteners, tapered-edge seams, butted seams, inside corners, outside corners—the precise order being important to avoid disrupting a flat seam when working the corners. We each slid a bucket of joint compound along as we worked, the rhythmic harrumph of pails scraping above and below marking the hours.

The next day, an impromptu tour sprang up, Hands showing off our progress to Axia, who had asked him about it during lunch. Hands detailed our work, allowing her to labor under the misimpression that we had erected the frame and poured the foundation, a falsehood none of us worked too hard to correct.

Hands's attitude toward Axia improved once we accepted as true his innocence in the matter of Mr. Malagon and Smurf, so that four or five days in, Axia was taking her meals at Figs and Hands's table. Hands even developed an avidity for astronomy once Axia coaxed Lindy into showing her the sky from the community center roof. We all became junior astronomers, electing to spend free time night after night huddled around Lindy and Axia, amazed by what amazed them.

Axia sat in on our poker games too, bluffing with an earnestness that fooled us every time. Had we been playing for real money and not poker chips, she would've bankrupted us all.

That Friday, the smoky fragrance of barbecue drifted through our windows as we changed out of our filthy work clothes for dinner. The source of the smell was not the kitchen but a barbecue pit Axia and the sophomores had dug. Axia and the sophs had moved fast to carve a pit into the lake bed, the idea sparked by an unopened bag of charcoal briquettes in the pantry. We were too enchanted to tell her the briquettes were for the Open House; that Mr. Hancock would not be present to strike up the celebratory barbecue lessened our guilt. So, too, did the chicken brushed with a homemade barbecue sauce that lured us in with the sweet taste of honey only to stab us with the heat of jalapeño. "My own recipe," Axia said. We tried to convey its tastiness, but our eyes watered and our lips burned if we stopped eating, so we grunted our approval.

"What was your high school like?" Figs asked, chomping on a plump chicken leg.

"It was nothing special," Axia said. "Not like where you guys go." She described her teachers, some good, some bad. "I didn't hate it or anything," she said.

A game of truth or dare started up as the coals died out. Roger asked Warren, "Truth or dare?" hoping Warren would answer,

"Dare," so Roger could dare him to kiss Axia, but Warren didn't oblige. Roger thought for a minute and then asked, "What's the *real* reason you disappeared?"

Warren laughed. "I already told you."

"The *truth*," Roger reminded him.

A refrain of "Yeah" went around the barbecue pit.

Warren laid his hand across his heart. "I swear I told the truth," he said, loving the attention.

"Tell them what you told me," Axia said.

Warren blushed. "Well, I . . ."

"Out with it, weasel," Roger said. Warren could take a little ribbing, and it felt good to let out a good-natured laugh at his expense.

"Answer me this," Hands said to Axia. "Did he dance naked with the Indians?"

Axia spit out a mouthful of soda, the spray dousing the briquettes, a wisp of smoke rising on contact.

"I just said that I didn't care if I didn't go back," Warren said.

We had hoped Warren's admission would be something hysterical, something lighthearted to stoke our good time, but instead what he said sobered us and we stared ruefully into the desert night.

Lindy broke the silence. "Why not?"

"I don't know," Warren said. "I wasn't out there long, but I liked the simple lifestyle. There weren't so many . . . questions. It seemed to me"—he looked at Axia for reassurance—"that that other life is about labor and not about always trying to figure things out. That's all."

"True, true," Axia said. She nodded herself into a reverie, and some of us looked away embarrassedly, as if we were spying on her getting dressed.

"Don't sweat it," Hands said, throwing an empty soda can at Warren. "You'll never figure anything out anyway."

We loved Hands for bringing us back around. In turn, our guffaws brought Axia back, and we continued with the game, hoping one of us would choose dare, until it became another game not to, each of us not wanting to grant another the privilege. Instead, the night was saturated with earnestly rendered truths and half-truths (as well as some outright lies), each of us trying to impress Axia by telling a tale on ourselves, gauging the success of our stories by how hard she laughed, or by how well we elicited her sympathies.

A smaller game was being played on the outskirts of the circle. Figs was anticipating his turn, glancing furtively at Hands, who sensed something was up. He doubted Figs had the nerve to ask him the truth about Mr. Malagon as a part of the game, but as the right to ask someone "Truth or dare?" worked its way back to Figs, Hands announced that he was turning in for the night. Lindy followed, the next casualty in what was a slow drift of tired souls, Figs and Warren trying to outlast each other in a bid to be alone with Axia.

The sight of Mr. Baker's truck drawing near inspired a current of panic through 1959 Regis Street; we weren't unprepared for Mr. Baker's inspection—we'd applied the skim coat of compound the day before—but we had not thought through what we would say to Mr. Baker's inevitable questions about Mr. Malagon.

Without flinching, Figs shifted his paper mask down around his chin and met Mr. Baker's truck, hailing him like a long-lost relative.

"Howdy," Mr. Baker said, waving back. "How's she lookin'?"

"I think you'll be pleased," Figs said, a master at making someone feel regal. "We've followed your instructions exactly."

Mr. Baker shaded his eyes, looking for Mr. Malagon.

"Oh," Figs said. "Mr. Malagon had to run out for some supplies. He said if he missed you that we should pay extra attention to your instructions for phase three."

"What did you run out of?" Mr. Baker asked.

Figs gave a hearty laugh. "Kitchen supplies." He glanced back at the community center as if to prove his point, Mr. Baker looking over his shoulder too. "And toilet supplies."

"Okay," Mr. Baker said. "Let's have a look."

A rare hush fell over the house as Mr. Baker worked his way from room to room, Figs following close behind. After pointing out several crowned seams—the result of too much compound spread over a taped section—that would need sanding, as well as several cracked seams running like lightning down the wall ("Compound dried too fast," Mr. Baker said) and a cracked corner bead, Mr. Baker lectured us in the art of sanding, texturing, and painting—the finishing touches we would apply before the Open House.

"First," Mr. Baker said, wiping his brow, "is that you must wear paper masks when sanding. I want you to write that down in capital letters." He paused while we took down the warning. "Do you have the telescopic poles for raising a plastic wall?"

Mr. Baker looked to Sprocket for the answer, but before Sprocket could reveal that Hands and Roger had commandeered the poles to use in a spontaneous volleyball game a couple of nights ago, a forceful spike of the soccer ball by Roger buckling one of the poles, Hands said, "Yeah, I saw them in the back of the supply shed."

Sprocket nodded idiotically to corroborate the misinformation.

"Good," Mr. Baker said. "Just make sure the ends of the poles are buried in plastic before you wedge them into the floor and ceiling. Nothing like having a plastic wall come loose and wrap around you while you're working." Mr. Baker laughed as if it had happened to him more than once.

The previous class had had the luxury of electric sanders, but an accident had resulted in their removal (and the removal of a finger, according to legend), so they'd been replaced by manual pole sanders. Mr. Baker ran through the different sandpaper grits we'd need—"one-twenty grit for coarse work; one fifty for finer work"—showing us how to move our hand along the wall in front of a hand sander to scout out areas needing sanding.

Mr. Baker cautioned us against sanding the face of the drywall and about the dangers of oversanding. "If you oversand, you'll have to reapply the third coat of compound, and another skim coat," he said. We took this advice seriously, promising to defeat any temptation to erase a scratch or dent in the taping completely. "Just enough so it won't show through the texturing and the paint," Mr. Baker said.

Next we listened to the procedure for what sounded like the best part of the job, the knockdown roller finish we'd have to apply to the walls and ceilings before painting the whole shebang. "Most textures are applied with a hopper and an air compressor," Mr. Baker said, "but there are a couple of ways to texture a wall by hand, and one is a knockdown roller finish. Its name gives you a clue as to how it's applied. First you roll on a light coat of joint compound with a paint roller, then you take a trowel and follow by applying even pressure"—Mr. Baker pressed the flat of his hand against the wall at an angle and dragged it down the wall—"to knock down the peaks created by the roller. Very simple. The key is not to press too hard, or load the wall up with compound." He looked at his watch and then out the paneless window at the community center. "How long do you figure till he gets back?" he asked.

"Not sure," Figs said, stepping up.

"What about the other one?" Mr. Baker asked. "What's his name? Hancock?"

Figs froze. He hadn't accounted for Mr. Hancock's absence, as Mr. Baker had hardly said more than hello to him. "He's . . . sick," Figs said lamely. "He's lying down."

Hands instinctively supported what Figs had said. "Stomach virus," Hands said.

Mr. Baker grimaced. "I thought this project required adult supervision," he said.

"Mr. Malagon really hasn't been gone that long," Figs said.

Mr. Baker looked at his watch again. "I've been here for close to an hour," he said. "Maybe an hour and a half."

"I think I saw him pull around behind the community center," Figs said.

We craned our necks to look, but all we saw was Adam Kerr flinging a bucket of dirty mop water out the back door.

"I'm not sure when to schedule the final inspection before the Open House," Mr. Baker said. "When is it?"

"The twenty-ninth," Hands said.

"What is that? A Wednesday?" Mr. Baker asked.

We guessed that it was.

"Does Mr. Malagon have your phone number?" Figs asked. It took all his will to contain his desperation. "He has a mobile phone. He can call you with the information when he gets back. I'll make sure."

"Yeah, I'll remind him," Hands said.

"Would Mr. Hancock know?" Mr. Baker asked. "I'd like to clear it up before I go."

"He's awfully sick," Figs said, "but c'mon, I'll take you to him. We'll ask."

None of us dared to breathe, uncertain of what Figs was up to.

"I'll go with," Hands said. "I want to ask him something too."

The three started out for Mr. Hancock's residence, making it as far as Mr. Baker's truck before a shrieking pierced the air. Mr. Baker raised his sunglasses and squinted at the display on his pager. "Shit," he said, forgetting Figs and Hands for a moment. We watched from the house as Mr. Baker made Figs copy down the phone number from the decal on the passenger-side door of Mr. Baker's truck, Figs's promise to have Mr. Malagon or Mr. Hancock call him fading as Mr. Baker started the engine.

"Tell you what," Figs yelled. "If they don't call, that means all's well."

It was hard to tell if Mr. Baker was nodding in agreement or if he was shaking his head, insisting someone call. Figs and Hands deliberated on the subtleties of Mr. Baker's head movement all through the dinner hour. Figs was convinced it was fine, that Mr. Baker was surely overwhelmed with more-important responsibilities. "So what if he does show up a few days before the Open House?" Figs asked. "By then, it'll be over. We'll be done."

Mr. Baker showing up before Open House was not what worried Hands. "What if he calls Randolph when Mr. Malagon doesn't call, to find out if he is supposed to do an inspection before the Open House?"

Figs suggested they wait a few days and then call themselves, telling Mr. Baker that Mr. Malagon asked them to call, a ruse for our benefit, Figs and Hands not letting on that Mr. Hancock's mobile phone was inoperable. "Or we could call after hours and leave a message," Figs said. Figs did his best to satisfy Hands that they had options, and time, but Hands knew Mr. Baker could single-handedly ruin their chances of completing the fellowship. The idea of having wasted the summer *and* not getting credit for the fellowship drove Hands's fears. He remained unconvinced by Figs's arguments and sought him out during free time to try to convince him otherwise. He checked in on Lindy, who was hosting the nightly sky-watching party on the roof of the community center, but Figs was not among the crowd. He stuck his head in on a poker game between me and Assburn and Sprocket, who asked him if he wanted to sit in. We told him that we hadn't seen Figs since dinner. Hands wandered Regis Street to its end, thinking Figs might have gone back to the construction site, though the site was too dark at night to see.

A light in Axia's living room drew Hands's attention. He kicked through a mound of gravel that had been built on the sidewalk by the wind, scattering the pebbles. As he raised his hand to knock on the door, he leaned over and peered through the window. His fist dropped when he saw Figs and Axia on the couch, Axia practically sitting in Figs's lap. Figs's hand bounced on Axia's knee as he spoke, and she laughed as Figs finished whatever it was he was saying.

Heat burned across Hands's forehead. He stomped back down the walkway, blinded, a portrait of Axia sitting on Figs's lap projected everywhere he looked. He was on the precipice of homicide when he summoned me from the poker game, though I put up a small fight—"The best hand I've had all night"—but the bloodthirsty look in Hands's eyes communicated that he was ready to yank me away from the table, and so I folded the four aces and king and followed Hands outside. His litany of grievances against Figs had a violent timbre, Hands straining his voice as we strolled along Garden Lakes Parkway.

"Loyalty is the only thing one friend can offer another," he said. "Disloyalty should be treated accordingly."

He'd regained his breathing, his hoarse voice scarcely above a rasp. Our legs ached; we'd walked miles around the lake bed. "Keep it quiet until the morning," was my parting advice. Hands didn't say anything that night, or in the morning, either, instead moving out of his room and into the house next door, Mr. Malagon's old residence.

The sound of hammering woke us, Hands deafened by the pounding as he repaired the doorframe of his new house, not hearing our calls as we passed by on our way to breakfast.

Chapter Twelve

We did not curse the sun as a heat wave gripped Garden Lakes, though the heat persisted well after midnight, dropping only a few degrees as the moon waned. The unbearable stifle distracted us from the truth that Hands was not merely repairing the damage done to Mr. Malagon's residence—a notion we commended as prudent, seeing how our parents would be arriving in a week and would ask questions—but had moved his belongings into the house, rehanging one of the plywood sheets we'd nailed over the broken windows that had slid to the ground.

There were those of us who guessed at the reason for Hands's relocation, but confirmation came only when Hands—who would one day lead his family's sixth-generation brewery to ruin by distrusting his chief financial officer, whom he considered a rival for his wife's affections, engaging in endless, meritless litigation against the CFO that ended with a huge judgment against the brewery—circulated a private invitation to a select few for a housewarming of sorts on Wednesday night after dinner. The invitations were proffered by an unlikely source—Hands had chosen Kerr and Laird to discreetly deliver the announcement—and Roger threatened to punch Laird during breakfast when

Laird tried to whisper in his ear. Those of us who had been invited wondered who else had been so privileged. The only certainty was that Figs would not be in attendance, a certainty unwittingly aided by Reedy, who happened upon Figs in his search for someone to take a look at the air conditioner attached to his residence, which had apparently frozen and shut down.

Figs fetched a hammer and a flathead screwdriver from the supply shed and descended on the air conditioner like a paramedic, Reedy right on his heels. Figs's quick reaction was an extension of the mode he'd been in all day, a manner triggered by his lust to impress Axia. Not even Hands's ditching out morning construction could shake Figs's focus. If he had to carry the team himself, he would. And Axia would have a front-row seat to his heroics.

The full roster convened in Hands's living room: Roger, Lindy, Sprocket, Assburn, and me. Kerr and Laird hovered near Hands, not realizing that their usefulness had expired.

Hands got right to it. "We've got a problem," he said. "We've all sacrificed our summer to be here, and now we have a situation that puts that sacrifice in jeopardy." We knew what Hands was referring to. Hands continued his tirade without mentioning Axia specifically, couching his argument in terms of her residency being a corruption of the rules. "Like Mr. Malagon said, we must have cohesion. And part of being cohesive is following the rules, regardless of what the rules are. If the rules said it was okay to have visitors, we wouldn't have to meet like this."

"It's not right to just turn her out," Laird said, mistakenly presuming he was an equal member of the committee.

Hands continued as if Laird had not spoken. "I'm only interested in what we're all interested in," he said. "I want our parents to roll in here next week and see that we've accomplished what we set out to accomplish, and then I want go home and enjoy what's left of summer. Is there anyone who disagrees with that idea?"

We did not disagree with Hands's thesis, though the idea seemed to us a reiteration of the case he'd been making since Axia arrived.

In later testimony we would swear that no stratagems were designed that night, no plan of action called upon, a truth that was subverted by the fact that by breakfast the next morning, Garden Lakes was swirling with innuendo that Figs and Axia were a couple and that Figs was granting Axia haven for wholly personal reasons. Certain of us would not repeat the rumor, but others actively promoted it, Roger and Hands the loudest voices in the choir. Figs's absence from breakfast lent credibility to the accusation.

The heat forced us to retreat to our residences halfway through the morning construction, Roger and Hands calling off work in Figs and Warren's absence. We dropped our sanding equipment where we stood, assuming we would begin again after dinner, racing against the gloaming to finish, not knowing we wouldn't return to our positions until that Saturday.

Figs, who would one day cover up an embezzlement at his firm, shifting the blame to an innocent department head at his father-in-law's insistence, resulting in the department head's firing, passed time at Axia's. He'd forgotten about his promise to call Mr. Baker and did not worry about the consequences, firmly believing one of two things would happen: that by his not calling, Mr. Baker would have excuse enough to dodge any reprimand, or that Mr. Baker's busy schedule would overtake his memory about the final inspection. A third principle guided Figs's confidence: A final inspection before Open House would serve only to point up the mistakes—it would be too late to repair any flaws.

Instead, Figs whiled his time in conversation with Axia about how best she could serve the community. He did not want to presuppose that Axia would be content with the kitchen and laundry duties—his parents interchanged these responsibilities in his own house, and he knew that it was insensitive to consider kitchen work womanly—and he ran down the gamut of our chores so Axia could pick and choose. It became evident, though, that Axia was not interested in helping with the construction ("I don't mind doing errands, but I'm not good with tools") or with the classwork ("I wasn't a good student").

"I'm fine in the kitchen," she said.

Figs knew that Axia's contributions would be vital to the unprecedented credit they would receive at Open House. He delighted in the idea of Principal Breen and Father Matthews learning about Axia, and how Axia had pitched in under his leadership. Figs was composing a speech about assimilation in his head, in case the administration tried to level a case against Axia.

Having missed breakfast, Figs was the first to arrive for lunch. The rest of us drifted in whether we were hungry or not, desperate to escape our caged existence. The air in the community center was not as cold as that in our residences, and the heat killed our appetite. We sat in front of plates of uneaten sandwiches, opting for liquid lunches, lining up at the soda machine to refill our glasses, which we stocked with ice.

Hands sat at one of the tables positioned under an air-conditioning vent, most of the roster from the night before filling the remaining seats. He appeared relaxed, despite the heat. Kerr and Laird were nearby, taking turns holding their hands against

213

the window, one counting until the other drew his hand back, shaking it as if it were on fire.

The whispers that Figs was trying to sabotage our fellowship had reached him via Reedy, who had been recruited by Roger. Reedy promised to follow Roger's instruction to spread the word that Axia was Figs's girlfriend, but he was so curious about the information that he had to confirm it with Figs.

Figs approached Hands's table.

"Can I talk to you for a minute?" he asked.

"Sure," Hands said.

Figs searched the faces at the table. "Privately?"

Hands did not move to get up. "You can say it to me here," he said.

"You sure?" Figs asked. He hid his trembling hands in his pockets.

"I don't see why not."

Figs rocked forward as Sprocket wheeled by behind him. "What is this about Axia being my girlfriend?"

Roger, who would one day be court-martialed for taking a platoon of men in Iraq AWOL and killing one of them after the soldier had been wounded by enemy fire, begging him for a mercy killing, couldn't control his snickering.

"Is she?" Hands asked. "I didn't know. Congratulations."

As Figs began to refute the claim, Axia appeared, rubbing the sleep from her eyes.

"Uh-oh," Roger said. "The missus."

A sharp laugh went around the table. Figs would later wish that he had called Axia over to dispute the gossip, though what he wouldn't admit to anyone was that he secretly liked the idea and couldn't bear to hear the contrary, especially in front of witnesses.

"It's a lie," Figs said quietly, hoping Axia would not hear.

214

"The only lie I'm aware of is yours about the grocery truck driver finding Warren," Hands said coolly.

Warren looked up from his ham sandwich at the mention of his name. He grabbed his lunch and corralled Axia, who was looking for a seat under the air-conditioning. "Help me in the kitchen," Warren said, leading Axia out of the room.

"Better watch out," Hands said. "Warren's after your girl."

Some of us laughed as Figs turned away. Cantu darted out of the kitchen carrying a jar of pickles, and Figs called out to him.

"Yeah?" Cantu set the pickles down cautiously.

"Come over here," Figs said.

As Cantu waded through the room, Figs addressed the crowd. "Many of you no doubt heard the story I made up about Warren's rescue," he said. "I want to apologize to everyone for making that up. Most of you know me well enough to appreciate that I try to do the right thing. Which is what made me come up with that story. I wanted to . . ." Figs struggled for the words to explain what he'd hoped to accomplish with the lie without exposing the sophomores to ridicule by divulging their fear or their thoughts of desertion. "I wanted to ease everyone's minds." Figs looked down at Hands. "The same reason I went along with the story about seeing Mr. Malagon that first morning," he continued. "I knew it was wrong to lie, but I was persuaded that it would put everyone at ease. So I went along with it."

Hands scoffed.

Figs motioned at Cantu, who had been leaning against the wall. "I think Cantu might have something to say about that."

Hands tensed up, realizing that Cantu would corroborate what Figs had said. He regretted not covering this with Cantu, maybe getting Roger to lean on Cantu if he refused. Hands was about to confess that he'd had a hand in the lie about Mr. Malagon

215

when our attention was diverted out the window. We stood as a coyote rambled onto Garden Lakes Parkway, its furry head hung low, tongue wagging. Kerr and Laird stepped back from the window, and the coyote registered their movement, raising its head. Its ear twitched uncontrollably, and the coyote took a few steps toward the community center and then collapsed, its fur ruffling like grass as an arid desert breath swept over it.

Bagging the coyote and hauling it out to the front gates for trash collection was the day's only event, a task Roger handled eagerly. Lunch had left a pall in the air and we languished in our rooms, speculating about if we would finish the work on 1959 Regis Street or not, or if we would receive credit for the fellowship once Randolph realized that Mr. Hancock and Mr. Malagon had left us stranded. The circumstances were so extraordinary we had no way of knowing.

Figs debated disclosing to Axia the rumor circulating about them. It wouldn't be long before she heard it—if she hadn't already—but Figs couldn't decide if it was better for her to hear it as he had, by accident, or if Figs should be the one to give it voice. He worried that she would believe he was the origin of the rumor, but he also did not want to report the lie only to witness her derision at its ridiculousness. The dilemma tired him, and it was when he mounted the stairs to his bedroom that he noticed Hands's empty room, the bed stripped bare, the dresser drawers hanging open like tongues stuck out in scorn.

Figs was awakened later by a knock on his bedroom door by Cantu and Reedy, their backs soaked with sweat. He wondered how long he'd been out. "The air conditioner quit again," they said. With one foot still in slumber, Figs stood on the mattress in Hands's room and shut the air vent, the slats giving a high-pitched whistle. Figs closed the door and followed Cantu and Reedy to their residence.

All the houses along Loyola Street were shut tight except for Reedy and Cantu's. "We had to open the windows to get a breeze going," Cantu said.

The sun had begun its descent, though the temperature held. Figs stood over the air conditioner without seeing it, wondering what time it was and which part of the schedule was being violated. He hadn't really fixed the air conditioner the time before, he knew, the unit whirring to life when Figs had banged it with a hammer. He beat his fist against the metal siding again, but this time the air conditioner did not cooperate.

"It's dead," he told Reedy, following Reedy inside, where Cantu, Kerr, and Laird lounged shirtless on the couch. "You guys will have to move into Mr. Hancock's place."

The idea bristled the sophs. "No way, man," Reedy said. "If he comes back and finds us living there, he'll freak out."

Figs hadn't considered the idea that Mr. Hancock would return. He wondered when he'd ruled it out as a possibility. That Mr. Hancock would reappear after being gone for weeks was incomprehensible, but not impossible. What *if* others believed Mr. Hancock would return? Would it be enough to keep focus for one more week, until Open House? Figs filed the idea away.

The sophomores continued to refuse to move into Mr. Hancock's residence, so Figs told them to bunk in his and Hands's old rooms. "I'll take Mr. Hancock's place," Figs said.

"What will we do about beds?" Cantu asked.

"Can they be moved?" Figs asked.

A short investigation revealed the beds to be too awkward to move down the hall, around the corner, and down the stairs. "What about just bringing your mattresses?" Figs asked.

"Sleep on the *floor?*" Reedy asked.

"Wouldn't it be easier if we moved into Quinn's old place?" Kerr asked.

"Well," Figs said. It wasn't clear if the sophs were suggesting that they should move in *with* Axia, or if Axia should be displaced so they could take possession. He suppressed the surge of jealousy he felt at the idea of the sophomores bunking with Axia. "I'll be right back," he said.

Figs found Axia lounging on the couch in the front room of her residence, flipping through one of his old handouts, the lesson about FDR, intermittently using the handout as a fan to whisk away the warm air. "I came by earlier, but you were sleeping," she said. "Hardly anyone came to dinner."

"Was Hands there?" Figs asked, wishing he hadn't.

Axia shook her head.

"How many were there?"

Axia let the handout slip to the floor. She sat up and yawned. "Ten or twenty that I saw," she said. "I sat with Phillip."

"Phillip?"

"The kid in the wheelchair."

Figs convinced himself that Sprocket would not be a host for the gossip infecting Garden Lakes and turned his attention to the matter at hand.

"Listen," Figs said. "I was thinking. There's an empty house down the street that you might be more comfortable in. It used to be a model home and it's a lot . . . nicer."

"This is good enough," Axia said. "That stuff doesn't matter to me. I'm used to living in a tent, remember?"

"I just thought you'd like it better down the street," Figs said, scrambling. "There's a tub."

"You don't say," Axia said, reclining.

218

"Yeah," Figs said, sensing he had her on the hook. "The furniture is nicer too. And the bed is a king, I think."

"Nice furniture. King-size bed. A tub," Axia said, ticking off the amenities on her fingers. "Sounds like a hotel suite."

"There's other nice things too," Figs said, though he couldn't remember what.

"I don't know," Axia said coyly. "I'm settled in here."

The last of the sunlight faded and Figs shut the blinds on the living-room window, catching a glimpse of Lindy, who was headed out to the lake bed, his telescope tucked under his arm. He held his hand up to the air-conditioning vent. "It doesn't feel very cold," he said.

"I just turned it on," Axia answered.

"You should leave it running," Figs said. He went to the thermostat and turned the dial down to seventy. "It'll take a couple of hours before it's cool in here."

Axia shrugged.

"You know," Figs said, struck by inspiration, "the air-conditioning has been kept low in the house down the street. You'll sleep better over there."

"Okay, okay," Axia said, exasperated. "I give. Let me get my stuff."

Figs clapped his hands together. "Great. I know you'll like it more. It's the house on the other side of the community center, the first one on Loyola Street. I'll meet you over there in a few."

Figs skipped out of Axia's house, pepped at being able to solve yet another problem. As he broached the walkway leading to the sophs' house, ready for the accolades due him for arranging their release from the torrid prison, he heard Reedy yelp. Figs sprinted the final distance, throwing open the front door. Had he been in the company of others, the scene would've been one of hilarity: Cantu poised above Reedy's partially shaved head with an electric razor, a bald Laird jumping around in the background while Kerr looked on. Reedy touched the nick above his ear. "It's nothing," Cantu assured him, continuing. The living room was covered in their hair.

"What's this?" Figs asked, remaining calm. Calmness was the means to managing any situation, he knew.

"It's too hot for hair," Reedy said, keeping his head down.

"Want us to do yours?" Laird asked.

"Whose razor is that?" Figs knew none of the sophomores were old enough to shave.

"Found it at Mr. Hancock's," Laird said.

Figs wondered about this looting, afraid to ask.

"Axia is moving out of Quinn's," Figs said. "You can move in whenever you want."

"She moving in with you?" Cantu asked. He razed the last stripe of hair from Reedy's scalp.

Figs shook his head. "Make sure you sweep up when you're done. And return the razor. Mr. Hancock's stuff should stay in his house." He shut the door on Laird's question—"Why?"— and turned to find Axia on the sidewalk in front of Mr. Hancock's residence.

"This one?" she asked, pointing.

Figs helped Axia settle in. Mr. Hancock had left his residence impeccably clean; only the mess of ungraded quizzes on the kitchen table (some blown to the floor by the free-roaming air-conditioning) and a pair of bedroom slippers in the upstairs bathroom suggested Mr. Hancock's absence was accidental. Figs again contemplated whether or not Mr. Hancock would materialize, and while he ultimately believed otherwise, he vowed to work on the explanation as to why Axia was living in his house,

220

just in case. Over the years, he'd built a storehouse of unused explanations he'd prepared rather than be caught off guard by anyone over anything.

Yelling brought Figs and Axia to the window. Cantu's and Laird's and Reedy's and Kerr's shaved domes bobbed down the street as they carried their duffel bags stuffed with clothing and bedding. Each had his towel slung over his shoulder, so that they appeared like a party headed for the beach.

"What's happening?" Axia asked.

"Not sure," Figs said, hoping that would be the end of it.

"Where are they going?" she asked, peering through the blinds. She watched the sophs as Figs paced behind her. "You know," she said, whirling around, "if you wanted me out so they could move in, you should've just asked."

"Their air conditioner broke," Figs said by way of justification.

"Why didn't they want to move in here? Is it *haunted*?" She laughed at her joke, though the smile was only temporary.

"They're afraid of Mr. Hancock," Figs said. "They think he might still come back."

"Could that happen?" she asked.

"No," he said. "I doubt it."

"I still don't understand why you didn't just ask me to move," Axia said.

"I . . . ," Figs started. He didn't know the answer himself.

"All that about the furniture and the air-conditioning," she said. "I thought something was funny."

"Listen, I'm sorry," Figs said.

"No you're not," Axia said, a menace creeping over her face.

"What?"

"You're not sorry. You're just saying you are."

221

Axia crossed her arms.

"No, really," Figs said. "I'm sorry."

"Say it again."

"I'm sorry."

"Again."

"I'm sorry."

"Again."

Figs lowered his head. "I'm sorry," he said softly.

Axia smiled. "See? You meant it that time."

Hands and Roger followed on the heels of the sophomores as they entered Quinn's old residence without knocking.

"Fuck's going on here?" Roger asked.

"Figs told us we could," Cantu said.

"There are no sophomores allowed on Regis Street," Roger said.

"But Figs said—"

Roger cut Cantu off. "It doesn't matter *what* he said."

"Where is Axia?" Hands asked, bemused.

"She moved into Mr. Hancock's," Reedy said.

"What happened to your heads?" Roger asked.

"Never mind," Hands said. He turned to Roger. "C'mon, we'll clear this up."

Hands and Roger exited in a haste, leaving the sophomores in confusion. Hands halted. "Let's let this go until morning," he said.

"I think we should fix this now," Roger said.

Hands nodded. "I agree with what you're saying," he said, "but it might be to our advantage to let this ride until morning. You'll see."

"I get you," Roger said.

Hands knew that Roger did not "get" him, that Roger didn't have the mental fortitude to know that the sophs on Regis Street could be traded for Axia's expulsion, the larger picture. But he let Roger believe that the morning would bring outrage and that the sophs would be booted back down to Loyola Street. Hands would ride that sentiment too, though it was not his primary objective.

The morning did not bring outrage, though. Only relief. Overnight, the heat had escaped, rolling on to terrorize another populace, and though the temperatures were still in the low seventies when we woke, we rejoiced. The morning brought purpose, too. Figs and Warren led a troupe including Sprocket, Lindy, and Axia to the construction site after breakfast, Sprocket outfitting each with the tools necessary for applying texturing compound. A hodgepodge of sophomores joined Figs's crew, taking up paint rollers.

Kerr, Cantu, Reedy, and Laird abstained from the sophomore work detail, volunteering for kitchen detail, hoping to avoid the cleave among the fellows, an unspoken split audible to those sensitive enough to perceive it. The four might've joined Figs's crew, but Roger and Hands had not decamped with the others, Hands holding court in the dining hall.

The conversation at the table swung from talk of the construction site to discussion of the daily schedule. Hands appeared in a jovial mood, so much so that he kidded Roger about needing a haircut. "Maybe Reedy will cut it for you," he joked. The strained frivolity influenced Roger's reaction, a smile instead of the expected threat of pummeling Roger normally extended at such a personal remark.

The mood soured appreciably when Hands railed against Figs's moving Kerr, Cantu, Reedy, and Laird onto Regis Street. "Who gave you that right?" Hands's voice carried into the kitchen, but the four sophs pretended to be oblivious. "What's next?" he asked in mock exasperation. "We got sophomores living with the fellows, outsiders living in the faculty housing. Principal Breen is going to shit himself when he finds out." Hands persisted in his argument, testing our reaction to the accusations leveled at Figs. "A total disregard for the rest of us," he kept saying.

Our reaction was sufficient enough for Hands to spread the indictment against Figs globally, Roger and Hands and Assburn servicing the allegation about the sophomores living in Quinn's old residence and Axia camping out at Mr. Hancock's. The slur did not take hold, though, as Figs had leveled the information in a preemptive strike during construction, explaining that the whole maneuver was initiated by the sophomores' air conditioner going kaput. The explanation satisfied Figs's crew, so that when Hands approached Figs at the midmorning break, Figs shrugged. "Doubt you could make it without air-conditioning," he told Hands.

"That was just a lie," Hands said. "The air conditioner works fine."

Figs and Axia had been tardy to the break, Axia fussing with clots of joint compound that had tangled her hair. Not even Reedy's testimony that the air conditioner was indeed broken assuaged the conspiracy talk. "See for yourself," Reedy said, not looking Roger in the eye when he said it.

"Why don't we," Hands said. He led all interested parties to Reedy's house for an inspection. The investigation would prove inconclusive, though, as the air conditioner lay splintered into pieces, the twisted fan grate sprouting near the unit like a new species of cactus, the inner coil stretched out lengthwise on the ground, the compressor missing.

Figs's crew took up the construction again after the break, Figs boldly inviting Hands and the rest of us to join him. "We could use the help," Figs said disingenuously.

Hands waved Figs off and Figs shrugged, filing out with the rest of his posse in tow. The visit to Reedy's had agitated Hands (who did not know that Roger had destroyed the unit, hoping to pin the blame on Figs), and Hands suggested we take to the lake bed to scrimmage. "We're still having the Open House match, right?" Hands asked.

"You bet your ass," Roger said, standing up from the table.

Practice consisted of little more than kicking the ball back and forth, Hands showing off a couple of new moves he intended to debut at Open House. "Check this out," he said, instructing Roger to pass him the ball. Roger kicked the ball along the ground, and Hands pointed his toe at it, the ball rolling up Hands's shin to his knee; he used his knee to bounce the ball to eye level, then whacked it with his forehead. The ball sailed back toward Roger, who caught it with his hands.

"Holy shit," Assburn said. "That was cool."

Hands sent Roger to fetch Kerr, Cantu, Reedy, and Laird, and they joined in.

In the distance, we could hear the cheers from the compound fight that had erupted when Axia playfully slapped a gooey handprint on Lindy's back. The fight spilled into the front yard, Figs trailing, calling for order, which was reestablished when the bucket of compound being used for artillery ran dry, most of the grenades landing wide of their marks.

Figs and Warren were engrossed in a conversation about how to convert Hands and the others back to the schedule when they were stopped by Roger, who barred the entrance to the classroom. Behind Roger, the rest of the fellows and sophomores had taken their seats. Sprocket dug into the box of handouts Hands had exhumed from Mr. Malagon's closet, doling out stacks to the first person in each row.

"Problem?" Figs asked.

"Class time," Roger said.

"That's why we're here," Figs said. He stepped in Roger's direction, but Roger didn't budge.

"Class is only for those who swear their allegiance to continuation," Roger said. He spread his arms across the doorway.

"That's mental," Warren said.

Figs called out to Hands, but Hands ignored the call. We fidgeted as Roger gave Figs and Warren the same spiel he'd given the rest of us before permitting us to pass: Attending class meant voting for continuation, and a vote for continuation was a vote to expel Axia. "None of us want your little girlfriend around here," Roger said.

Figs protested weakly that Axia was not his girlfriend, but Roger was unmoved.

"You in or out?" Roger asked.

"This is ridiculous," Figs said. "We agreed she would leave the day before Open House."

"We who?" Roger asked, dropping his arms.

"We," Figs said. "Me and Hands. Hands, tell him."

Roger's arms shot up again. Hands turned and stared at Figs.

"Wrong, wrong, wrong," Roger said. "The only thing we agree on is that your girlfriend must go. We're all about finishing this fellowship and getting credit." He hesitated before shutting the door on Figs and Warren, allowing them one last chance to change their plea; but Figs and Warren would not accede, their eyes searching the class for a friendly face before the door slammed shut.

***

226

At the start of sports, Hands was picking through the sophomores as Figs and Warren walked onto the playing field.

"What's going on?" Figs asked. The question was meant for
Hands, but Roger answered as he selected Cantu and Laird.

"We're choosing new teams for the Open House match,"
Roger said, ignoring Figs. "It'll be me, Hands, Assburn, and this
group of sophomores. The rest are with you."

"Hey, wait a minute," Figs said. He took a step in Hands's
direction, but Roger blocked his path. "I need to talk to Hands,"
he said. Roger refused to move and Figs shoved him in the chest.
Roger cocked his fist, but Hands grabbed him from behind.

"What do you want?" Hands asked. "Isn't it enough that you're
trying to ruin our fellowship? What else?" Hands's eyes flared.

"No one is ruining anything," Figs said.

A circle formed around Figs and Hands, the unmistakable
sign that violence was imminent.

"Everyone here has voted for continuation," Hands said. "You
made your choice."

"What the hell are you talking about?" Figs asked. He took
another step toward Hands, and Roger reflexively stepped
toward Figs.

"You know what the hell I'm talking about," Hands said.
"Either you're with us or you're against us."

A strong smell of orange blossoms blew across the field.

"Quit wasting our time," Roger said.

"You can do what you want," Hands said, "but she's not part
of Garden Lakes, so keep her out of the way. We don't want her
in the dining hall or in chapel or in class, distracting us from
what we've set out to do. And that goes for this"—he gestured at
the field—"and the construction site. Those of us who are serious
need to focus."

The sound of a horn directed our attention away from Figs and Hands. A burgundy-colored LTD floated along Garden Lakes Parkway, its driver waving madly. The LTD glided to a stop near us.

"Excuse me," the driver said. "Can you tell me how to get back to the freeway? I'm turned around." A heavyset woman sat staring at us from the passenger seat.

"Go through the gate and turn right," Warren said. "You have to go about fifteen miles. Then you come to a fork. Left for Phoenix and right for Tucson. You'll see the freeway soon after that."

"Thanks." The driver pulled on the bill of his cap. "What're you fellas up to, anyway?" he asked. "You live out here?"

We waited for someone to answer. Roger telegraphed our punishment if we spoke up about our situation.

"Just a little game of soccer," Figs said, holding his hands out to receive the ball. After a delay, Hands passed it to him.

"Where's the field?" the driver asked.

Figs pointed a thumb at the lake bed.

"How you play on that?" The heavyset woman shifted to get a better look.

"We make do," Figs said. He leaned in the driver's window. "This is a sharp car," he said. "Is it new?"

"Hell, no," the driver said. "I wish. They quit making these things."

"Man, coulda fooled me," Figs said, masterfully slipping into slang. "This is a beaut."

"Thanks," the driver said. "Thanks for saying so."

"You're welcome," Figs said, pushing off the car. "We better get back to our game. Big stakes!" Figs laughed, and the driver laughed too. The heavyset woman smiled and the car drifted away.

"Good luck!" the driver shouted to us. He swiped the hat off his head and waved it in the air as he screeched the tires around the parkway. The LTD slid through the front gates like a speedboat gliding ashore. We watched the right-turn signal blink twice and then the car disappeared.

Figs drop-kicked the ball over our heads, staring down Hands and Roger. He turned and walked away, Warren following dutifully. The ball rolled up onto the island and came to rest under the withering palm tree. Hands yelled for Cantu to get the ball, instructing the others to pick a captain in Figs's absence.

We battled well into the dinner hour, Hands driving aggressively toward the goal every time he touched the ball, second only to Roger, who sent 50 percent of his kicks sailing high and wide. Sprocket would call, "Out," and one of the sophomores would track the ball down and throw it back into play.

Our play on the lake bed suspended time, allowing us to suppress our individual feelings about what had transpired between Figs and Hands. More than a few of us disagreed with Hands's hard-line stance; while we agreed that continuation was necessary to validate our commitment to Garden Lakes, we also felt there was room for Axia and thought that any repercussions brought by the administration—*if they even found out about Axia*—could be successfully argued against.

None of us would give voice to these thoughts, though, preferring to mutter them in parties of two and three on the sidelines during play, and later at dinner, employing the Randolph Backcheck before whispering any dissent. Sprocket, however, would act on his conscience, passing Figs and Warren copies of Mr. Malagon's handouts along with the corresponding exams. "I'll file them away with the others," he said. "No one sees them after I grade them anyway."

Figs and Warren would involve themselves in an act of subter-fuge too, sneaking meals from the dining hall with the help of a core of sympathetic sophomores.

"If I have to live like a prisoner, I might as well leave," Axia said, pushing away her plate of goulash and asparagus.

The truth in Axia's statement spooked Figs, who sat on the edge of her bed. "You can't do that," he said. "Then they'll win."

Axia shrugged. "What do I care if they win or not?"

Figs hadn't considered this. Axia had no stake in the outcome. She could blow through Garden Lakes as easily as she'd blown in. "Where will you go from here?" he asked.

The look on Axia's face told Figs he'd called her bluff; she didn't really want to leave, and Figs let himself believe that he was part of the reason why, though he knew it could've been anything. He didn't have a clue what it meant to live by your wits and imagined that chancing upon a situation like the one at Gar-den Lakes was rare.

Axia set the untouched dinner on the nightstand. "Not sure," she said.

An idea popped into Figs's head. "My neighbor has a guest house he might let you live in," he said.

Axia smiled. "You a real estate broker too?"

"No," Figs said, blushing. "But he's old and needs someone to take care of him." The layout of the guest house flashed through Figs's mind, he and Hands having spent a week living in it when they house-sat while the neighbor was away. "It's just an idea."

"It's a nice idea," Axia said, yawning. She kicked off the bed. "I'm going for a walk," she announced, intimating that she was going alone.

"Be careful," Figs wanted to say as Axia tied her shoes, but he didn't want to frighten her. While he worried about how far

Hands and the others would go to intimidate Axia, he knew she could handle them in ones and twos. He also knew that any misbehavior would result in the nullification of the fellowship. Figs would make sure of that.

Figs loitered in Axia's room, too wired for sleep. He'd kill some time with Lindy, who had taken the community center roof as his permanent observatory, animating the night sky with stories, Warren occasionally supplementing the tales with information we'd learned in textbooks but had long forgotten.

Figs's enthusiasm for the idea was brief, however, as he spotted not Lindy but Roger on the roof. He watched as Roger raised a pair of binoculars, sweeping the development in slow arcs. Roger aimed the binoculars in the area where Figs stood, and Figs backed farther into the shadows.

From then on, we manned the daily schedule with clockwork precision, moving in two distinct teams as effortlessly as if the work had been assigned as such. Indeed, we ran on two separate but simultaneous schedules—Hands and his team took to the playing field after breakfast to run drills, while Figs and his crew took the early shift at 1959 Regis Street, then the whole routine swapped after the midmorning break. Meals were staggered, so each team ate in a half-empty dining hall, everyone scavenging the kitchen for themselves, pairs of cooks pooling their expertise to concoct dishes other than peanut butter and jelly sandwiches, or plates of spaghetti dowsed with parmesan sprinkles dumped from the economy-size green canisters in the pantry. Figs and Warren continued to refuse classroom instruction—and Sprocket continued to smuggle them the packets and tests—but the rest of us assembled for the vital component of the fellowship, the classroom remaining silent except for whoever was taking a turn reading aloud from the handout. Axia continued to drift behind the scenes, spending the bulk of the day inside her air-conditioned room ("catching up on my rest," she called it) and passing the evenings with Figs and Warren and Lindy, the three engaging in various entertainments—most involving cards or dice or the telescope. And while it was true that a disharmonious note rang in the air, it played in the background, and from the vantage of our last weekend at Garden Lakes, it looked like we would make it.

In retrospect, the events of that Saturday night were the seeds from which we would reap out-and-out failure.

By all accounts, the evening started to ebb until Kerr produced the bottle of cabernet he'd secreted from the case Mr. Hancock had brought. Many times he'd thought to offer it, but he was glad he'd waited, sensing the moment was finally right. Kerr and Cantu were passing the bottle when they were paid an after-hours visit by Hands and Roger and Assburn, who were looking for Reedy. The search was called off, though, when the fellows discovered the contraband. Roger requisitioned the bottle from Kerr, who ceded it with a mild complaint. Hands and Roger and Assburn passed the bottle, Hands abstaining because of his allergy, an affliction that astounded Cantu.

A rattling sounded. "Party favors," Assburn said, producing the bottle of Lindy's painkillers Lindy had assumed he'd lost the day after returning from the emergency room. Years later, Assburn's fondness for pharmaceuticals would fuel his decision to smuggle counterfeit gaming systems from Canada, resulting in his icy death as he plunged through the frozen lake somewhere near Detroit, in an effort to raise enough bail money for his best friend.

The living room of Quinn's former residence grew boisterous, and the bottles of wine and pills circled. The pills spread a thick fog through Hands's brain, dulling his senses and draining the stress of the preceding days. In addition to shepherding the fellows and sophomores through their final days at Garden Lakes, Hands knew he would have to find ways to give Roger some command without giving him too much. He'd made a step in that direction by giving Roger leeway with the soccer team, even looking the other way when Roger screamed at any player that made a foul or a bad shot; but he wanted to make sure Roger understood the leeway had been bestowed upon him, and by whom.

Hands's warning about keeping Axia out of sight had been successful too. If he thought about Figs and Axia spirited off somewhere, laughing and fucking around, he became so angry his thinking muddled. Whether or not he would be friends again with Figs, he couldn't say. Hands's command of the situation at Garden Lakes—and the recognition he would receive from the faculty and others—would go a long way in equalizing what Hands perceived as a power differential in their relationship.

As he passed the bottle of wine to Roger, he realized that he hadn't imagined hearing Figs's name. He heard it again, this time ferreting out the source: Laird was trying to be heard over the din, asking something about Figs.

"What?" Hands asked, raising his voice. Laird seemed very far away.

"Do you want to know the real story about Figs?" Laird asked.

"What story?" Hands asked.

"About what happened in Mazatlán. At Rosa's," Laird answered.

Hands and Roger and Assburn exchanged looks.

"How do you know about Rosa's?" Roger asked.

Laird glanced around nervously. "Everyone knows."

"Yeah?" Roger asked. "And what does everyone know?"

Hands diffused the atmosphere with a laugh. "Who cares if everyone knows?"

A smile spread across Laird's face. "Yeah, but I know what *really* happened."

Roger coughed. "Tell it or shut up," he said.

Laird settled back, recounting what we all knew by rote about that night at Rosa's.

"What was it like?" Laird asked, making us wait. "Was it cool?"

"Don't get sidetracked," Hands said.

Laird reveled in his station as master storyteller for a moment longer, then said, "There weren't any *federales*."

Laird laid out what he knew: that Figs had taken advantage when the heavy at the door left his post, and run screaming into the house, scattering those inside and those in the backyard, Laird's older brother among them. "He goes to Trevor Browne," Laird said. None of us knew Laird at all, let alone that his older brother went to public school. "He saw everything."

We sat waiting for more details, the truth about that night stirring our hunger, but that was all Laird had to tell. The reality of Figs's elaborate lie sank in as the bottle was passed around.

"Faggot," Roger exhaled. "I knew it."

Hands stood and bolted for the door. In retelling the story for the administration, he would omit that he'd been high and would declare that he'd simply needed some fresh air. That Roger mistook Hands's action as an advance on Figs's house would not exonerate those who besieged the residence, dancing and chanting, "*Federales! Federales!*" the chant amplifying, punctuated with the sound of shattering glass. Not even the administrative inquiry could bring to light the identity of the hurler.

***

It was around this time that I began to feel my loyalties shift. I'd fallen in with Hands's bunch instinctually—Hands knew of my dislike of Figs and had invited me to that first meeting with the others. But that meeting seemed to me to be the first step toward putting affairs at Garden Lakes back on the right path. I did not sense that Hands wanted to do Figs harm. Conversely, I recognized Hands's ambition to lead the fellowship to its glorious conclusion, and given my choice, I preferred it be Hands rather than Figs who claimed the crown.

I was even willing to overlook the weaknesses in Hands's administration. Certainly, he couldn't be held liable for Roger's rough behavior; Hands's surrounding himself with lunatics like Roger was a matter of chance. And as far as I was concerned, the fault lay with Roger, whom I considered an asshole. I dreamed lasciviously violent dreams about smashing Roger upside the head during sports, or leading a gang of vigilantes against him. Roger's heartlessness inspired the kind of cruelty we imagined only the depraved felt.

I had no opinion about Axia. For the most part, Axia kept to herself. Other lusty feelings did not make their way into the official record. And while I was reluctant to say so publicly, I could understand Figs's point about assimilation. Mr. Malagon spoke often of the need for tolerance—no one in his class was permitted to talk over someone else, himself included—and the claims Figs had made about inclusion struck a chord with me. Still, I was reticent to align with such a risky enterprise. What if, upon learning about Axia, the administration voided our fellowship? Any appeal would be undermined by fraternization. There were others who felt similarly, though we were too cowardly to express it.

The undignified ruckus that Sunday night moved me a step in Figs's direction, though.

I looked out my window as Roger led the charge on Figs's residence, Kerr, Reedy, Cantu, and Laird behind him. Roger bade his lieutenants to kick in the door, but as many times as their feet bounced off the front door, the lock held. I imagined Figs cowering inside, fearful of the glazed look in the sophs' eyes. Kerr and Reedy disappeared, Laird and Cantu sticking close to Roger, who was hunting for rocks large enough to hurl at the double-paned windows donated by a local glass company. Kerr and Reedy reappeared with a hammer from Sprocket's supply shed—which Sprocket would discover ransacked the next morning. Kerr handed Roger the hammer and he busted out the front-room window. Hands looked on as the sophs entertained themselves by tossing rolls of toilet paper up and over the house, the strands billowing in the hot desert breeze.

The chanting began again, but the riot eventually succumbed to thirst, everyone opting for a raid on the dining hall. I sensed that they did not want to confront Figs anyway and was relieved when they dispersed, Roger lingering, glancing at Figs's door as if daring it to open.

My attitude changed, however, when I learned of the smashed telescope at breakfast. A group whose complete membership was never verified had set out from the dining hall to spread the word about what had happened in Mazatlán. The group came upon Lindy and his telescope in the lake bed. Lindy would wait until he was securely ensconced in the administration's bosom before he would name those he remembered from the assault. He told about how Roger had knocked the telescope to the ground and how Hands had held Lindy back while Roger stomped the instrument into uselessness. Lindy remembered yelling, hoping someone would hear and come to his aid, but his yells were quieted by Roger's fist, which landed squarely in Lindy's chest, knocking the

236

wind out of him. (It was not this assault but the one on Mr. Baker that led to Roger's expulsion from Randolph.)

While Lindy stayed silent about the attack the next morning, it wasn't hard to piece together that Roger was behind it. And because Hands and Roger moved in tandem, the assumption that they were in on it together was hard to ignore, though it would come out later that Hands hadn't so much participated as allowed it to happen, turning his back on Lindy, as he did Figs at Summer Griffith's party. Not that anyone objected on Lindy's behalf. Instead, we privately assured him that we would take his side of the matter should he choose to pursue the issue. This cowardly turn did not sit well with your faithful columnist, and for all these reasons, I convinced myself to jump ship and throw in with Figs.

I would not get a chance to exercise my decision, though, as my mind would be decidedly changed again the following morning.

To his credit, Figs was able to function as if nothing had happened, though he did skip breakfast, electing instead to finish the knockdown roller finish, the final step toward completion of the work at 1959 Regis Street. He had to outlast the chiding for only three more days. He would work to repair the damage over the summer, first with Hands and then with a few key fellows that would back him up at the start of senior year. The reclamation of his credibility lay in the fellowship, he knew, a fact Figs could not later reconcile with his actions that Monday morning.

The rest of Figs's crew reported to the construction site, and while no one had the courage to challenge Figs about his lie, whispers of "*Federales! Federales!*" rose with the wind. Whether Figs heard or not no one would ever know, but it was the only rationale for what happened next.

Roger saw it from the playing field, training Mr. Magalon's binoculars on the construction site. He had arrived with Hands for breakfast with the binoculars around his neck, and they spent the morning zooming in on us, Hands providing commentary on our food's progress as we chewed and swallowed. The binoculars were not as unnerving as Hands's and Roger's freshly shorn heads gleaming under the fluorescent lighting, hurrying us through our bowls of cereal.

Through the lenses of his binoculars, Roger saw Figs yank a panel of Sheetrock from the far wall in the living room.

Lindy and Warren reacted first, racing into the living room.

"What's happening?" Warren asked.

Figs looked at Warren like he wondered who he was. "What?"

Warren pointed at the displaced drywall. The others gathered around the vandalism. Play in the lake bed ceased, and Roger and Hands passed their binoculars around so the rest of us could see the commotion in the living room. And while we could not hear what was being said, we understood the look on Warren's face as he chastised Figs.

We raced to the construction site. Figs's explanation—that the piece had been hung improperly—did not convince many. "Why didn't Mr. Baker catch it?" Roger asked when told, quieting Figs.

"I saw it," Warren said, bailing Figs out. "I didn't mention it because I wasn't sure. But it wasn't sturdy. It had a"—Warren chopped his hand through the air—"dent in it."

Warren's corroborative testimony only temporarily mitigated the feelings of sabotage, feelings that intensified when Figs disappeared for the balance of the day, disabusing me of any notion about changing allegiance. Roger's transgressions appeared small when matched against the pettiness Figs had exhibited.

Even if I felt strongly about my complaints about Hands and Roger, Figs's ship appeared to be sunk that afternoon.

My renewal of faith in the other side would not last long, however. In hindsight, it is not hard to understand the actions taken by some that afternoon. But I was as baffled as the other fellows by the second wave of vandalism in the living room of 1959. Hands's convenient evacuation from the vicinity as Roger pulled down a second panel of Sheetrock implicated him. Hands knew that he would need plausible deniability, and there were rumors at lunch that Figs had wrecked the entire living-room wall. Only those who had observed Roger and his minions—Laird, Reedy, Cantu, and Kerr, their bald heads bobbing in unison as they kicked in a wall—knew the truth, though no such witnesses could be found.

The anatomical view of insulation and wiring sprouting from the living-room wall brought the application of the finish to a halt.

"End of the line," Warren said. "We need to call Mr. Baker and get some more drywall."

"No can do," Hands said, shaking his head.

"Give me Hancock's mobile phone and I'll do it, then," Warren persisted.

"I can't," Hands said, hoping to leave it at that. But Warren pressed him, following Hands out of the dining hall at lunch. "It's broken, okay? It doesn't work."

"I don't believe you," Warren said.

Hands turned on Warren. "I don't care if you do," he said. "Why don't you ask your buddy?" Hands said. "He knows all about it."

Warren did not ask Figs about the phone, though. That Figs was complicit in a conspiracy over Mr. Hancock's mobile phone would've proved too much for even Warren to bear, and he persuaded himself that he did not want to know, preferring the impression that Hands was hoarding the device for his own use.

An afternoon spike in temperature drove us indoors, our energy sapped by the heat. It was reasonable to say that we, including yours truly, were overcome by recent events, too. An awful taste developed in my mouth, my mind muddling whenever I tried to get straight what was what. It was impossible to know where virtue lay, and I was adrift, overwhelmed by hopelessness, surrendering to the certainty that it didn't much matter what I chose to believe or whom I chose to follow: The fellowship had been consigned to failure, maybe as early as Mr. Hancock's departure—maybe from the beginning—and that inevitably ushered in a flood of indifference that washed over us all.

Under the cover of night, I saw Laird and Reedy and Cantu and Kerr in the community center doorway. They disappeared inside one by one and then reappeared in formation, each carrying sacks of purloined food, their skin glowing under the streetlights.

Warren wanted to know what the joke was. "I don't get it," he said when Figs told him. "Where'd she go?"

Figs was too angry to repeat what he'd told Warren, that Hands had expelled Axia in the middle of night—he'd been hearing murmurs that Hands was putting Roger up to something and guessed that it was Axia's removal, confirmed when Figs knocked on her door for breakfast to find her gone. The idea that Axia had up and left on her own was inconceivable. That she had no ties to Garden Lakes, or to anything, really, was a concept that Figs couldn't grasp. A concept he *could* grasp was malice. He swore to meet Hands's malice with malice, whatever the cost. Warren bolted for Axia's, blind with rage, wanting to see for himself.

A blast of humidity greeted Figs as he followed in Warren's wake. He gasped when he saw Mr. Baker's truck parked nose-first in front of the construction site. He shaded his eyes and watched as Hands and Roger and Mr. Baker stood in front of the exposed living-room wall. Hands shrugged several times while Roger pantomimed how the panels of drywall had been pulled down. Figs hoped Hands was negotiating with Mr. Baker for more drywall—there was still time to mend the wall and slap up the finish, though barely—but he refused to join the negotiations. Hands would see how he'd taken him for granted all these years.

Figs scanned the development. Most everyone was at breakfast, he knew. He looked at the sky, the coming cloud cover visible beyond the rooftops on Regis Street, and headed for the dining hall for something to cure his hunger. He passed Warren asking anyone he encountered if they'd seen Axia. No one had.

Eventually Warren changed tack and went after Hands, whom he spotted ducking inside Roger and Assburn's house. Warren kicked in the front door, calling out Hands's name in anger. Roger and Assburn and Hands jumped in surprise, Roger pushing Mr. Baker—whose hands had been amateurishly tied with rope, his mouth sealed with duct tape—quickly up the stairs, Assburn following. Warren exited just as quickly, convincing himself he hadn't seen what he'd seen so when asked, he would say he knew nothing about it.

Roger threw Mr. Baker facedown on a bed in an empty room, instructing Assburn to close the blinds. Mr. Baker's initial protest had been reduced to grunts and moans. Assburn watched while Roger wound the tape around Mr. Baker's ankles.

Roger had enlisted his help during breakfast. He warned Assburn not to tell Hands, who promised he wouldn't. Everyone in the dining hall looked out the window in disbelief as Mr. Baker's truck cruised down Regis Street. A beat passed before Hands stood, knowing he had to do something, not wanting Figs to reach Mr. Baker first. Roger followed, pointing at Assburn on his way out the door.

The selection emboldened Assburn, lifting his wilted spirits. He had all but resigned himself to being a pariah at Randolph. His attempts to remake his reputation had failed, and he knew that once senior year started, there would be little room for maneuvering. But then Roger anointed him. He followed Roger to 1959 Regis Street, escorted into the upper echelons, or so he imagined. Even Quinn would have to accept him now, he supposed, which was a relief, since Assburn had destroyed Senator Quinn's pen out near the Grove, demolishing the emblem of his shame with a large, flat rock.

Assburn was so enamored of his elevation that he could not impartially judge whether holding Mr. Baker down while Roger tied Mr. Baker's hands behind his back was a building block to respectability or not. The point was he'd been called into action and he'd served. Not even Mr. Baker's screams and calls for help could diminish the merit Assburn was earning.

Hands knocked on the bedroom door and entered, surveying the landscape as Mr. Baker wriggled on the bed. "What's the plan?" he asked.

"You tell me," Roger said.

A moment passed and no one said anything, the three standing around the bed, staring at its occupant. "I have to think," Hands said.

The clouds rolled in as Warren straggled out past the Grove. He expected to find Axia hiding out, on the run from Hands and Roger and the others, remembering what she'd said the night before about "wandering some more." He'd been delighted when Axia reappeared downstairs, wanting to go for a walk, the poker game having dissolved into boastful card tricks. The night was muggy and rife with desert insects, but Warren refrained from complaining, influenced by Axia's cool. They talked about nothing in particular, mostly about how stressed out everyone seemed. They looped around Garden Lakes Parkway, cutting east to tramp through the undeveloped land. Warren asked if Axia was interested in moving to Phoenix, offering up the spare room at his house (he was convinced his parents would not mind). She laughed and told him it was the second such offer she'd received. Warren's ears burned when she told him of the guest house next door to Figs.

"It's sweet," she said, "but I don't think I'll be moving to Phoenix."

"Why not?"

Axia answered with a shrug and a smile, and Warren knew right then that she would not come to Phoenix; or if she did, she would not stay for long. He appreciated her not saying "It's just better . . ." or "I could never . . ." His admiration for her tripled. She'd decided to live life a certain way, and with fidelity to that way of life. He was jealous of the clarity he imagined such a decision brought. You would do this, but not that. He imagined there were ups and downs—as with anything—but that there wasn't as much uncertainty because you weren't always entertaining all the possibilities, struggling to come out on top. He thought about how unambitious he was before enrolling at Randolph Prep, and he shuddered at how he'd been infected.

Warren's anxiety dwindled as they walked well into the early-morning hours. Cool air rushed through the quiet development as they retired to their houses, and as Warren said good night, he pledged a transformation similar to Axia's. He would ask for her help and guidance, and wherever Axia ended up in the world, they would share this bond.

Now, as he searched for Axia, lightning crackled overhead, thunder booming around Warren as he continued south, fighting the moist air that tried to blow him backward. He didn't know for sure that he was traveling in a straight line, but he intuited that he was moving in the right direction. He'd seek out the family of olive farmers if need be. Maybe she had returned to them. If not, maybe they knew something about where she might've gone. Warren took refuge behind an outcropping. Sheets of hot rain blew across the desert, the ground wet with puddles, deepening until they ran together. He closed his eyes, letting the rain soak through his clothes, imagining a misty curtain parting to reveal Axia.

He opened his eyes, disappointed.

Hands crouched on the end of the bed in the room adjoining the one where Mr. Baker was imprisoned, listening to the monsoon as it rapped against the side of the house. The sky outside his window was dark gray, matching his mood. Roger's jumping Mr. Baker still seemed unreal. He took no comfort in telling himself that he probably couldn't have stopped it. But he hadn't tried, and he knew it would be his undoing. He replayed the morning in his mind, dreaming of a different outcome.

"What happened here?" Mr. Baker had asked.

Hands could hear his voice, whiny and small, telling Mr. Baker it was an accident.

"Doesn't look like an accident," Mr. Baker had maintained. He'd inspected the precision with which the panels had been ripped out.

"We were hoping to get a little more drywall."

Mr. Baker didn't hear the request, though, instead demanding to know where Mr. Malagon was. Hands wished for Figs's presence right then, which doubled his regret. On the field or on the court, Hands relied on his instincts, which never failed him. If a defender twice his size bore down on him, or if he sensed he could intercept an errant pass, his mind and body moved at will. But to his chagrin, the gift was only physical. Mr. Baker's questions begged for some mental and verbal dexterity he didn't possess. He worshipped this quality in Figs, but confessing this to Figs would not imbue Hands with the gift, so what was the point? Figs had enough people wrapped around his finger; Hands refused to become another. The day before, when Figs was on the ropes, Hands had stayed in the shadows during the chanting, hiding behind Roger and Assburn and the others, but the release had been as euphoric as if he'd been leading the barrage. Finally, finally, Figs's reputation had proved permeable. He didn't really care about Figs's lie, but he knew the ramifications of such a lie, and no matter what happened thereafter, Figs's days at Randolph would be humbler.

"Seriously. Where is Mr. Malagon?" Mr. Baker had asked.

Roger had come out of nowhere, lunging. He and Mr. Baker fell to the ground, Roger overpowering his prey with stupefying quickness. Then Assburn appeared and the two strong-armed a dazed Mr. Baker into their house. Hands would have to convince the others that the abduction was Roger's idea. He could count on Assburn to back up the assertion. Roger had lassoed Assburn as a henchman on his own; it would not be hard for Hands to sell his innocence to Assburn. He would offer Assburn the inclusion that everyone was determined to withhold from him. Assburn had walled himself off by wearing his desires so openly, Hands

245

thought, so that the others made a game of denying Assburn acceptance. Regardless, Hands would make the first offer; he would promise Figs's friendship too, though Hands knew that some rehabilitation of his own friendship with Figs would be required. The idea repulsed him—he'd never truly be friends with Figs again, and he questioned their friendship going all the way back to Julie Roseman. He'd granted Figs absolution, but had he meant it? His boarding the bus to Disneyland so long ago, before he learned about Figs's betrayal, resonated as the last sunny moment of their friendship. And now rather than make a principled stand against Figs, Hands knew he'd have to fall back in line, too weak to withstand what he knew would be Figs's manipulation of everything that happened at Garden Lakes.

The storm raged as Hands balanced two columns in his mind: those who would be on his side and those who wouldn't. Thunder echoed above. The cascade of air-conditioning falling on Hands's shoulders trickled to nothing, the electricity flowing through its veins cut off by the storm. The lights flickered and then went dark. He slipped downstairs, braced himself for the deluge, and then dashed from the house.

Reedy burst in, a wild look in his eyes, startling Roger from his lookout on the stairs. He had heard Hands leave and expected his quick return, wondering where he was going. Rain pooled under Reedy's feet as he stood in the doorway.

"Shut the damn door," Roger said gruffly, still freaked out by the sight of Reedy, his bald head slick with rain.

"Laird's got a snake," Reedy blurted out.

Roger eyed Reedy. "What do you mean he's got a snake?"

Reedy poured it all out about how Laird had been lying down and about how a snake had crawled up in his bed, coiling on his chest. "They do it to get warm," Reedy added. "Laird wanted me to get you. He wants your help to get it off him."

"What does he want me to do about it?" Roger asked, though there was no way he wasn't going to go, flattered that they'd thought of him in their moment of panic.

"I don't know," Reedy said. "He just said to get you. He said to hurry."

Roger glanced up the stairs and thought to make an excuse, but because he didn't yet know what would be done about Mr. Baker, he followed Reedy into the rain, splashing through the loch that had formed along Regis Street.

Assburn watched out the bedroom window as Roger followed Reedy to a house on Loyola Street. He'd heard muffled voices in the living room and wondered what was going on. He suspected he was being set up to take the fall for Mr. Baker, who was struggling facedown on the bed, his hands wound behind his back with duct tape. His suspicion had been bred when he saw Hands run out the front door toward the dining hall. It *was* near lunchtime, Assburn thought, but why hadn't Hands asked if he wanted anything, or offered to relieve him of his command? Assburn sneaked downstairs. He flicked a light switch on and off. Nothing. He slid open the window above the kitchen sink to admit fresh air into the fetid house, but the steamy air did little to comfort him.

He momentarily mistook a loud bang for thunder, realizing his mistake when Mr. Baker bound down the stairs, his keys in hand, a small piece of duct tape still stuck to his cheek.

Roger tapped on Laird's door. He could feel Reedy's breath on his neck, but the sick feeling in his stomach trumped his annoyance. The door was opened cautiously by a soph wearing a look of panic. Roger was surprised to find the room packed with sophomores, a bald circle arranged around Laird, who lay stiffly in bed with his eyes closed. A coiled bulge under the covers rose and fell with Laird's shallow breathing.

"You have to whisper," Kerr said.

Roger trod carefully toward Laird, who opened his eyes. Reedy fell back, blending into the gallery.

"What is it?" Roger whispered. The air in the room was stagnant, fired by the mass of sweaty bodies.

Laird whispered something Roger couldn't hear.

"What?" Roger asked, his voice threatening to rise out of a whisper.

A chorus of "Shh!" went around the room.

Laird rolled his eyes and whispered again.

"I can't hear you," Roger whispered.

"Maybe you should lean in," Kerr whispered.

Roger kept his eye on the coil, listening for the telltale rattle that signaled the snake's agitation. His breathing became measured, his heartbeat slowing. Roger bent down to Laird's ear but shot upright when Kerr tapped him on the shoulder. "Be careful not to bump him," Kerr whispered. Roger scowled, but Kerr didn't notice. He bent down again, putting his ear next to Laird's lips, the coil eye level now.

"If you rip the covers off, I'll roll the opposite way," Laird whispered in a halting voice.

Roger frowned. "It won't work," he mouthed.

Laird rolled his eyes again and took a deep breath, the snake rising under the sheets. Roger backed away, a look of terror on his face.

"What did he say?" Kerr asked in Roger's ear.

Roger repeated the plan to Kerr in a hushed tone.

"I'll help," Kerr whispered. He went around to the other side of the bed and pantomimed that Roger should take a corner of the sheets.

Roger shook his head. "It won't work!" he whispered loudly.

The room filled with shushes.

"On three," Kerr whispered, grabbing the sheet in one hand. Roger gripped the other side. "One . . . two . . ."

Roger clenched the sheet tightly. A rivulet of sweat leaped off his forehead.

"Three!" Kerr yelled, whipping back the sheet. Roger tried to lift his arm, but the room spun away from him as he passed out from fear and stress and the heat, the coil of garden hose on Laird's chest falling to the floor as the room erupted in laughter.

Lindy couldn't believe his luck. He realized he'd have more time to operate than he'd ever dreamed as he witnessed first Hands and then Roger bolting out of the house, followed by Mr. Baker running for his truck, Assburn in step behind until Mr. Baker reached his truck and peeled out. Something was up, but he'd have to find out about it later. He knocked for good measure—it was possible someone was loafing in the house, staying out of the rain—but there was no answer. He slipped inside, leaving wet footsteps on the stairs.

The house was in some disarray. All the doors had been blown open, as if a tornado had roamed the halls. Panicked that either Hands or Assburn or Mr. Baker would return, Lindy pillaged Roger's room with the efficiency of a burglar. It didn't take him long to locate what he'd come for: The job journal was at sea in a drawer of unrolled socks. He plucked the booklet out and cleared a place on top of the dresser to write. He used the plunger end of his pen to trace over Roger's handwriting. He practiced

Roger's disconnected capital printing, lines flaring on the *E*s and *F*s, *T*s that crossed with a dot, *R*s that looked like *P*s. He traced over a half page about corner beads and then clicked his pen, ready. He found a space in the margin and wrote, "Mr. Morgan is a fag," the slur matching Roger's handwriting perfectly. The famous episode about Roger transferring out of Mr. Morgan's Advanced English class, complaining to Principal Breen that Mr. Morgan's grading was too harsh, would complement the slur nicely.

Lindy tucked the job journal away in the top of Roger's closet so he could easily find it again during the Open House. He started at what he thought was the sound of someone downstairs, but what he'd really heard was the deafening quiet: The rain had ceased pelting Garden Lakes, the gray clouds that had concealed sunlight rolling away, the winds blowing their last breath as the monsoon passed.

Some of us would remember inspecting the water damage to one of the sophomore houses on Loyola Street when we first heard the sirens that afternoon, others would remember eating lunch in the dining hall when the first traces of blue and red painted the air. Still others would conveniently forget the answer to the question. Our collective confusion would be a source of consternation for the administration as they spent the fall semester trying to sort out the details.

Your faithful columnist would prove to have the clearest memory of events, becoming invaluable as the police waded through the alibis and plots. Figs fingered Hands as the mastermind of Mr. Baker's kidnapping, having heard about Hands's involvement from Warren, but Hands had a rock-solid alibi. I'll tell it to you as I told it to the cops: Hands was on the roof of the

250

community center with yours truly, watching the storm gather through binoculars, when Roger attacked Mr. Baker. Hands's alibi forced Mr. Baker to retract his positive ID, landing the blame solely with Roger and Assburn, neither finding an ally among us.

The truth, of course, is that I had no account of Hands's whereabouts at any time that day; and while I was averse to providing him with an alibi, Figs's eagerness to sacrifice him to the police changed my mind. I admit to succumbing to the urge for revenge. The opportunity to do to Figs what he had done to me in denying me the friendships that I so desperately coveted, as he had Assburn, was not likely to present itself again, I knew. It had taken the help of my neighbor, Mr. Chandler, an alum, to gain me admittance to Randolph, and I recognized it as my last chance at any sort of equal footing, or at least at putting some distance between my peripatetic past and my future. All the shuttling between distant relatives after the gas leak exploded my childhood home in California and stole my parents away before I could know them, a life of transfer before I even understood what it meant. I was just the kid who lived on the wrong side of town, who hadn't gone to any of the middle schools or junior highs the others did, who didn't appear to have parents. But it wasn't going to happen at Randolph, I knew by then. If he were being honest, Assburn had known it long before Garden Lakes too. All through life, people like Figs just decide. The American dream about upward mobility is a myth, save for the incremental movements of some under the watchful eyes of the few.

To my credit, I wavered. The police had separated us into groups—fellows pointing at one another as they spoke, sophomores shrugging or crying as the policemen accused everyone of everything—and it was by chance that Hands and I were

251

cordoned off under the palm tree in the lake bed. Mr. Baker accompanied the police officers as they made the rounds, and when Mr. Baker laid eyes on Hands, he gesticulated wildly, saying, "There's one!"

The nearest officer, a rotund man whose uniform was losing its battle to the heat, asked Hands if he knew anything about the assault on Mr. Baker. Hands shrugged, the gesture agitating the policeman. "I asked you a question, son," he said. "Did you assault this man"—he pointed at Mr. Baker—"along with the others?"

Maybe I let him sweat it out a minute. Or maybe that's just a story I tell myself to ameliorate the regret for my original sin, which has only led to a life of prevarication and an alienating superiority that has haunted me since. Many stories went around that day and for months and years after, the truth obscured and then lost, which is what compelled me to undertake this confession. The price of lying seemed affordable then. All I desired in exchange was friendship, to break free of my transfer-student status, to find acceptance among some faction of my new peers, a group that had until then resisted my ingratiation, the exception being the He-Man Becky Haters Club, which I'd uttered as a joke to Jason, the other transfer student, whom I counted as my only friend, powerless to reverse the chain of events that led to poor Rebecca Clement's embarrassed exit from our lives. Forever after I disavowed any suggestion that it was me who was the inspiration for such awfulness, until I was convinced that it was someone else.

As it adjusted for inflation over the years, my lie that afternoon at Garden Lakes was steeper than I could've calculated. "He was with me," I said. The alibi satisfied the officer and cast doubt in Mr. Baker's confused mind. He muttered that we all looked alike, while reiterating his confidence in his identification of Roger and Assburn, both of whom would be expelled. I hoped for Assburn that his expulsion would bring about the second chance he'd been denied, much as my emancipation earlier in the school year made it easy for me to forego my senior year, freeing me. I never knew. The search continued for more perpetrators, interrupted briefly by the caravan of parents, summoned by the police, who raced to Garden Lakes to look for their children.

It would be some time before we realized that what they were searching for was gone.

Acknowledgments

My thanks to

Josephine Bergin
Rebecca Boyd
Heather E. Fisher
Pete Hausler
Dan Pope
Michael Rosovsky
David Ryan
Lavinia Spalding
Jonathan Wilson
Stephanie Duncan and everyone at Bloomsbury
Clarkes, Gilkeys, Kaliens, and Cottons
Mary Cotton and Max

About the Author

Jaime Clarke is a graduate of the University of Arizona and holds an MFA from Bennington College. He is the author of the novels *We're So Famous*, *Vernon Downs*, and *World Gone Water*; editor of the anthologies *Don't You Forget About Me: Contemporary Writers on the Films of John Hughes*, *Conversations with Jonathan Lethem*, and *Talk Show: On the Couch with Contemporary Writers*; and co-editor of the anthologies *No Near Exit: Writers Select Their Favorite Work from 'Post Road' Magazine* (with Mary Cotton) and *Boston Noir 2: The Classics* (with Dennis Lehane and Mary Cotton). He is a founding editor of the literary magazine *Post Road*, now published at Boston College, and co-owner, with his wife, of Newtonville Books, an independent bookstore in Boston.

www.jaimeclarke.com
www.postroadmag.com
www.baumsbazaar.com
www.newtonvillebooks.com

By Jaime Clarke

VERNON DOWNS

www.bloomsbury.com/JaimeClarke

"*Vernon Downs* is a gripping, hypnotically written and unnerving look at the dark side of literary adulation. Jaime Clarke's tautly suspenseful novel is a cautionary tale for writers and readers alike—after finishing it, you may start to think that J. D. Salinger had the right idea after all."

—TOM PERROTTA, author of *Election, Little Children,* and *The Leftovers*

259

"Moving and edgy in just the right way. Love (or lack of) and Family (or lack of) is at the heart of this wonderfully obsessive novel."

—GARY SHTEYNGART, author of *Super Sad True Love Story*

"All strong literature stems from obsession. *Vernon Downs* belongs to a tradition that includes Nicholson Baker's *U and I*, Geoff Dyer's *Out of Sheer Rage*, and—for that matter—*Pale Fire*. What makes Clarke's excellent novel stand out isn't just its rueful intelligence, or its playful semi-veiling of certain notorious literary figures, but its startling sadness. *Vernon Downs* is first rate."

—MATTHEW SPECKTOR, author of *American Dream Machine*

"*Vernon Downs* is a brilliant meditation on obsession, art, and celebrity. Charlie Martens's mounting fixation with the titular Vernon is not only driven by the burn of heartbreak and the lure of fame, but also a lost young man's struggle to locate his place in the world. *Vernon Downs* is an intoxicating novel, and Clarke is a dazzling literary talent."

—LAURA VAN DEN BERG, author of *The Isle of Youth*

"An engrossing novel about longing and impersonation, which is to say, a story about the distance between persons, distances within ourselves. Clarke's prose is infused with music and intelligence and deep feeling."

—CHARLES YU, author of *Sorry Please Thank You*

"*Vernon Downs* is a fascinating and sly tribute to a certain fascinating and sly writer, but this novel also perfectly captures the lonely distortions of a true obsession."

—DANA SPIOTTA, author of *Stone Arabia*

Selected by *The Millions* as a Most Anticipated Read

"Though *Vernon Downs* appears to be about deception and celebrity, it's really about the alienation out of which these things grow. Clarke shows that obsession is, at root, about yearning: about the things we don't have but desperately want; about our longing to be anyone but ourselves."

—*Boston Globe*

"A stunning and unsettling foray into a glamorous world of celebrity writers, artistic loneliness, and individual desperation."

—*Harvard Crimson*

"*Vernon Downs* is a fast-moving and yet, at times, quite sad book about, in the broadest sense, longing."

—*Brooklyn Rail*

261

By Jaime Clarke

WORLD GONE WATER

www.bloomsbury.com/JaimeClarke

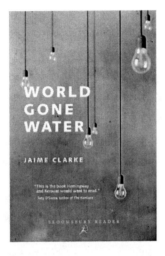

"Jaime Clarke's *World Gone Water* is so fresh and daring, a necessary book, a barbaric yawp that revels in its taboo: the sexual and emotional desires of today's hetero young man. Clarke is a sure and sensitive writer, his lines are clean and carry us right to the tender heart of his lovelorn hero, Charlie Martens. This is the book Hemingway and Kerouac would want to read. It's the sort of honesty in this climate that many of us aren't brave enough to write."

—TONY D'SOUZA, author of *The Konkans*

"This unsettling novel ponders human morality and sexuality, and the murky interplay between the two. Charlie Martens is a compelling anti-hero with a voice that can turn on a dime, from shrugging naiveté to chilling frankness. *World Gone Water* is a candid, often startling portrait of an unconventional life."

—J. ROBERT LENNON, author of *Familiar*

"Funny and surprising, *World Gone Water* is terrific fun to read . . . and, as a spectacle of bad behavior, pretty terrifying to contemplate."

—ADRIENNE MILLER, author of *The Coast of Akron*

"Charlie Martens is my favorite kind of narrator, an obsessive yearner whose commitment to his worldview is so overwhelming that the distance between his words and the reader's usual thinking gets clouded fast. *World Gone Water* will draw you in, make you complicit, and finally leave you both discomfited and thrilled."

—MATT BELL, author of *In the House upon the Dirt between the Lake and the Woods*

"Charlie Martens will make you laugh. More, he'll offend and shock you while making you laugh. Even trickier: he'll somehow make you like him, root for him, despite yourself and despite him. This novel travels into the dark heart of male/female relations and yet there is tenderness, humanity, hope. Jaime Clarke rides what is a terribly fine line between hero and antihero. Read and be astounded."

—AMY GRACE LOYD, author of *The Affairs of Others*

CPSIA information can be obtained
at www.ICGtesting.com
Printed in the USA
LVOW09s1402201017
553169LV00004B/80/P